TOUCH OF HEARTACHE

Stay in Touch

JOY PENNY

Crimson Fox
PUBLISHING

Touch of Heartache by Joy Penny

© 2017 by Joy Penny. All rights reserved.

Published by Crimson Fox Publishing and Joy Penny.

Crimson Fox Publishing, Turner, OR

www.crimsonfoxpublishing.com

Cover photo by VitalikRadko via DepositPhotos. Cover design by Berto Designs.

ISBN: 978-1946202574

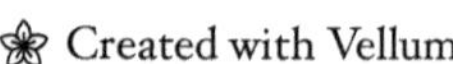 Created with Vellum

CHAPTER ONE

Lilac had been sitting on her big news for days—well, more like hours, but it certainly felt like days. She'd wanted to tell Gavin almost immediately, but she hadn't been in the mood for one of his mood-killing—though well-intentioned—lectures, and waiting until Brielle and Pembroke joined them seemed like the smarter idea. They'd act as a buffer for Gavin's paternal instincts coming to fore and then she wouldn't have to repeat herself to each one individually.

Besides, she wanted her college life to go out with a bang. And boy, would this be a bang.

She hadn't eaten much of her farewell-cafeteria-food lunch. Instead, she opened her mouth, about to deliver the news, when she noticed Brielle staring down at her lunch tray as if it were the ashes of a recently-lost pet. "Are you crying?" she asked, the wind knocked out of her sails just a bit. "Bri, are you actually *crying?*"

Laughing, she looked at Gavin and Pembroke, hoping to share her amusement with them, but one was blowing his nose and the other was trying to touch up her makeup. *Okay,* everyone *is crying...*

"Just because some of us are made of stone doesn't mean the rest of us aren't going to miss this place," said Brielle, her mouth full of a tater tot she was chomping with *way* too much relish.

Sometimes Brielle really got on Lilac's nerves. But not today. No, she wouldn't let her get to her today.

"A college is but four walls and a roof, my dear," Lilac said, putting some of her high school drama teacher's advice into effect by gesturing grandly as if about to deliver a Shakespearean monologue. "Albeit four very *expensive* walls and a roof, but walls and a roof nonetheless. No graduation is going to take away what this place means to you." She put her palm to her heart. "You'll always find it here."

Gavin gave Lilac such a mischievous grin at that, she could have recited what he said next if she'd been so inclined. "In your ginormous boob?" he asked.

"Har har," retorted Lilac, whapping his shoulder. Gavin was the only one she'd ever let get away with talking to her like that. He had a heart of gold and was as sweet as a grandma—to everyone except her. But that's why she knew she was his best friend. Suddenly hit with the realization that she wasn't going to be seeing her bestie every day from now on, she started playing with her food, mushing the greasy tater tots into one corner of her tray. *It doesn't matter*, she thought. *This is just how life goes. We'll never not be friends. You can't get stuck in the past.*

She nodded to herself more than to anyone in particular. "I don't know. I think it's about time we move on. Crappy French toast and tater tots served on a divided tray? What are we, middle schoolers or soon-to-be-independent adults?"

"Says the soon-to-be elementary school teacher," said Brielle between sips of her orange juice. "Get used to these," she added, pointing to the crumbs left in the squares on her tray.

Ha! The perfect segue. Thank you, Brielle's need to rub things in.

Lilac shrugged. "Maybe someday. Maybe not. I don't have to anytime soon."

Pembroke spoke up then—Lilac had almost forgotten she was even there. "What do you mean?" she asked. "Aren't you going to be teaching at Jacobson Primary this fall?"

"Nope." Lilac dug into her scrambled eggs with glee. *Let them chew on that*, she thought, taking her time to swallow her food.

"*Shut up*," said Gavin as he nudged her. "Are you serious?"

"Would I joke about something like that?" Lilac grinned, doing her best toddler-caught-breaking-Mommy's-favorite-lamp impression. Then she laughed. *On second thought...* "Don't answer that."

Brielle practically threw her fork down on her tray before crossing her arms. "When were you going to tell us?"

Ah, Brielle. She'd been Lilac's roommate the first two years of college before Lilac had spent a semester her junior year in Spain. When she'd come back, she'd wheedled her daddy into splurging on an apartment off-campus for her and Gavin. Not because she hated Brielle or anything, but because she'd preferred spending time with Gavin. And frankly, after she'd come home from living in another corner of the world, Gavin—with his broader horizons, his love for big cities—had seemed like more sophisticated company.

Brielle cradled her head. *Cradled* her head. Like what Lilac did was any concern of hers. And what was *she* planning on doing that was evidence she had her life any more together than the rest of them? Job hunting. While working her high school job, cleaning for old folks and snobs with cash to burn and slobs too lazy to do it for themselves. True, Lilac's mom and daddy usually hired cleaners after throwing one of their soirees or when they'd be gone for a while—which was pretty often. But there was something about having strangers going through your house on that kind of intimate level that gave Lilac the willies. But that was what Brielle had to show for herself. Going through other peoples' garbage.

"Don't have a conniption over it," said Lilac, shrugging as she gently placed her own fork on the table. "Something better came along."

"Better than a job offer?" asked Gavin, studying Lilac like she had a screw loose, but grinning devilishly nonetheless. He knew her too well. He might not have approved of everything she did, but... "A *paying* firm job offer, I might add?"

Therein lay the crux of the matter. Sweet Gavin, smart and hand-some and ready to take on the world... But the world wasn't so ready to take him on. He'd gotten what could lead to the job of his dreams —in marketing, which, if she were being honest, Lilac thought dull and a waste of his talents—but he had to start off as an unpaid intern. If Gavin hadn't already known some friends in Chicago whose couch he could crash on until he started raking in the big bucks, there was no way he could have pulled it off. All because he was gambling on being hired by summer's end. He had nothing to fall back on, no one else to turn to if that didn't pan out. There was his grandma, but she lived in such a small town, Lilac had thought she'd phased through into another dimension—a dimension where people dug holes and only peeked out from under their rocks to spit out a strange sense of pride in their vitriol and hatred—the one time she'd gone with him there. Even though Gavin's grandma was a peach, there was no way Lilac would abandon Gavin to that place once more. No, if things didn't work out how Gavin hoped they would, she'd find a way to let him come stay with her and Aunt Frankie.

Clearing her throat, Lilac tapped her fingers on the table, trying to shove all thoughts of unpleasantness aside. "I repeat: Something better."

"Did you... get a job offer abroad?" Pembroke didn't even try to hide her gasp as Lilac snorted.

Poor girl. Lilac knew Pembroke had been envious of her time in Spain—not because she'd wanted to go to Spain, but because her own plans to study abroad in Japan had fallen through. Lilac really had no idea what Pembroke planned on doing—that girl was quieter than a nun who'd taken a vow of silence. She didn't even remember how exactly Broke had started hanging out with their group. It had had something to do with Gavin, of course. Easily two-thirds of Gavin's day was devoted to taking care of others. Sometimes Lilac hated the fact that she had to share him.

"I *wish*," she said, thinking about how nice it might have been to live in Spain long-term—or to live anywhere stylish, really. But she'd only ever pictured herself lounging around in a Spanish villa, and Daddy had been quite clear he wasn't going to fund an extended vacation. As if he ever did anything *but* go on extended vacations himself. "About the only thing that would guarantee me that is a job teaching English, and I don't think a change in venue would make enough of a difference when I really wanted a... change in job."

There. She'd said it. The whole and honest truth she'd been keeping even from herself for far too long.

Leave it to Brielle to shit all over that. "You're not going to be an elementary school teacher?" she asked, the acid practically dripping off her tongue. "After all the hard work you put into becoming one?"

"Maybe I wished I'd have taken a cue from you," Lilac said, forcing some friendliness she didn't feel at that moment into her tone. She loved Brielle—she really did. But sometimes... "And had studied something more useless so I didn't have to spend so much time in training and studying for my license."

"*Lilac*," said Gavin. He darted his gaze away and shook his head, as if he couldn't believe Lilac had gone so low.

But it was true. Brielle had a history *and* a philosophy major, and what was she going to do with those degrees? *Nada*, apparently.

Brielle bit her lip and kept quiet, a glaze covering her eyes. Lilac had gotten her right in the gonads—metaphorically, of course.

"I'm serious," said Lilac, her defensive shields lowering somewhat. "All that wasted time just showed me... I'm not cut out to be a teacher."

"That's not true!" Pembroke spoke up again, and Lilac smiled. She was sweet, for sure, although she couldn't remember if Broke had even seen Lilac around kids much. She might have, though. Basically, anytime Lilac was around kids, she got into a zone and the whole world around her melted away. Time flew by alarmingly fast between breaking up fights over toy cars and dispensing hugs on demand.

"That's nice of you to say, sweet pea," said Lilac, ready to finally drop the big news. "But wait until you hear what I'm going to be doing instead." Shoving her tray aside, she leaned forward, as if ready to drop the juiciest piece of gossip imaginable. Only Gavin and Pembroke took the bait, though Brielle's eyes were still on her. "I'm. Going. To. Tildy. World," said Lilac, injecting pride into each word.

Brielle looked as if she'd been struck. "Wait, what?"

Yeah, yeah, it's not Disney World, thought Lilac, already ready to defend her choice. Growing up as a Tildy Tapir fan, Lilac knew just how rare it was to find someone who appreciated the happy-go-lucky cartoon tapir with quite the same fervor she did. All the other Orlando theme parks had nothing on Tildy World, small as it might be. She didn't care what her friends thought.

"Doesn't your aunt live in Orlando?" asked Gavin. Aunt Frankie and Gavin had hit it off big the few times they'd both been over to her parents' for a get-together. Two souls in harmony, like peanut butter and jelly.

"She does!" said Lilac. "And Mom and Daddy only *approved* of this venture because I'm going to move in with her, at least for the first few months. Not that I need their approval exactly."

Pembroke tucked a strand of her blue-streaked blonde hair behind her ears as she stared at Lilac, clearly completely lost. "But... are you going to be on vacation for *that* long?"

Okay, this was taking more to explain than Lilac had thought necessary. "It's not a vacation," she said, sighing and shrugging at once. "Well, not that I won't ever just hang out at the park or head to the beach. Kind of the whole point of relocating to Florida instead of even-worse-winters-than-here-like-that's-somehow-possible Minnesota." Lilac threw her hands up, ready to lay it all on the table. "Aunt Frankie knows someone who works at one of the resorts as a manager. She knew he was looking for an assistant manager and voila." She rotated her hand to gesture to herself. "I became available in an instant."

Maybe she didn't want to have any regrets. Was that so hard for her friends to believe? Something sharp tugged beneath her breast-bone, a little voice at the back of her head telling her she was headed for disaster.

"They hired you as an *assistant manager*?" asked Brielle, oblivious to Lilac's attempts to squash her own regrets. "Right out of college? With a degree that has nothing to do with running a hotel at all?"

Lilac smiled. Brielle of little faith. "What can I say? I'm a charming interviewee, even over Skype."

She paused, taking in the scene around her. *Okay, is everyone at this table now staring at my breasts?*

Lilac was no stranger to people staring at her double-Ds, but she expected more from her friends of all people. She cleared her throat, eager to stop associating her figure with her success. She'd worked hard at preparing for that interview, even if—especially since—it had all been last-minute. "And I'm just in training to start. Earl was especially keen to hear about my experience with elementary school children since running interference between the resort's childcare center and the management office would be a big part of my duties."

Gavin made a face like he'd just sniffed sour milk. "You're working for a guy named Earl. *Earl*."

Lilac dismissed him, waving a hand. "He could be named Billy Bob Jimbo for all I care if he got me a job in Florida."

"I don't know," said Gavin, injecting something sly into his words. "There's just something ominous about a guy named Earl."

"I'll behave," said Lilac, smacking her fist into his shoulder. "It's a thin-haired, chubby-faced man old enough to be my father named Earl. And I'm sure there's a Mrs. Earl."

"Hasn't stopped the type before," said Gavin, that beleaguered-dad-about-to-lecture tone in his voice clearer than ever. He exchanged a look with Brielle and something silent passed between them, as if they'd spoken about Lilac and men many times before.

They probably had, the traitors. Gavin better not have told her that Lilac's tastes usually strayed toward the older gentleman. In theory anyway, if not in practice yet. But not this guy regardless. Charming, he wasn't.

"Stop being such a drama queen," said Lilac. "So *anyway*, enough about me." *Time to steer the conversation away. Far away.* She wasn't going to end her college experience arguing with her closest friends about things that didn't even really concern them. "Pem, what about you? I know Brielle's got a plan for the summer until she finds that *amazing job* that awaits her, but you've never let us know what you have planned. Did you ever find anything?"

Cue Pembroke shutdown. "No. Not really."

"What?" said Gavin, clearly surprised but still gentle. "A catch like you, with honors in biology? There wasn't any lab or something that would take you?"

Staring at her lunch tray like it was her toast that had posed the question, Pembroke shrugged. "Nothing local, anyway."

Ah. Pembroke had been a commuter—a resident of this college town since the day she'd been born. Japan had been her one shot at widening her horizons just a bit. But even now, as she was about to cross that stage tomorrow and graduate college, she apparently had no interest in broadening her horizons. Lilac never could understand people like that. "And you can't move because…?"

Pembroke snapped her eyes up at that. "I didn't apply to any jobs outside the area," she said curtly, as if that were the end of it.

Gavin wouldn't let her shut the conversation down. "Well, maybe you can think about med school or nursing school. They need medical professionals everywhere."

Lilac couldn't picture Pembroke as a doctor or a nurse—she had no personality to speak of. She knew Brielle and Pembroke bonded over all their TV shows and geeky movies, but she had never gotten into that herself, so she hadn't been able to follow along. Still, those types of conversations seemed to be the only reason Pembroke ever came to life. Little help that would be in a medical emergency, though.

Pembroke nodded and Lilac decided to throw her a bone and

pivot the discussion. "Well, good luck with whatever you decide." She was more certain than ever now that she'd made the right decision. Sure, Minnesota was still a new place to move to, but Florida? Beaches and sunbathing, year-round heat and the cuddly cute tapir named Tildy. She was going to be living the dream—her childhood dream come true.

Gavin mumbled something about "trouble at 3:00," and Lilac's feet floated back to the floor. "Is it 3:00 already? I thought all our parents weren't coming until after dinner anyway." They were all coming for one last hurrah, a grade-wide graduation dinner and campus tour followed by the ceremony tomorrow morning.

Brielle jumped to her feet, her attention drawn over her shoulder. "Right. Thanks for the heads-up. See you guys tomorrow!" She gathered up her tray and left.

Lilac supposed Brielle might be so busy with her mom and sister's arrival that she hadn't planned to sit with them at dinner. All the better. Both sets of Lilac's grandparents were coming and she knew that between them, her parents, and Gavin and his grandma, there wouldn't be room for any more.

"I hate that guy," said Gavin, wiping his hands with his napkin and shaking his head.

"What guy?" asked Lilac.

Gavin nodded in Brielle's direction and Lilac witnessed Brielle storming off angrily toward the cafeteria doors with a lanky, gangly guy in a Hershey's T-shirt hot on her tail. "Oh. The ex?" said Lilac, only half-sure.

"Daniel..." said Pembroke, who stared a *little* too intensely after them as they vanished from sight. *Ew*, thought Lilac. Was Pembroke—*Pembroke* of all people, who hadn't so much as glanced at a boy in all her four years here—checking out that skin-and-bones jerk? That made for two women in Lilac's circle with no taste. Not to mention, he was younger than them. Not her type at all. All her college relationships had been short and sweet—they'd scratched an itch, but they hadn't really done much for her. But seeing as how the only older men in her social circle here were professors—which, *no*, despite any leers she may have detected coming from that way on occasion—it had been frat boys with commitment issues or nothing. Good thing she hadn't cared about any of them committing.

"Why can't he leave her alone? Honestly." Gavin let out a breath as if Brielle's love life affected him deeply. "He's such an asshole."

Pembroke's face flushed and she stood, gathering her own tray. "Yeah," she said, almost as an afterthought. "So I... I'm going to get ready for my dad," she added, not meeting either Gavin's or Lilac's eyes.

"See you later, sweetie," said Gavin, as if she were a kindergartner. Not that Lilac could blame him. She often found herself acting like the tiny blonde-with-blue-streaks was a kid as well.

"Bye," said Lilac, and Pembroke mumbled her farewells before retreating to the dishwashing station to deposit her things.

"So," said Gavin, inching his chair back so he could pivot to face Lilac entirely, one elbow on the back of the chair, his other hand clasping his wrist.

"So," said Lilac, grinning and echoing his posture.

Gavin batted his eyelashes. "When were you going to tell me?"

"I just did."

"Yeah, you *sprung* it on me. That's cold, Li."

Lilac pouted. "I just didn't want to repeat myself," she said, then turned to say, "*¡Hola! ¡Felicitaciones!*" to a couple of other senior girls from her advanced Spanish classes who'd walked by and wished her the same.

Gavin rolled his eyes at her as he waved and smiled at a group of guys and girls who sat down a table away. "Lilac Townsend, a woman of few words. Hates to have to repeat herself—especially when it comes to juicy gossip." He didn't drop the friendly, greeting smile off his face or even turn to look at Lilac the entire time he spoke.

"Stuff it," said Lilac, who went to playfully slug his arm. Instead, she gave him a big hug. "I'm going to miss you, Gavvy."

She'd never call him that in front of the others. It was too embar-rassing. But whenever she was alone with Gavin, she could feel her defenses melting.

"I'll miss you," said Gavin, running a gentle hand down the length of her blonde hair. It came down to her mid-back when not tied up, though she usually preferred a bun. Today she hadn't been dressed to impress. Just her school sweatshirt and pajama pants. She'd look smarter by the time her family arrived. The family who had shaken their heads and sighed but had all said, "That's our Li" when she'd told them about Florida, as if "impulsive" and "reck-less" were her middle names. Grandma Violet had put the blame all on "Daisy Francesca," or "Aunt Frankie," as she preferred Lilac to call her (she insisted so because she wanted to buck the Townsend-women-flower tradition), who had always been a wild, impetuous child, as her grandparents liked to remind her. Lilac liked that about Frankie, though.

"Am I... doing the right thing?" asked Lilac, almost afraid to ask.

"You're asking me *now*?" said Gavin, a hint of humor beneath his words. "Now that you've already gone and committed to it?" He winced as he said that, as if remembering that she'd committed to Minnesota, too, and he grabbed her by the upper arms, pushing her gently away. "*Have* you committed?"

"It's all done," said Lilac, struggling to meet his eyes. "I've burned my bridges in Minnesota—they weren't happy to have to scramble to find someone else, and then there was the matter of the educational grant they'd offered me for taking the job last year, but Daddy paid it back and then some—and I have my plane ticket. I'm leaving Monday morning."

"So you've known about this new job for a while," said Gavin, pinching his lips into a straight line.

"No," said Lilac, honestly. "It all went down yesterday."

"Li," said Gavin, shaking his head. "That's... Wow."

Lilac pulled away from him. "I knew you wouldn't approve."

"What do you care if I approve or not?" There wasn't a hint of anger in his words—in fact, there was encouragement more than anything. "You have to do you, Lilac."

"This *is* me," said Lilac. She dared to look back at Gavin and he didn't seem angry or shocked or anything. This was why he was her best friend.

"Then you go be you," said Gavin. He smiled. "And clear me some room on Frankie's couch because the second I have some free time, I want to work on my tan alongside you."

Lilac bopped his nose with one French-manicured finger. "You can sunbathe with me, but I'm going to slather you with sunscreen," she said. "Melanoma, remember?"

Gavin laughed. "You think I'm going to be on a sunny, Florida beach and let *you* slather sunscreen on me?" Shaking his head, he grinned deviously. "I'm going to bump into my true love there and ever-so-innocently ask *him* for help reaching my back, thank you very much."

Lilac chuckled and wiped her eyes, realizing tears had started to form there. "All right," she said. "But he better have a hot, single father who'll lather me up too."

"No thank you and ew," said Gavin, shaking his head. "You and your daddy issues..."

"Don't call my taste in men that!" Lilac shuddered. "Especially when I'm going to see Daddy today." She paused. "Okay, don't say anything about me saying *Daddy*," she added, knowing full well how calling her dad "Daddy" creeped Gavin out. But she couldn't help it. Daddy had always been "Daddy" to her.

They stared at one another, a silent showdown, each waiting for the other to comment further. Then they both laughed. Leave it to Gavin to boost Lilac's mood, to help her shove those doubts all the way deep down where they belonged.

CHAPTER TWO

It may have been five o'clock somewhere, but here, it was ten in the morning and Lilac's entire family was drinking. *If I don't get past airport security soon,* thought Lilac, *I might not make my flight.* Despite the fact that she and practically her entire family had arrived hours in advance. Her mom and daddy had insisted they make a day of it. They were off to the Caribbean themselves, an impromptu trip born from her mom's envy of Lilac heading for a sunnier clime. Her mom's parents had to catch a flight home to Rochester. Her daddy's parents lived in the same town as her parents during the summer months and New Mexico during winter. So they weren't going anywhere, but they'd tagged along, too, and now the seven of them sat around a rather cramped table in a restaurant at the Hilton connected to one of O'Hare's terminals. They'd finished eating ages ago, but everyone cradled a drink they kept nursing at the rate of one sip per half hour. Lilac had already downed hers ages ago and had refused a refill, her nerves a bit on edge. This was a *good* thing, damn it, but she always did get nervous even before good things happened.

"Cheer up, princess." Her daddy raised an eyebrow as he lifted his shot glass to his lips. "You look like you're on your way to a funeral, not a theme park."

"*Rodney*!" Lilac's mom shook her head as she stirred her martini for the dozenth time.

"What?" asked Papa William, laughing. "Afraid the next time we're all together like this we'll be missing one family member?"

"That's not funny," snapped Lilac's mom, but she was fighting to keep a smile from cracking her lips. "Besides, you're hardly an old man. You've got time yet."

"Oh, so it's my number that's up next, is it?" Papa William raised his shot glass in the air. "I'd better drink to that. To us old people."

"You'll drink to anything," said Nana Abigail, her pearl bracelet slipping down her arm as she moved to fan herself with the dessert menu. "And I'd appreciate you not calling us 'old,' dear, despite appearances." She reached into her purse, bringing out a compact to touch up her already-perfect lipstick. Nana Abigail was like a supermodel—if supermodels were allowed to get white hair and wrinkles.

"If I recall, Lilac always got nervous before traveling," said Grandpa Matthew, who took up more than his fair share of the small table with both forearms laid out in front of him. The shock of white arm hair against his tanned skin marred by the scars from melanoma surgeries urged Lilac to rifle through her carry-on to make sure she'd packed her SPF 50.

"There she goes," said Grandma Violet, as if everyone was in on some joke. "Checking to make sure she remembered every-thing. Honey, you've done that already. Four times since we sat down."

Lilac clutched her bottle of sunscreen, feeling her palm go clammy, and let it go as a feeling of relief washed over her. "I just want to make sure," she said. "I don't know when I'll be able to get back here, so I don't want to leave anything important behind."

"Your mother or I can always send you anything you've forgot-ten," said her daddy.

As if they're ever home. Her daddy had inherited a sizable fortune from his grandfather at the age of twenty-one, as had Aunt Frankie. Technically, her daddy considered himself a stock trader or something, but Lilac knew he hadn't worked an 8-5 in her lifetime. Her family had had a successful business once—long ago. But her grandpa had retired decades early and sold the company to someone more interested in running it. Someone who probably didn't have quite as big of an investment fund to fall back on.

Lilac also had one somewhere, funds overseen by her daddy, who had his accountant handle Lilac's taxes. But she wasn't going to while away her days doing nothing. Her daddy hadn't seen the irony in insisting she not do as he did, that she not just lounge around Spain for a few more years. To be fair, he never stayed put in one place long enough to need more than a tourist visa.

"I know," said Lilac, bringing out her phone, "but you might not be home for a while yet."

"Not at the table," said Nana Abigail, snapping her compact shut. Lilac noticed it wasn't from the cosmetics company that had been responsible for the Mahoney fortune. That stuff was probably too cheap for her grandma.

"Yes, Nana," said Lilac, slipping the phone back into the front of her bag. She'd just wanted to check the time—and she supposed she did have enough time left. Her leg bounced under the table.

"Excuse me," said Lilac. "I'm going to the bathroom."

"Say you're 'powdering your nose,' dear girl," said Grandma Violet. "I swear you're not even in Daisy Francesca's house yet and she's already rubbing her crassness all over you."

Lilac plastered a faltering smile on her face and headed around the bar. Instead of turning toward the restaurant bathrooms, though, she stopped, looking toward the terminal entrance. *Just for a few minutes*, she thought, digging her phone out of her purse.

Gavin was busy moving to his temporary apartment—it was Memorial Day, so he didn't have to work yet. Brielle was probably not that busy and Pembroke... Who the hell knew what she was doing? But did she really want to reach out to either of them right now? She didn't need to hear any of Brielle's lectures and when had she ever solo-texted Pembroke?

Group text it was. Lilac looked around for a good spot. It was crowded today—one of the reasons why the waitress kept giving her family the stink eye for taking up a table for so long, she was sure—but she managed to find a spot by one of the glass walls that afforded her a good view of some of the planes in the background. Not any from the airline she was riding, but whatever.

She put her bag down and squished it between her sandaled feet, digging through for her compact mirror and making sure there were no flyaways in her hair. It was overcast in Chicago, but she grabbed her sunglasses anyway and put them carefully atop her head, checking again to make sure the movement hadn't rustled her hair. With her flowery, off-the-shoulder blouse, she was going for the "Florida" look—and who knew if she'd have the time and energy to pose once she got there. She held her camera above her, making sure she got some of the planes in the image, and smiled, flashing a peace sign at the camera.

So nervous but sooooo excited! she typed in a group text to Gavin, Brielle, and Pembroke. Satisfied with how the picture had turned out, she uploaded it to Instagram as well for all those other friends who rarely texted her to see. *Starting a new chapter in my life*, she typed. *Goodbye, cloudy skies!*

Once she posted it, she caught sight of the time again and her heart practically leapt out of her throat. Though she knew she was being overly cautious, she felt like she needed to get past security like *now*, but she couldn't very well go without giving everyone their goodbye hugs. She grinned as she saw an emoji thumbs up and a wacky face from Gavin in the text—of course, neither Brielle nor Pembroke had bothered to comment yet—and she stuffed the phone into her bag, practically running back toward the restaurant. At one point, her left sandal flew off and she had to run back to collect it, apologizing profusely to the older woman in a business suit whose rolling suitcase the shoe had whacked. She was almost at the restaurant, though, so she just carried it and limped the rest of the way, coming upon her mom and grandmas at the front of the restaurant.

"There you are!" said her mom. "We couldn't find you in the bathroom, so we were about to send in the National Guard."

"I went to another one," she said, gesturing over her shoulder. She really did have to go, too, but she was going to have to wait until after security now.

Grandma Violet took Lilac into a one-armed hug just as her daddy and grandpas exited the restaurant, Papa William tucking his credit card into his wallet—they'd probably all dueled it out to decide who would pay.

"Hugs and kisses for Grandma," said Grandma Violet, kissing her on each cheek. Lilac could feel the lipstick left behind and went to rub it off with her palm, although she smiled the whole way. Grandma Violet grabbed her tightly by both shoulders. "Now, don't you let Daisy Francesca talk you into doing anything unseemly."

Lilac rolled her eyes. "Aunt Frankie isn't like that, Grandma. She's just... eccentric."

Grandma Violet scoffed at her daughter's nickname as Grandpa Matthew demanded a hug from his little "all grown up Li-Li," and she gave him butterfly kisses as well.

"We'll let you all get going," he said as Grandma Violet hugged both her son and daughter-in-law. "Stay in touch!" he called, nodding to Lilac's other set of grandparents and wrapping an arm around his wife before heading toward hotel parking.

"Don't you have to leave at 12:40?" asked Lilac's mom, blowing a strand of dyed platinum-blonde hair out of her face as her fingers flew over her phone.

Lilac jumped, shoving the shoe back onto her foot. "Yeah, we should get going!"

"Not so fast," said Papa William. "We all have to go to different terminals, so let's say our goodbyes here."

Lilac turned around, her legs still bouncing, and hugged and kissed her other set of grandparents. Nana Abigail bristled a bit and went to check her makeup as soon as she broke away, but she smiled to find her foundation unmussed. "You'll love Florida, honey," she said. "Make sure you get plenty of beach time in."

"I will," said Lilac, already on to hugging her mom.

"Congrats again, sweetheart," said her mom, shoving her phone into her purse and taking Lilac's face in both hands.

"*Mom*," said Lilac, her eyes flitting back and forth to see if anyone was watching.

"Oh, cut your mother some slack," she responded. "My baby's going off into the big, wide world..."

"And she better be on the lookout for big, bad wolves," said her daddy. He took over from his wife and swung Lilac in his arms, letting out an exaggerated *oof* and cradling his back after he put her down. Lilac could feel her face flush, but she gave her daddy a peck on the cheek anyway. "My little girl's not so little anymore," he added.

"Well, *that's* flattering," sniped Nana Abigail.

"Mom," Lilac said, looking from one parent to the other and taking a hand from both. "Daddy. Thank you for everything."

"I mean it, princess," said her daddy, grabbing his wife's and his bags. "If any beach bum gives you trouble, I want to be the first to hear about it. I'll have a fist with his name on it."

Nana Abigail's eyebrows arched as her husband and son-in-law exchanged a look and laughed. Lilac wondered if her grandpa had had a fist or two for her daddy back in the day.

"Bye!" said Lilac, shuffling off. She walked backward a few steps, her view of her family growing hazy through the tears.

"You've got this," she told herself as she turned around.

And for the length of the mostly uneventful flight, she did.

Lilac couldn't believe she'd fallen asleep on the flight, but she'd had trouble sleeping the night before. All the excitement over graduation and saying goodbye to Gavin and everyone else for the foreseeable future... True, she hadn't seen them when in Spain, either, except for that time her parents had paid to send Gavin there to join her for spring break, but she'd known then she was returning to her friends, to her routine in the fall.

She didn't know anyone in Florida except for Aunt Frankie.

...And whoever had left a piece of paper with a phone number and the message, "Call me, hot stuff?" on it on her lap when she'd been asleep.

Ew. Lilac crumpled the paper in her fist but thought better of it, afraid of some overly aggressive guy taking it the wrong (or *right*, really) way. She stuffed it into her pocket, her eyes darting to and fro for some hint, but she doubted it was either of the hyper twenty-something women sharing the row with her—or at least, they certainly didn't seem to be concerned with her reaction. She stood, opening the overhead bin and shoving aside a suitcase to get to her bag.

"Need help?" asked a silver fox in a suit who'd stepped up from the row beside her.

Wow, thought Lilac numbly. "Sure," she said, feeling her voice shake as she stepped aside to give him room. "Thank—"

She bumped into someone as she moved back and whipped around to apologize. "Hey," said an orange beach bum in a tank top and swim trunks. His baby face made him look anywhere between twelve and twenty, but he stared at her above chubby cheeks, his gaze flitting between her face and her chest.

Oh, crap. No. Not you.

"Did you get my note?" he asked.

Of course it was you.

"Miss," said the handsome man from behind her. "Your bag."

Lilac spun around to take the bag from the man who held it out to her just as a beautiful middle-aged woman appeared from the row behind him and wrapped her arm around his waist.

Of course. Taken. "Thank you," she said, nodding her head.

"Can you guys not hold up the line?" shouted someone from the back of the plane.

Lilac turned back around to see the front of the plane nearly deserted in front of her except for the kid who looked ready to walk out the airport and dive into a pool.

"So, uh, I'm Benji—" started Beach Bum.

"*Excuse me*," said Lilac, who had to shove him aside, smacking him a little with her bag.

He cleared his throat, the word "bitch" just *barely* audible. Lilac walked faster, making sure to snatch the paper out of her pocket and toss it into the garbage can as she exited into the terminal. She followed the crowd in front of her, considering running to the bathroom but afraid that Beach Bum was not too far behind her and might linger outside the door. She hated thinking like that, but she was alone. Even in Spain, she'd usually had someone from her host family or *universidad* with her. She bypassed the baggage claim because most of the stuff she wasn't just storing at her parents' was being sent via UPS by Grandma Violet. She pulled out her phone and switched it on to see where Aunt Frankie was waiting for her. There were a lot of notifications from her Instagram photo and Brielle at least had chimed in with *Have a nice flight!* in their group text.

There was a voice mail from Aunt Frankie—*Argh, she always finds it easier to talk than text*—and Lilac started to listen to it just as she spotted the wildly waving pale arm near one of the doors.

"Aunt Frankie!" shouted Lilac, slipping the phone back into her bag and jogging the rest of the way. She stumbled once. *Darn sandals.*

"My favorite niece!" said Aunt Frankie, taking her into her arms. Lilac knew she was supposed to point out she was Frankie's only niece, but she had grown wearisome of that game.

Grinning, Lilac pulled back from the hug and took a good look at her aunt. It'd been months—since Christmas—since she'd last seen her. She'd dyed her usual pixie cut gray-and-ginger hair a deep auburn and she looked twenty years younger than Lilac knew her to be. "Love the hair," she said, and Aunt Frankie pretended to fluff it.

"Thanks," she said. "You look fabulous. More and more like a model every time I see you."

"Thanks," said Lilac, a rush of heat flooding her body. Maybe it was just her body trying to compensate for the chill of the A/C.

Beach Bum Benji walked through the doors and headed out onto the sidewalk, sparing a scathing but leering glance her way as he passed. Lilac tried to ignore him, letting Frankie take her by the hand.

"No luggage?" she asked.

"Grandma's sending most of my stuff this week," said Lilac.

Shaking her head, Aunt Frankie took her sunglasses off the top of her brow and slid them over her eyes. "Don't be surprised if your boxes arrive with five thousand bottles of sunscreen. Even though I already have quite a stock from her over the years. Your grandma thinks it's the perfect gift for a Floridian for every special occasion. Too bad she could never convince Dad to wear it."

That reminded Lilac sharply of her own fears of getting melanoma. She gently took her hand from her aunt's and dug into her bag, grabbing her sunglasses and her own bottle of SPF 50.

Aunt Frankie crossed her arms as Lilac started applying the sunscreen to her elbow. "I see she's got you trained already."

"It's got toner in it," said Lilac. "I don't want to stick out like a sore thumb in the Florida sun." She paused halfway through lathering up one of her arms. Her aunt was pretty pale. She probably burned instead of tanned.

"That's what these are for, dear," said Aunt Frankie, pulling a sunhat out of her tote bag and affixing it to her head. The brim was so large, it cast a shadow over her entire upper body.

"I'll have to get one of those," said Lilac, her skin already flush with the prickling of sweat. She stared out at the sky, so blindingly bright even with her sunglasses on. "And maybe polarized lenses."

Aunt Frankie laughed and fished her car keys out of her tote. "Come on, Ms. UV-Ray-Battle-Ready. Let me whisk you away to my bungalow before you turn to ashes in the sun."

Lilac caught Beach Bum Benji lowering his phone from his ear and pointing it in her direction, something like mischievousness on his expression as he snapped a pic of the "scenery" behind her. She shoved the bottle of sunscreen back into her bag and fell in step behind her aunt, no longer caring much whether or not she was protected from the sunlight.

CHAPTER THREE

Lilac had had exactly twenty-five minutes to enjoy the jam-packed and colorful views of sunny Orlando before she'd arrived at her aunt's house, and then she'd spent the whole evening catching up with her aunt and learning just a little more about Earl Stevenson, the guy Aunt Frankie had met through his wife, Tara, who had a yoga class with Frankie. Gavin had made her laugh with a side-by-side photo of his new digs, one of a window overlooking Lake Michigan and the other of a pile of clothes on the ground in front of a closed door. Apparently, his new roommates had been *in flagrante delicto* when he'd moved in and hadn't exactly rolled out the welcome mat.

They'd been texting about it all night, going off the group text into a private conversation. Even now, in the passenger side of Aunt Frankie's car on Tuesday morning, Lilac texted to Gavin.

Morning. I know you're probably getting ready for work. (Me too. No rest for the wicked, right?) Good luck! You'll be amazing.

She put the phone back on her lap, not really expecting him to text back, before taking in the sights around her. They'd left residential territory for the most part and were now smack-dab in tourist city. Souvenir shops full of Disney and Tildy merchandise you could pick up anywhere else in the world—or maybe you couldn't, maybe they weren't exactly licensed goods—tried to outdo each other with the lowest prices and restaurants from the fast food staples to the "dessert restaurant" claiming it was better than sex all competed for her attention. There were palm trees crammed in small strips dividing traffic or between lots on occasion, but for the most part, the town made use of every available inch of land.

She hadn't often spent time out here, outside of all the theme parks, when she'd come before. True, they'd always met up with Aunt Frankie—either at a park or at her house—but they'd never lingered outside the gates for long.

Lilac's phone buzzed as Aunt Frankie continued to explain the best route to the park. "This is where you'd turn to go to Disney," she said. "And we already passed Universal. But for Tildy World, you'll want to make sure you get over in time to merge onto this road here." Aunt Frankie bit her lip as she looked over her shoulder and alarmingly kind of forced her way into an already-forming line of cars. They got honked at in return and Lilac winced, checking her phone for the message.

You, too, Li. Watch out, Ms. Tildy Tapir. Lilac Townsend is here to rock your world!

Lilac smiled and Aunt Frankie cranked up the A/C. Lilac had only had a few hours to sort through all her things at her parents' house, but she'd made sure to leave the winter wear she'd stocked up on for life in Minnesota behind. That had left just a few light-weight blouses and dress pants to manage in the Florida heat and she'd only packed a couple of each in her carry-on. Aunt Frankie had helped her steam out the wrinkles the night before. Now she was wishing she'd left the blazer behind, as she could feel the sweat soak through three layers of clothes, if you counted the bra—and she always counted on that thing to hold up all that heft she carried in the front—and that was despite spending virtually all of her time since waking in air conditioning. She didn't remember sweating like a pig whenever she'd visited as a tourist, either, but she'd worn mostly sundresses and shorts and tank tops. Whose bright idea was it to require formal attire from staff forced to toil in a place that reached steaming-vegetables temperatures?

So did your roommates ever at least say hi? typed Lilac.

She stared out the window at the sky, still bright even with her sunglasses on and the car visor down.

Yeah, typed Gavin. *Sort of. They came out of their rooms with bedheads and a guy who'd given one of them head overnight, all four of them acting like I had done them a great disservice by daring to walk around and turning on the coffee maker this morning.*

You told me Ryder was bald. How did he have bedhead?

He didn't. I just thought it sounded good with my setup. Situational humor and all that.

Fail, typed Lilac. *That's about as bad as dorky dad jokes. Gavin has got no comedy game.*

Always back to Daddy with you, isn't it?

Lilac grimaced. *Anyway... Enough about the sex lives of those who are getting some right now.* She frowned. She didn't remember the last time she'd gotten some. It couldn't have been *that* long ago. There was that cute Omega Beta Chi boy she'd done on occasion throughout her time at school. He had to have been the last. But man, that had been back in early April. Had she really been so focused on the end of the school year that she'd "neglected" to take care of those needs?

And Brielle had always insinuated that *Lilac* was the one batting off guys with a stick. True, Brielle didn't always draw the eyes of guys when standing next to her—the brunette was definitely beautiful, just not as curvy or as approachable—but she'd seen that little minx with a drink or two in her, her inhibitions flown. She had always been the aggressor with that creepy ex of hers, always the one asking for the booty call. And it was hard to outdo a guy like that when it came to libido.

Did I tell you there is, in fact, a Mrs. Earl?

Poor woman, wrote Gavin, as if he knew a thing about the man.

"Lilac, not to sound like your mother—my god, I don't want to sound like *my* mother—but are you paying attention? Rodney told me we have to get you a car and charge it to him, but I wanted to bring you the first week or so to make sure you know the way."

Like a student caught with her phone out, Lilac jumped in her seat, sending a quick *TTYL* before shoving the phone back into her purse. "Right," she said. "Sorry."

She stared at the highway sign, trying to commit it to memory. Sure, she'd be able to GPS the best route, but she did appreciate having Aunt Frankie free to guide her. Frankie had her inheritance and probably some kind of funds keeping her afloat, but she occupied her time crafting jewelry and selling it on Etsy. Lilac doubted she made enough that way to support her lifestyle, but it was what made her happy, and with the inheritance, that hadn't really been a concern. Lilac wondered if she'd be one of the few in her family to work a traditional job for more than a couple of years, if she'd ever make enough to afford to support herself without reaching into those investment accounts and incurring fees and paying taxes that she didn't fully understand on the withdrawals.

Still, it felt good to have that there as a backup. Good to be without the student loans that Brielle, Gavin, and even Pembroke bitched about. Just a fresh, clean start and all the world ahead of her.

"There it is," said Aunt Frankie. "Little Lilac's favorite place on Earth."

As Tildy's cheerful grin and waving blue-gloved hand poked out above the "Welcome to Tildy World, Turn Here!" sign, Lilac's heart fluttered, and she felt for all the world like a wide-eyed, innocent child again.

"Ah-one and ah-two, wave your hands and make your dreams come true!"

Lilac stood on quivering legs, tightly clutching her purse in front of her knees with both hands. The sweat dripping from her palms made it difficult to hold on to the strap. She'd made a quick dash to the bathroom after kissing her Aunt Frankie on the cheek and thanking her for the ride, doing her best to touch up the flyaways that had become a permanent part of her hair in this heat, then taking her blazer off and running it under the hand dryer to evaporate some of the moisture. Of course, now it felt warmer than ever on her, but it had seemed like a good idea at the time. And she had made a point of standing beneath an air vent while she waited for the receptionist to page Mr. Stevenson, which put her right in line with a screen playing old Tildy Tapir cartoons, a couple of kids sitting on the floor and staring vacantly at it. One little girl with her hair in two pigtails clutched a worn Tildy Tapir plush—it had to have been a hand-me-down, as it looked just like Lilac's old treasured one, which ought to have been arriving in her boxes sometime this week—and Lilac thought vividly of her own childhood spent staring at the same thing.

"Don't you want to watch a princess movie?" her mom had often asked, holding up a collection of Disney DVDs.

Lilac shook her head. Mama always asked that right at the good part when Tildy Tapir reached her hand out to save Silly Sandgrouse from falling off a cliff.

"I'm here!" Tildy said. "Reach out and wish hard enough—your dreams will come true!"

"You've seen that movie five hundred times, I swear," said her mom, tossing the DVDs onto the coffee table with a sigh. "Yesterday, she asked me if Tildy and Silly could come to her birthday party. I had to tell her they aren't even real, but I don't know if she believed me..."

"Oh, let her be," said her daddy. He looked up from his laptop then to reach forward and ruffle Lilac's hair. "There's nothing wrong with letting her dream, is there?"

"Miss Townsend," said someone from behind her in a deep, burly voice. "It's so nice to finally meet you!"

She turned around, a smile plastered onto her face. "Mr. Stevenson," she said, extending her hand toward him. He stepped closer, taking her hand with both of his and shaking it vigorously.

"Please," he said, "'Earl' is fine."

"And call me 'Lilac,'" she said. "Thank you again for extending me this opportunity. I really appreciate it."

"No, I appreciate *you* freeing up your schedule like this to fill in on such short notice." He held tightly to her hand as he grinned at her, his eyes flicking down and up a few too many times. "But come on," he said, turning and only then finally letting her hand go. "Let's go to my office and we can get started."

"Okay," said Lilac, slipping her purse over her shoulder and wiping the moisture from her palm on her pant leg. She thought she caught sight of the woman behind the reception desk smirking at her as they passed the counter, almost as if to say she'd caught her in the movement, but the woman's attention was quickly diverted by a man in a Hawaiian T-shirt who left his family and a mountain of luggage behind to approach her.

"Tent Tildy is the only official resort of Tildy World," said Earl as they wove through tourists throughout the lobby. Lilac probably knew everything he was about to tell her, like the fact that the guests there were officially called the "campers," but she kept her mouth shut. "We may not match the size or number of resorts they have at those *other* theme parks, but we like to think we have even better service, better amenities." He stopped suddenly and Lilac almost crashed into him as two kids ran across his path.

"I'm so sorry!" said a beleaguered woman running a few steps behind them. "Colin, Embry!"

Earl laughed. "No problem at all, happy camper." Tent Tildy was about as far from a camping experience as you could get, but the entire place was decked out like a wilderness lodge or a camping site, with decorations like fake campfires and plastic pine trees peppered throughout. It was supposed to be like the camp-site where Tildy, Leah, and Silly had spent most of *Tildy Tapir: The Grand Adventure: The Movie,* Tildy's first and most popular feature-length adventure. Lilac remembered shouting at her mom that Tildy and Silly *were* real after all the first time they'd set foot inside.

"Those young campers might just be on their way to Tildy's

Tots," said Earl, pointing down the hallway through which they'd vanished. "The daycare center. I might be needing you to show off your childcare expertise and run to and from there," he said, and Lilac smiled, trying to project a confidence in her "expertise" she didn't quite feel. Earl ran a hand under his chin.

"Maybe I should introduce you," he said, "then we can head to my office and sort out the rest of your duties once we get there." He made a sharp turn, retreating through a dark hall lit with glowing stars all over the ceiling and walls to make it seem like a starlight sky. Lilac got goosebumps as one of the lights lit up across the ceiling—a shooting star. She remembered this hallway and the way it had made her feel. She even remembered being sent to Tildy's Tots. After checking in, you had to crawl through what looked like a tent flap in a hole in the wall to get inside to where the video games, TV screens, and crafting tables were. Earl nodded at the woman behind the reception desk and she nodded back, but she kept her attention focused on the mom of the two rambunctious kids who were practically salivating at the prospect of climbing through that tent hole. Earl opened a door painted to look like just part of the overall mural of a stream and mountains on the wall and stepped inside, ruining the perfect illusion of the picture as he did. Lilac felt a small, ridiculous twinge of jealousy toward the kids at the idea of not crawling through that tent flap hole. As if she'd expected employees to get inside that way.

"Tanya!" said Earl, cupping his hands over his mouth as he dodged a couple of boys running to dive into a ball pit.

"Hey!" said an approaching woman with a deep brown complexion and black-and-purple hair. She was wearing what could only be called a "camp counselor" Tildy Scout uniform and she made Lilac envious of her polo shirt and cargo shorts, even if she had to wear a ridiculous handkerchief scarf around her neck. Her gaze followed the little runners. "No jumping into the balls!" She turned back to Earl, blowing a strand of hair out of her face. It was only eight in the morning and she looked as if she'd been working for half a day. "What can I do you for, Earl?"

Earl smiled and Lilac was sure she saw his eyes rest on Tanya's well-toned legs for just a moment before she put her hands on her hips and cleared her throat. "This is Lilac, the girl I told you would be starting today," he said, reaching behind him and placing a hand behind Lilac's back, shoving her forward. His hand lingered there an uncomfortably long moment, his fingers wrapped around her side as if they were intimate acquaintances instead of a boss and employee who'd only just met.

Don't say anything, she thought. She clutched one hand into a fist and reached the other out toward Tanya. "Nice to meet you."

Tanya shook hers quickly and Earl's hand finally fell from her side. "Same," said Tanya. A woman wearing a marker- or paint-stained apron over her Tildy Scout uniform jogged up to Tanya and asked something about the new shipment of construction paper. Tanya told her to check the back.

"Ah, I'm not sure if we replenished any of your supplies yet," said Earl, rocking on his feet. "Mei left so quickly—hardly gave me any notice—and it's been a hassle trying to pick up things where she left off, let me tell you." Lilac noticed a slight quirk to Tanya's brow as she stared down at Earl. "But Lilac here will get everything you need in quick order, I'm sure." He reached around and patted Lilac's shoulder. She was about to step aside slightly to weasel out of his way when his phone buzzed. "Excuse me," he said, lifting his hand and holding up his finger. He headed toward a corner as he raised the phone up, using his free hand to cover his other ear. Between the Tildy Tapir cartoon playing on the big TV screen and the sounds of kids laughing and shouting, it was certainly hard to hear.

"Hope you last longer than all the other assistant managers," said Tanya. She gazed over her shoulder as a door in the back corner opened up. "We could use some stability and structure around here." Before Lilac could ask any more about that, Tanya excused herself as she headed back toward the opening door, through which Silly Sandgrouse—or more accurately, a person in a

Silly Sandgrouse suit—stepped out, his wing looped through the arm of a woman dressed like a Tildy Scout camp counselor.

"Hey, kids!" shouted Tanya, cupping her hands over her lips. "Look who's come to visit you!"

A bunch of the kids squealed in excitement and jumped up, rushing toward the back corner.

"Don't run!" said one Tildy Scout.

"Form a line!" said another.

But kids were already running toward Silly, the nearest fighting to seize hold of his legs.

"Hey, hey!" Tanya clapped her hands together. "The line is over here! Don't you go scaring off poor Silly with all your love and affection. You know he's sometimes shy."

The kids backed off, some hanging their heads and stomping over toward the wall. When everyone was settled, Tanya extended her hand toward the first one in line and guided her toward the mascot.

Lilac smiled as she watched Silly interact with the girl, tapping her on the back of her head to surprise her and bending down to hug her and poke his long beak amidst her hair. She giggled as her hair stood up and fell back down over and over like a waterfall. "Let's take a picture!" said one of the Scouts.

Lilac checked over her shoulder, but Earl was still on the phone, laughing and pacing back and forth in his dark corner of the room. Something drew her attention: a small sniffle barely audible under all of the noise. A little boy sat in a dark corner behind her, opposite Earl's, a little girl crouched beside him. He kept wiping his face.

Lilac walked over, putting her purse on the ground and sitting on her legs beside him. "What's wrong?"

The little girl who'd been touching the boy's shoulder stared up at her. "Who are you?"

"Lilac," she replied, extending her hand toward them. "It's very nice to meet you."

The girl studied the hand but eventually let go of the boy's shoulder to shake it. The boy just hugged his knees against his chest. They both had the same wavy, brown hair, the same peach complexion with freckles spattered across their noses. "I'm Willow," she said. "This is my brother Landon." She looked to be about eight and her brother was maybe four or five.

"Hello, Willow and Landon." Lilac shifted so she hugged her own legs to her chest in a posture that echoed Landon's. She sat close but not too close, allowing him the personal space he needed. "I'm sorry you're so sad," she said. "I'm just wondering if you want someone here with you. I'll just sit quietly if that helps."

To Lilac's surprise, Landon started bawling and rolled into her, wrapping his arms around her.

She jumped but quickly wrapped her arms back around him, stroking his head. "I'm here," she said, not sure what else to say.

Had some kid been mean to him? She wasn't sure if he was crying over something like a stolen toy or if he felt ill. "Do you feel sick?" she asked. True, she didn't want to catch anything so early into her new career, but she wouldn't get out of this hug before Landon was ready for the world.

"He's fine," said Willow. "He's not... really. But he's not sick."

Nodding, Lilac patted his head again. "Do you want to talk about it?"

Landon shook his head as he buried it against her shoulder. She could count on snot stains in addition to the sweat stains now, but she really had no plans on wearing this dumb blazer to work again anyway.

"He just misses Mommy," said Willow, tracing her index finger on the carpet beneath them.

Lilac patted his back. She knew about kids having separation anxiety when going to school—she supposed it was the same with daycare. Lilac wondered if his mom was an employee at Tildy World or if she'd dumped her kids here this early in the morning to gallivant around the park and enjoy it adult-style, with alcohol and golfing or one of those adult-only retreats. Her own mom and daddy had done that a few times.

"I'm here," Lilac repeated. "And look, Silly Sandgrouse is too!" She shifted her shoulder to try to point over toward the crowd of kids.

Willow snorted. Lilac was surprised such a young child could snort. "Silly Sandgrouse isn't real."

"I'm looking at him right now," said Lilac. "He sure looks real to me."

Landon stopped sniffling and shifted his head just a bit to stare at the sandgrouse, who was dancing now with a boy, both of the kid's hands clutched tightly in the tips of Silly's oversized wings. "Nolan," said Landon.

"What?" Lilac asked.

Willow shrugged and kept tracing invisible designs in the rug. "He thinks all Silly Sandgrouses are Nolan," she said. "It probably is. Nolan says only one can be in each section of the park at a time."

"Who's Nolan?" asked Lilac, confused.

"Our brother," answered Willow matter-of-factly. "And we're not babies. We know he and his friends are inside the suits. He told us."

Good going, older brother, thought Lilac. She thought "Tildy Scouts," the quirky name for employees of the Tildy World resort and theme park, were sworn to secrecy about these things, especially when it came to kids.

"Well, I still think he's real," said Lilac. She watched as the line to see Silly grew shorter and kids dissipated back to the play stations throughout the room.

"Hey," said Lilac, "why don't we go see him?"

Willow shrugged.

"I'll show you why I think he's real," said Lilac.

Willow laughed but stood up. "Okay." She reached a hand back toward her brother. "Let's go see Nolan."

"You mean *Silly*," said Lilac, standing and walking behind them.

"There you are," said Tanya. She bent down and ran a finger under Landon's chin. "Are you feeling better yet, honey?" She stood and almost seemed to exchange a glance with Silly Sandgrouse. *A glance with a costumed mascot.* "Landon was feeling blue this morning," she said. "But Willow's so good at cheering him up, aren't you, honey?"

Willow crossed her arms across her chest and huffed. Lilac laughed a little to think of the little surly girl as the example of cheerfulness.

Dropping Lilac's hand, Landon ran toward Silly, hugging him. "Nolan!" he said, rubbing his head over and over on the creature's tummy.

"This is Silly," said the Tildy Scout who'd walked in beside him.

Landon glared at her as if to say she was an idiot and she actually backed off.

"See?" said Willow. "Even a four-year-old knows Silly isn't real."

Landon turned around and reached a hand out toward Lilac. "Pretty Lilac," he said, "just like Mommy. She's nice to me."

Lilac took his hand. His fingers were so small in her palm. She smiled awkwardly at Silly and chuckled when she realized how tall she'd become since she'd last posed for a picture with the sandgrouse. They were almost the same height now. "Willow and Landon keep telling me Silly isn't real," Lilac said. "But I don't know. You look real to me."

Silly reached a fluffy wing out and wrapped it around Lilac, pulling her into a hug with the little boy. Lilac laughed and hugged him back with her free hand. Then Silly pulled away and pecked her cheek with his spindly beak.

"I think Nolan likes you," said Willow in a conspiratorial tone.

"You mean *Silly*," said the Tildy Scout escort again.

"Sure," said Willow. She reached a hand up over her mouth, but Lilac was certain she saw the edges of a wide grin.

CHAPTER FOUR

Some of the guys Nolan worked with would tell you that the best part of working the suit—the Silly Sandgrouse suit in Nolan's case, but there were others like Tildy Tapir herself and Leah Llama—was the cute women who were interested in posing with the mascots and giving them a hug, oftentimes a glass of wine or a martini in hand. The tipsier they were, the handsier they tended to be, but Nolan had never been a huge fan of those moments. He had to keep acting in character as he squirmed his way out of pinching reach and he'd even had one brazen young woman pose for a picture only to grab him by the junk just as the phone flashed. She had been grabbing "Silly" by the junk, you see, as if that were utterly hilarity. He wished she'd have known that sometimes there were women inside that suit, too—although he doubted someone so shameless would care, really.

Besides, it was the women who'd often dealt with worse, like the frat boys—especially if they wore a human character costume like Queen Animaliao and had their faces and figures on full display.

"He's back," said Cheryl as she sipped her water through a straw. Her head for the "Queen Animaliao's ball" version of the Tildy Tapir mascot rested on a table on the back wall beside

Nolan's standard Silly Sandgrouse one. The ball versions of the characters were often deployed at the same time as the standard ones, so long as they were never seen in the same room at the same time.

The employee break room was the only place in the building they were allowed to remove their suits—unless they wanted to get fired, of course. If anyone had to go to the bathroom before it was time for their break, they had a signal for their Tildy Scout caretaker. Three bops on the Scout's right elbow and a tap on their own heads. Then the caretaker would make some in-character excuse to the gathering crowd and take the mascot by the arm, guiding them back to the nearest break room. None of the other break rooms in the park proper were as big as this one at Tent Tildy, though, so most employees congregated here during longer breaks. Plus, there was food here.

Nolan hated having the resort shift in lieu of being out in the park because Earl, the resort manager, didn't take kindly to mascots taking more than their allotted breaks. Yet the resort shift was what he got more often than not.

"Who?" asked Nolan, his thoughts unfocused as he realized Cheryl was waiting for him to respond.

"Grabby McGrabberson," answered Cheryl, staring Nolan down over her straw as if he were the densest man on Earth. She still had her body suit on, though Nolan had taken his top off to cool down. "He has a season pass and I swear he takes off work in the middle of the week at least once a month so he can have Tildy relatively to himself." She looked over at Jo, dressed to the nines in her Queen Animaliao costume, her long, purple wig affixed tightly atop her page-cut brown hair. Many of the women who worked the characters kept their hair short because it was too hot in all those layers otherwise. "He's the freak who loves feeling up Tildy. Like, he doesn't even know if there's a guy or a girl in there. He's felt up guys in Tildy before. Why can't he just focus on those curves on display in the Queen A costume? When I'm not in it, that is."

"Thanks," said Jo. "I get enough of that, thank you. I also get kicks in the shin from the kids who are still mad about *that one time* Queen Animaliao was possessed and locked up Tildy in the castle dungeon. They shut their ears to any protests that 'I' was under a magic spell." She took dainty bites of her sandwich, looking for all the world like the queen she was playing, even when on break.

"So what's this I hear about Silly stealing some sugar?"

Eddie, dressed in sparkly pastel blues as Prince Beastly, Queen Animaliao's human consort, slipped in beside Nolan and Jo, a plate loaded to the brim with pasta, veggies, and even a sandwich. Nolan felt a bit nauseous looking at it. If he ate that much in costume, he'd hurl.

Shrugging while sipping his water, Nolan then grabbed a carrot stick from Eddie's plate and munched on it.

Eddie unfolded his napkin and tucked it carefully over the front of his regal regalia. He wasn't dumb enough to get sauce on his pasta, but you didn't want to get a crumb on the human outfits in particular, even if they were dry cleaned on a daily basis. "Angie told me. At Tildy's Tots?"

Everyone at the table stared at Nolan, and he gazed over Jo's shoulder to spot Angie, his Tildy Scout caretaker for the day, across the room and eating nonchalantly with the other Scouts. *Traitor.*

"You got some sugar at... Tildy's Tots?" asked Cheryl, incredulously. "One of the kids' Tildy Scout caretakers, I hope?"

"As opposed to a child?" asked Nolan incredulously, although he wasn't angry. Cheryl just liked to tease like that. "I don't know who it was. A new woman in a suit."

"A mom?"

"No," said Nolan, taking another carrot. "She works here. With Earl."

"Ugh," said Jo and Cheryl at once. Jo added, "Poor woman."

Nolan felt something in his stomach sour and he put down the rest of his carrot. He'd eat like a bird tonight—look it up, he'd tell anyone who ever doubted his phrasing, birds eat more of their body weight than horses—but when he was actually in character as one, it was all he could do to get some water down. But he needed it. He wore a sheen layer of sweat in that mascot costume.

Earl really is a sleaze on top of being a jerk, isn't he? thought Nolan. There were whispers.

Eddie bumped his arm. "So is she hot?"

"Who?"

Rolling his eyes, Eddie spun his pasta around his fork. "Your grandma! Who do you think? The girl you were canoodling!"

Jo spurted some of her tea out, causing Cheryl to jump back to protect her costume—not that it was anywhere near the line of fire. "Who says 'canoodling'?" asked Jo.

"I'll show you what that means, my queen," said Eddie, wiggling his eyebrow. "Betwixt the royal sheets of the royal bedchambers."

"La la la, not hearing this," said Cheryl, covering her ears with her fluffy hands. "Queen Animaliao is chaste and pure and her boytoy is just for eye candy."

Maybe so, but Jo and Eddie had left their chaste days behind months ago. Everyone knew they were banging each other.

Nolan shrugged, sipping on his straw until the echoing sound of his empty cup made his whole table jump. "I don't know. I couldn't see clearly. But I think she was... better than average." Like he was about to gush over a woman being hot in front of two women.

"Wow," said Jo. "That might be the highest praise you've given a girl since I've met you."

"Nolan's in love," said Cheryl and Nolan winced. He couldn't hear perfectly through his mascot suit, but he had heard what Willow had said in front of that new girl and he'd seen the woman laugh it off but her face had reddened even so. Leave it to his kid brother and sister to let the hot new girl know who was inside that suit, too, and now she had a name.

But it was just a hug and a fake little kiss atop her head. Was that so weird? He hugged kids and adults all the time. A "kiss" in a suit was just like a fluffy stuffed animal bonking you.

It was just... He hadn't seen Landon look so happy in a while. He'd smiled when he'd looked back at her, had said she'd reminded him of their mom.

He still didn't know what to do about Landon. Their dad was no help. He didn't even believe Landon fully remembered their mom, and he refused to recognize there was any problem. Maybe Landon *had* been too young when she'd died to fully remember her. She hadn't looked much like that hot new girl at all. But he remembered the feeling of warmth and comfort and support their mom had always provided.

"She was just nice to Landon and Willow is all," said Nolan. "So I had Silly give her a big peck and a hug."

He'd been looking for his brother and sister as soon as he'd entered Tildy's Tots. It was hard to see much beyond a few feet, though, so he hadn't noticed them until they'd come toward him, Landon's hand in the woman's. Tanya had introduced her to "Silly" and Angie as Earl's new assistant manager once the kids had gone off to play, but they'd left shortly thereafter.

"What's Willow doing at daycare instead of school?" asked Cheryl. Nolan was grateful for the change in topic. He hadn't gotten *too* good a look at the new girl through the mesh over his eyes, but it'd been hard to miss her curves. Pair that with her business suit and Nolan had felt himself melt.

Not that he had told Angie that. She'd drawn her own conclusions based on a plush-beak kiss.

"Suspended," said Nolan, clearing his throat.

"Yikes," said Jo. "Little wicked Willow strikes again."

"*Dude*," said Eddie, cocking his princely head at Nolan. "What'd she do this time?"

"Hit some boy," said Nolan. He tapped a finger on the table. "Busted his lip."

Tsking, Cheryl bit her own lip. "What does your dad think?"

"He doesn't care," spat Nolan. "As long as he doesn't have to stay home from work to watch her, he couldn't care less." Nolan shrugged. "We get free daycare as full-time employees, so it was just easier to bring her here with Landon."

No one said anything about how that policy typically applied to the parents who worked there, not the older siblings, but everyone knew that HR had made an exception for Nolan when his mom had died and he'd asked to go from part-time to full-time.

Frowning, Cheryl finished slurping her water. DeShawn, her Tildy Scout caretaker for the day and their shift supervisor, was heading over, nodding at a few friends as he passed them. "No," whispered Cheryl. "It can't be time to go back. He can't make me!" She was clearly kidding, although a small part of Nolan knew the feeling.

Nolan grabbed a fresh towel from the rack behind him and passed it over to Cheryl. "Thanks," she said, grabbing it with her furry hand and dabbing it to her forehead. Her short black bangs were soaked and stuck to her pale brown skin. "You know, I never thought that coming to work at Tildy World would be so..."

"Backbreaking?" offered Eddie.

"Skeevy?" said Jo, taking a sip from her drink.

They were seasoned performers. Outside of this room, they were sure to offer words like "rewarding" and "enchanting" to anyone who asked.

"Moist," finished Cheryl, grimacing. She stood as DeShawn arrived at the table and exchanged greetings with everyone there. She pointed at Jo. "I'm Queen Animaliao next week, by the way. I don't care if I end up with my hands all over your boyfriend."

"You can try," said Jo, wrapping her hands around her boyfriend's back. "But I'm going to be his Tildy Scout caretaker."

Of course, thought Nolan. They always found a way to pair themselves together. DeShawn was their accomplice in that matter.

"Well, whoever's in Ball Tildy better watch out for McGrabber-son," spat Cheryl, putting on her head. She waved her furry paw at everyone.

"Next time that guy shows up," said DeShawn, scowling, "I'm

going to show him that Tildy Tapir has her own dreams—and they involve my fist in his face."

Nolan laughed. DeShawn wouldn't do anything. None of them ever could.

When they were performing, they were in character. And Tildy Tapir lived in a world where groping just didn't exist, so they all had to pretend they weren't bothered by it.

———

Nolan wrapped his shift for the day at five and took a quick shower to wash away the buckets of sweat. He knew Landon and Willow would be antsy, Willow watching the clock and promising their big brother would be there any minute now, but he hated making the drive home drenched in sweat. Even so, he knew there was little point in spending too much time drying off. Damp hair and a tinge of moisture worked to keep him cool in the humidity and would dry off within minutes anyway. Besides, when he started off in the extreme air conditioning of the Tent Tildy resort, his hair would practically ice over, prolonging the relaxing chill the dampness provided.

"See you tomorrow," said Angie in the corridor where the men's and women's locker rooms met up. She'd showered, too, and had slipped out of her Tildy Scout outfit into a slinky black dress. *Someone is hitting the town.* Nolan missed those days. Before he'd been in charge of his siblings for most of the day, he'd been too young to do much other than loiter with friends at the mall or game at a friend's all night. It'd been forever since he'd been on a date—at least a year. He hadn't felt like dating anyone seriously since the accident.

But even if he'd wanted to hit the town these days, who was there left to hit the town with? His high school buddies had all moved on to college and/or other parts of the country—a number had even gone to the college he'd had his own eyes on, had joined the fraternity he'd hoped to make the bulk of his college memories at. To tell the truth, he couldn't even stand to look at their social media posts.

He was jealous. He didn't want to be, he loved his brother and sister—and despite his irritation with him, his dad. But he still resented them needing him just a little. He even resented his mom for leaving them—as if she'd had any choice in the matter.

Sometimes he really hated himself for thinking such things.

"You have class tonight?" asked Angie, slipping a tote bag at odds with her nightclub dress over her shoulder.

Nolan nodded. "Not until nine, though. I have to get the kids home and fed first."

Angie offered him a faltering smile. "You're so responsible, Nolan." It was supposed to be a compliment, he was sure, but the truth was, he didn't *feel* responsible. It had all just sort of... happened. The summer after he'd graduated high school. He'd withdrawn from the college of his dreams and enrolled in a few classes per semester at the local community college instead. With the loss of their mom's income, their family couldn't afford to pay the bills, let alone offer any support for Nolan's tuition. Tildy World offered a partial tuition reimbursement program for full-time employees going to school in-state, so it had just been the smart thing to do.

But Nolan was tired of doing the smart thing. "Thanks." He stuffed his hands into his pockets. "Have a nice time tonight!"

Angie had already fished her phone out of her bag and waved back at him, heading toward the employee parking lot.

Nolan checked his own phone and jumped at the time. Landon would be beside himself by now and Willow probably wouldn't be much help.

He decided to take a short cut through the offices off-limits to the guests, or "campers," he supposed his bosses would prefer he say. He made it through nearly without notice—other than that one administrative assistant old enough to be his grandma who always waved when he went by and shouted, "Hello, sweetheart!"— when he turned one corner and slammed into someone, sending a large cardboard box tumbling to the ground, markers and other coloring supplies spilling everywhere.

"I'm so sorry!" said a woman just as Nolan shouted in surprise and then said, "Sorry!"

The woman was already crouched on the ground, flipping the box over and scrambling to pick up all the markers and pencils that still continued to roll across the narrow hallway. The top of her bright blonde head stood out against the deep navy of her blazer like a shining star amidst the deepest dark night.

Blonde hair. Dark blazer. Landon's friend. Nolan got on his knees beside her, grabbing the escaped coloring instruments in fistfuls. "My bad," he said. "I was rushing and I didn't stop to look where I was going."

"No, I... I couldn't see over the box." She looked up. A large strand of her golden-white hair had fallen out from her tightly-wound bun to dangle over one of her alarmingly-blue eyes. She smiled, although she looked exhausted. "I don't know these halls well enough yet. Oh, no, don't—Please!" She reached out toward Nolan's hand and winced as he dropped his handful of markers and pencils into the box. "I had that all organized." She spoke quietly, but it was clear she was holding back.

Raising his eyebrow, Nolan surveyed the hallway and the pencils and markers sprawled every which way. "I don't think it's organized anymore."

She laughed at that—an exhausted, if frustrated laugh.

"Uh-oh! Looks like a classroom of toddlers made their way through here!" One of the HR workers, Brad, Nolan thought, appeared from behind him and gingerly put the toe of one of his shoes down in a small space clear of markers as he made his way through the hall.

"Sorry!" called Nolan and the woman at the same time.

They stared at one another. "Just... Don't worry about it," she said again. "If you have somewhere you need to be—"

"I can help you with this first. It's the least I can do, considering I'm half responsible." Nolan reached a foot out to shepherd a huge pile of the coloring instruments closer to them.

The blonde watched and winced, but she didn't say anything more.

"So," Nolan asked, "how do we get this organized?"

The blonde stared down into the box and looked about to cry. "I guess we don't," she said, tossing a couple of markers in unceremoniously. She growled. "I was supposed to have dropped these off at Tildy's Tots and returned to Earl's and my office by now."

Nolan grabbed more markers and threw them in the box before reaching out a hand. "That's right. You're the new assistant manager. I'm Nolan. Nolan Gregosky." Tanya had said her name, but it'd been too hard for him to hear inside the costume.

"Lilac Townsend." She took his hand quickly and shook it up and down. Her skin was so soft and her shiny nails made her hand look like a hand model's. Actually, she looked like she could totally be a model... A curvy, businesswoman model. Nolan quickly tore his eyes away from her chest and back to the remaining markers, checking himself.

Lilac cleared her throat and he could hear her gathering other pencils and markers as they worked for a few moments in silence.

"What department do you work in?" asked Lilac. "Nolan... Are you... That is, back at Tildy's Tots—"

But before Nolan could answer, someone else said, "Wow. I didn't think I'd have you crawling on your hands and knees this soon."

Nolan froze and looked up, but Earl wasn't talking to him—naturally. He stared down at Lilac's backside. Nolan's gaze flicked there on instinct and he saw her blazer and blouse had come untucked and with the way she was reaching, the very top of her soft curves back there peeked through. Lilac seemed to feel the eyes on her there in that moment and snapped up, pulling her blazer down immediately. "I..." she started. "I'm sorry. There was a bit of an accident. I'm almost finished here."

"It was my fault," Nolan offered. He tossed the last of the

markers into the box and stood, standing between Earl's leering eyes and the blonde on the floor. "We ran into each other."

"I see," said Earl, lifting a mug to his lips and taking a step back. He seemed to sense a threat unsaid and Nolan didn't blame him. After what Cheryl had told him about Grabby McGrabberson, Nolan had no patience for men crossing lines today.

"Hey, Nolan," said Earl, diverting his eyes to a corkboard with reminders and notices affixed haphazardly across it. "Picking up the kids?"

Nice try, buddy, thought Nolan. *She already knows they're my siblings, not my kids.* He didn't know why, but Nolan got the feeling Earl had been trying to make it seem as if Lilac should have no interest in befriending a twenty-one-year-old "father." He turned around to help her lift the box, but instead of letting go, he took it from her. "Yeah. In fact, I can carry this for you to Tildy Tot's."

"Thank you," said Lilac through a faltering smile. "But I don't mind... I mean, it was asked of me—"

"Great," said Earl, slapping his free hand on Lilac's shoulder. "Then you can come back with me, Lilac, and we'll wrap up for the day."

Lilac smiled, but the movement didn't reach her eyes. She looked uncomfortable.

"Do you mind not doing that?" asked Nolan.

Earl's smile dropped immediately, but his hand stayed put. "What are you talking about?"

"She doesn't want your hand on her shoulder," said Nolan, lifting the box and gesturing toward the offending appendage.

Lilac went scarlet red and she stepped out of Earl's reach, his hand shifting casually to his side, his fist clenched. "No, it's..." She looked between Earl and Nolan, and Nolan could have sworn her eyes grew wider when she looked at him, her head cocked as if to tell *him* to knock it off.

Him and not Earl.

"I should go finish that spreadsheet," said Lilac, rushing back the way she came.

She didn't say a single word more.

Earl sipped his coffee loudly, a smirk on his thin, chapped lips. "Thanks for helping out," he said, ignoring everything else that had happened. "Brad, you sonova!" he said, staring over Nolan's shoulder as Brad appeared once more in the hallway behind him.

Nolan could feel his phone buzz and his eyes darted to the nearby clock on the wall. *Shit. I'm late.* He jogged the rest of the way, already rehearsing his apologies to his little brother and sister.

CHAPTER FIVE

When Lilac had gotten home that first day, she'd gritted her teeth and told Aunt Frankie about the amazing time she'd had at her new job over the Indian curry her aunt had made.

"I can tell it's run you ragged, though," Frankie had said. After they'd cleaned up everything together, she'd suggested Lilac make an early night of it while she went back to her crafts table. Lilac had logged on to Facebook and had found herself messaging both Brielle and Gavin. She'd told Brielle nothing but the good parts of the experience so far, of course, and Brielle had just chimed in with "that's great" and "wow" and "so happy for you." She'd had almost nothing to say about her own day back at work—not that Lilac had expected her to when working the cleaning job she'd had every summer for the past six years. Then Gavin had logged on and had had such a bad day at work, Lilac had gone quiet. Gavin almost never complained about anything. He almost always found the good in everyone. If this *Gabriel* who was his boss had inspired this much time complaining, he must have really, truly deserved it. Lilac had let him vent, had done her best to finally be the shoulder he could "cry" on since he'd asked it so infrequently of her, and she'd waited before she'd told him anything negative about her day, though she had been careful to phrase it all as merely a mild inconvenience. She was made of sterner stuff. She just had to keep pretending.

But surely it wasn't any more than any other harried young woman out of her depth in the big bad business world had experienced. She remembered her mom and both grandmas telling her horror stories of the short periods they'd worked jobs—Nana Abigail at her husband's own company. Even being the boss' girlfriend, and then wife, hadn't stopped the assholes from making comments.

In fact, Nana Abigail had always grinned when she'd talked about it, like she'd found the whole thing delightful, especially when she'd still elicited whistles visiting her husband at work well into her forties. Lilac shuddered and instinctively glanced down at her huge rack, finally free of her bra under a sweatshirt to air out for a bit until it was time for bed. Brielle had never understood why she'd had to wear a bra to bed as well, but Brielle had a modest B or C cup. She couldn't begin to imagine the strain these inconveniences caused Lilac. If she had Nana Abigail to thank for inheriting this mess, she wished she could turn around and say "no thank you." Besides the strain, there were the leers, the eyes that always drifted down. And she probably had nothing but more backaches to look forward to thanks to them.

Yes, Nana. It's so flattering to be valued for your boobs. One of these days, Lilac might have seriously considered reduction surgery. But she was too chicken to just yet.

It was late by the time Lilac had logged off—Brielle had logged off ages ago—after she and Gavin had shared complaints about their bosses. Earl for being a grating sleaze and Gavin's boss, Gabriel, for being a total stickler for the rules. After letting it all out, Lilac had slept like a log that first night.

Only to repeat it all the next day. And the next. Well, not quite *all* of it, thankfully. She'd steered clear of any hallway catastrophes, but she'd always felt one wrong move away from disaster. She'd been hugged by her little friend, Landon, more than once when she'd stopped by Tildy's Tots—Tanya had even said he'd kept asking for her—and she'd asked where his sister was, but she'd gone back to school. She hadn't asked about his brother, although every time she saw Silly Sandgrouse around Tent Tildy, she wondered... The comical creature did seem to recognize her, waving at her broadly with his wing, but *all* the mascots waved at her. That's what they did. Child or adult, Tildy and her friends welcomed you with open arms.

Still... She'd been too flustered to appreciate what he'd done for her in the moment—in fact, she was pretty sure that at the time, she'd mostly just been annoyed that he'd shined a spotlight on it—but the more she thought about it, the more she appreciated what Nolan had said to Earl. He looked sixteen, she swore, but he had to be at least eighteen since he worked during the school day, but regardless, he was certainly too young to be *totally* to her tastes, though she had to admit she'd found herself considering that he was good-looking more than once since she'd met him out of the suit. Whatever his exact age, she couldn't believe someone so young had had the balls to do that to the resort manager. But it had worked. Earl seemed to keep a wary, if still brittle, distance from her in the days since, though there was a time or two he'd hovered uncomfortably close behind her and reached a hand around her shoulder to show her something on her monitor or on a table.

But that was just how men were, according to people like her Nana Abigail. Especially men from an older generation.

Not the silver foxes in her head, though. Lilac imagined the man of her dreams—a lifelong bachelor, tired of traveling the world alone perhaps—coming in one day to sweep her off her feet. His eyes would stay glued to her hers, his hand would stay appropriately coy on the small of her back whenever they danced or he escorted her inside, he'd ask her to share her experiences living in Spain... And he'd never tell her how beautiful she was until she was certain he valued her as a person first.

But she knew she was deluding herself. Men like that didn't exist. And how many men that age weren't fathers or at least ex-husbands? If they weren't, they weren't the type to suddenly seek commitment, either. She didn't know if she was prepared to take all that on—and she didn't like being teased for her tastes. So to anyone but Gavin, the idea of dating someone her dad's age was a big, fat *no*. It was easy to deny her "Electra complex" as Gavin sometimes called it—which, ew, no, it was *not* about her own daddy—when her options seemed limited to someone like Earl. Even if he weren't married, she shuddered to think about it.

So far, Lilac wasn't sure there was such a thing as a decent boss out there. Both Earl and Gabriel, the surprisingly-young Chicago marketing firm CEO, had served as fodder for countless texts throughout the week with Gavin—though Lilac continued to fluff her side of things off as an annoyance rather than an obstacle.

"I've got a surprise for you," said Earl on Friday, clapping his hands together as he entered their shared office and startling Lilac. He clearly seemed to be waiting for her to respond, so she swiveled in her chair to face him, fighting her own lips to force a smile on her face.

That seemed enough to satisfy him. "You're walking over to Queen Animaliao's castle today—or you can take the shuttle out front of the resort if you want." He held up the keycard hanging from a lanyard around his neck and slipped it off, handing it to her. "Since your card is still being issued, use this to get in through the employees' entrance and go talk to Gyu-ri—she's in charge of the place. Tell her I sent you and I need the specs on the last few years of the Tent Tildy/Queen Animaliao's ball crossover event."

Lilac's heart thudded as she gripped the keycard in her hand. There was no way she was going to slide his sweat-soaked lanyard over her own head and she had no pockets in her dress pants and blouse to speak of. "There was a crossover event?" she said, letting her Tildy fangirl self fly. She'd never visited the park during such an event before.

Earl seemed to have noticed her genuine excitement bubbling to the surface because the grin he gave her was strong enough to ooze invisible slime. "We stopped a couple of years back. It required too much staff to be on duty, with people needed here to run the place and our own Tildy Scouts needed there to turn the Ballroom into a campsite." Clasping his hands together, he leaned one elbow on a filing cabinet. "But we've been talking about trying it again this fall. And you might be just the organized, productive assistant manager I need to get it all done."

Despite the just barely tangible ick factor of the messenger, Lilac felt something like pride shoot through her entire body. If she were being honest with herself, despite the rose-colored vision she'd painted for Gavin and Brielle when she'd continued to check in with them, she'd felt more like an assistant than an "assistant manager," and she supposed in some ways, she'd expected that, especially this early on. But wasn't the job supposed to entail *some* responsibilities? This was her big shot.

Queen Animaliao's ball had always been her favorite part of Tildy World. True, Tildy was always her favorite, but Queen Animaliao herself had been so beautiful, so poised, so regal. Unlike those other beloved women characters across the way, she was a *queen*, not a *princess*. And now, for the first time since she'd started here, Lilac would be able to set foot in that magical place.

"Okay," said Lilac. She smiled broadly. "Thank you. I'm excited to look into this!"

"Good. Good to see some initiative. Just don't dawdle," said Earl, crossing the room and leaning over her to snatch his empty, brown-stained mug off his table. His tie caressed her cheek and his armpit wrapped around the back of her head.

Lilac's insides went cold as she scooched out of reach.

Earl laughed at her as he straightened up and cradled the mug against his shirt pocket. "I need you here," he said, as Lilac scrambled to get up and push her chair under the table so she could be on her way. "But I sure as hell love watching you go," he added, just as she turned the corner.

Lilac could have gagged.

———

Since Lilac's shoes, though gorgeous, were not the best shoes for walking, she hopped on a resort shuttle headed toward the castle. Sure, there were a few extra stops along the way, but despite what Earl had said, despite what she knew the professional businessperson would do in her situation, she was in no rush to get back.

The Tildy Scout driver was hilarious, and although she swore she caught his eye more often than anyone else in the go-cart, she had no concrete evidence he was doing anything more than taking a look. She supposed she could live with that, especially since he was charming enough, if not more than "cute." When she arrived at the castle, with the footmen and women there to offer the go-cart passengers "assistance" disembarking their vehicle, Lilac felt, for just a moment, like a princess or visiting queen about to dance the day away. She stared slack-jawed at the grand entryway, which was smaller than she remembered, even if she'd been here as a tourist just last summer, and found herself swaying just a bit in place to the classical-style music echoing out from the Ballroom.

"Lilac!" squealed a high-pitched voice.

She turned around just in time to be preschooler-body-slammed by Landon, who wrapped his arms around her thighs and buried his face against her legs.

"Landon?" she asked, unsure why she was running into him here and not at Tent Tildy.

As if to answer her question, Tanya came jogging over from a group of small children lined up across the room against the wall. "Landon!" she said. "What did I say? Everyone has to get in line or no one is going in to the ball."

"I don't want to go to the dumb ball," mumbled Landon from Lilac's legs.

"Hi," said Tanya to Lilac as she approached. She glanced at the keycard in Lilac's hand. "Employees' entrance is over there." She pointed to a nondescript door with a keycard slot next to it, again painted to look like a part of a mural—this one of Tildy, Silly, and Leah dancing in their dresses and tuxedo. Tanya smiled. "I know newcomers can have a hard time finding it." She bent slightly to grab Landon gently by the arm. "Come on now. Leave Miss Lilac alone. She has work to do."

"No," said Landon, squeezing tighter.

Lilac laughed. She hadn't expected to make a lifelong friend with one small act of kindness. "What's wrong, kiddo?" she asked, patting his head.

"Nolan isn't Ball Silly," said Landon, pulling his head back to gaze up at her. "He's almost never Ball Silly."

Lilac wasn't exactly sure what that meant, but she nodded and exchanged a look with Tanya.

"He means he's usually in the regular Silly Sandgrouse outfit and isn't often posted here at the ball," said Tanya quietly. "But Friday's his day off, so he's not here at all today."

Lilac frowned, wondering why Landon had to go to daycare even on a day when his brother wasn't working.

"He has classes all day on Friday," said Tanya, as if reading her mind, but it was Landon she was talking to. She crouched beside him. "You know that, Landon. You have to let your brother to school."

"Why?" asked Landon.

"Your sister goes to school too—and you will too when you're big enough."

"No, I won't." Landon stuck out his tongue at Tanya and buried his head back against Lilac's leg. Tanya sighed and stood up, signaling to her fellow Tildy Scouts to go on without her. They led a bouncing line of children into the Ballroom.

"Everyone else is going to the ball," said Tanya. "That sure looks like fun."

"It's not," spat Landon. "I want to go home!"

"Your brother or dad will get you later," said Tanya. Her nerves were clearly getting a little frayed. She grabbed for his hand. "Now come."

"No!" He pinched Lilac's legs tightly and she actually let out a small gasp.

"Landon!" said Tanya, grabbing him by the torso and pulling him away from Lilac. He held tightly as long as he could, but eventually, she peeled him away. "No pinching!"

"Nooo!" screamed Landon, and then he shrieked. "Mommy!!" He reached both hands toward Lilac.

Lilac stood, frozen, not sure what to do. She'd known it was common for some kids to call teachers and other women "Mommy" on occasion, but it was usually on accident. This child seemed desperate—*desperate*—to believe it was true.

Tanya grabbed his hands and pulled them down. "Do you want to go to time out?" she asked, sternly, but not without patience.

"Nooo!" he shrieked again, this time kicking at Tanya.

"Timeout," she said and started walking away. She stopped suddenly and looked over her shoulder, letting Landon shriek and kick and slap at her, almost without being fazed at all. "Sorry about that," she said. "He's worse on Fridays when he knows his brother isn't here."

Nodding, Lilac bit her lip. "No problem." She watched as Tanya navigated through families who stared at the shrieking kid and took Landon outside. He kept shrieking, "Mommy!" and reaching toward Lilac whenever he could.

Once the echoes in the entryway died out, for some reason, Lilac drew the stares of all the tourists. As if she actually were his mommy and had dumped him on a daycare worker to deal with during his tantrum.

She straightened out her blouse, smoothing the wrinkles Landon had made there. She loved kids—she did—but she was more confident than ever that she'd made the right choice in opting not to spend her days being shrieked and kicked at.

But there'd been something in that boy's eyes that had made it clear this was no mere tantrum.

————

By the time Lilac plopped herself down in her room at her aunt's after dinner, she was in a good mood. Gyu-ri had been so nice, so excited at the idea of working with Lilac to plan the event again. She'd spent over an hour talking to her about it before loading her up with all the data about costs and attendance for the previous events and then she'd had another funny Tildy Scout driver on the shuttle ride back and when she'd gotten to the office, she'd been told by the administrative assistant they shared with a few of the other offices that he'd had to go home early—his wife had had a flat tire.

Lilac had never thanked the skies for someone being inconvenienced by a flat before, but she did it then. She wrapped up her other tasks for the day and even spent an hour poring over the documents Gyu-ri had given her and starting a draft of a proposal for changes to keep it all under budget this year.

Aunt Frankie had surprised her by telling her she was going to take her to get her new car tomorrow and they'd eaten out at a seafood restaurant that was beyond divine—Lilac wasn't sure even the places she'd been to in New England could beat its maple-glazed salmon. It had been Aunt Frankie's treat to celebrate her first successful week of work.

Utterly relaxed in a wicker chair with a plush paisley-patterned cushion in Frankie's guest room, Lilac logged on to video chat with her phone, calling up Gavin and then tagging Brielle and even Pembroke into the chat. *May as well check in with them.*

"Hey!" said Gavin, grinning like a chocoholic kid on Easter.

"Hey..." Lilac cocked her head. "What's gotten you in such a good mood?"

"I went on a date."

Lilac almost dropped the phone as she resettled it on its stand on her desk. "What?? With who?"

"Hmm... Maybe I should wait until I don't have to repeat myself." Gavin looked at the "dialing" screen calling Brielle and Pembroke. Pembroke didn't connect or she rejected the call or something. Brielle's kept dialing.

"*Fine.* Be coy," said Lilac. "I can fill the silence just fine. I was saved by a flat tire today."

"You were... huh?" Gavin leaned back against the couch in his roommates' apartment. "Did some handsome grease monkey save you and sweep you off your feet?"

"Very funny," said Lilac. "It wasn't *my* flat tire. Earl had to go home early to deal with his wife's flat and I had almost the entire afternoon blissfully Earl-free."

"Wow, a whole few hours without that creep breathing down your neck."

"He doesn't *breathe down my neck*," said Lilac, frowning. But dour thoughts weren't going to ruin the day's good mood. "But I mean... Okay, he *is* a massive pain."

Brielle joined the video call and Lilac decided to dump her right into the midst of it. "Bri! Help me!" She smooched the air as if in greeting.

"Miss Big Bazongas is being harassed by Earl," said Gavin. "Like that's such a big surprise."

Brielle looked to be sitting on a park bench on a sunny day—though it was early evening, Lilac supposed. Brielle squinted as she stared at the phone. "Earl?"

"The guy I work for at the resort. He's *this* close"—she pinched her fingers together in front of the camera for emphasis—"to like dropping a pencil in front of me and touching my butt when I'm bent over to pick it up, I'm telling you." She wouldn't tell them that she'd been halfway there—picking up markers she'd dropped herself and feeling him leering at her exposed tramp stamp area.

"Gross," said both Gavin and Brielle at once.

"But he's like... He's walking that line perfectly. Making me feel uncomfortable without ever giving me anything I can actually complain to anyone about." She sighed. "And actually, I don't even know *who* to complain to since he's my boss and I don't know who *his* boss is."

"Tildy Tapir," said Gavin. He was such a smartass.

"I'll be sure to file my complaint to Ms. Tapir, right before I hop over to Disney World like a traitor and tell Gaston how my best friend back home first thought he might be gay when he fell madly in love with his two-dimensional six-pack."

Lilac reached behind her for her metal tumbler she'd filled with raspberry-infused water and took a drink as Gavin and Brielle debated the merits of his unabashedly romantic love for a sexy cartoon.

"Gav always has the worst taste in men," said Lilac, raising an eyebrow at him.

"Says Earl's new girlfriend." Gavin gestured toward the screen with both hands as if to prove his point.

"Don't even." Lilac felt bold then, even cheeky. "Besides, if I'm going to be anyone's new girlfriend, it's going to be the guy in the Silly Sandgrouse suit."

Okay, so she hardly knew him. And she'd kind of been a bitch to him the one time they'd talked—but that had been all her. He'd caught her at a bad time. But in any case, he wasn't her type. Then again, he was clearly fatherly with his siblings, which kind of made her heart melt. And she hadn't been able to stop thinking about how he'd stood up for her to Earl, even if she knew she'd failed to show him her gratitude. He was so baby-faced and he *had* to be younger than her if he was still in school (barring it being graduate school), but he was cute.

And Lilac was in a silly mood, so she thought of her Silly Sandgrouse in shining armor.

"You're joking, right?" Brielle asked. Leave it to Brielle to let out all the air in Lilac's fun balloon.

She laughed anyway. "Only half-joking. He's pretty hot once you get that doofus head off."

"There are actual live Gastons walking around the much better park next door," said Gavin, holding a finger up to stop Lilac's automatic defense of Tildy World as the superior park before she could start, "and you're telling me Silly Sandgrouse is hot. Reality check, Li."

"So how's your love life, Gavin?" asked Brielle, shifting gears.

Lilac drank from her tumbler again. That was fine with her. Lilac wasn't in the mood to get all defensive about Tildy World again.

"Don't ask," she said, snorting. Gavin never had any luck with guys, so she was quite sure even this "date" he'd hinted at having wouldn't lead to much.

"That bad?" asked Brielle.

"That *good*," answered Gavin. He smiled.

"Okay, now I want to know more." Brielle seemed riveted. And Lilac needed to know what was up, too.

Gavin shrugged. "My roommates have a date here almost every night." He paused to count on his hands. "Okay, between them, there's been a guy here every night."

"You must be getting a lot of sleep with all that... activity," said Brielle, wincing.

Gavin looked like he was about to vomit. "Yeah, well... One of their 'dates' decided to hang on my couch with me before heading off to the bedroom."

Brielle's nose wrinkled. "Please tell me you didn't hook up with someone your *friend brought over to bang*."

Pretending to be shocked, Lilac gasped before giggling. Everything was so funny to her this evening. She wondered if it might have anything to do with the few glasses of Pinot Grigio she'd had with dinner.

But Lilac knew Brielle ought to know better when it came to Gavin. Since when did he ever "hook up" with someone after one date?

Gavin lifted one hand and then the other, pretending to "weigh" his options. "Is it really so bad if he didn't make it to the bedroom and decided to take me out for coffee instead?"

Still, Lilac couldn't help teasing him about it. "Aw, coffee. Not a drink. Not the bedroom, but coffee... Sure."

"I don't exactly have a bedroom to invite a guy to," said Gavin before lowering his voice. "Until I settle in permanently, I have to entice a guy to invite me back to his place."

Laughing, Lilac clapped. "So innocent, this one."

"Besides," said Gavin, rubbing a finger over his cheek, where a five o'clock shadow had taken root, "I'm not a one-night-stand kind of guy. So excuse me if I wanted to get to know him a little better."

Brielle seemed flustered. "How's the job, though? Think you'll have an offer by the end of the summer?"

Lilac shook her head as Gavin's face fell. *Poor guy.* "I don't know if I want an offer. I'm thinking of this as a resume-booster and hitting the classifieds in a few weeks to see if I can find something else in Chicago." He pointed over his shoulder with his thumb. "Otherwise, I'm just out of here."

"Oh, but what about coffee guy?" asked Lilac in an obnoxiously sweet voice.

"Shut it," replied Gavin, but he looked like he might crack a smile. Lilac loved seeing him so happy. It was too soon to tell if this would last, but he needed a pick-me-up like a little romance after all those texts he'd exchanged with Lilac.

"Why?" asked Brielle, not up for teasing. She and Lilac didn't often tease each other. "I thought you were really excited about working there."

"His boss is a huuuuugggeee asshole," said Lilac. "Like, we've been having a competition for whose boss is the bigger asshole all week."

Gavin pointed right through the screen at her face. "No, you win that, hands-down. If Gabriel starts grabbing my ass, maybe there'll be an actual comparison." He paused, contemplating what he'd said. "No, even then, you'd win. I don't know if Gabriel is married or not, but at least he's hot."

Lilac gasped. "Oh *my god*, you never told me he was *hot!*" Maybe it was just the wine, but that changed things, didn't it? Gruff, strict, and hot... Yummy.

"*Anyway*," said Gavin, clearly not agreeing that changed things at all. "Bri, you've barely told us what's up with you. How's your week been?"

Something strange flashed over Brielle's face. "Not much going on. I've been cleaning. I've applied for a few jobs. My sister and mom are at each other's throats just about every day." She shrugged. "I... Well..."

Lilac hugged a decorative pillow she'd grabbed from the chair matching hers to the side of the desk. "Oo, please tell me this is boy-related."

Gavin brought a finger to his lips and said, "Shush!" as Brielle squirmed in her seat. *Bingo.*

"It *is*!" said Lilac.

"Not really," said Brielle. "I mean, this guy I clean for is kind of super sort of gorgeous."

Gavin looked like he'd have to check the dictionary for that description. "'Kind of super sort of gorgeous...'" He chuckled. "That's even better than the compliments you first paid Daniel when he caught your interest."

Brielle crossed her arms and pouted sourly. "Don't remind me."

"Details, details!" demanded Lilac, pounding a fist against her pillow.

Brielle shrugged ever-so-innocently. "Nothing to tell. I clean for him. We had a misunderstanding the first day and I thought I would die from embarrassment, but... We're cool now, I guess?"

She's hiding something. "What kind of misunderstanding?" asked Lilac.

Brielle stared off into space and ran a finger over her cheek "He's in a wheelchair and he was grumpy about me seeing his comic book art and I just... sort of crossed some boundary with him? I don't know."

Gavin snatched his phone and his face went off-screen for a minute as he spoke. "Wait a minute. Archer Ward?"

Lilac was lost. "Is that some kind of codeword I'm supposed to know or... some zoning info?"

Brielle's mouth hung open. "How did you know?"

"Super hot, disabled, comic book artist, from your hometown," said Gavin, tapping his head. "I have a good memory for these kinds of details. Besides, he's only the current lead artist on *The*

Mystified. Kind of sort of a big deal in comics circles. Kind of." He was echoing Brielle's words back at her.

"I didn't know," said Brielle.

"Oh my god, Brielle's going to date a celebrity!" shouted Lilac.

"Kind of," said Gavin.

"We're not dating," said Brielle. Her brows furrowed. *She's keeping the juiciest parts to herself,* Lilac thought.

Lilac could feel the excitement bubble up through her wine-coated bloodstream. Then a thought struck her. "But if he's disabled, how would you two—"

"*Okay*," said Brielle, raising her voice. "Change of subject. Has anyone heard from Pembroke?"

What kind of segue is that? "No," said Lilac and Gavin at once.

"I DMed her earlier this week," explained Brielle, "and still, nothing."

"Ditto," said Gavin.

Lilac didn't think she'd ever spoken to Pembroke without either Gavin or Brielle there as well. Was this silence unusual? It hadn't occurred to Lilac that it would be. "I haven't reached out," she said, "but I included her on a few texts and she never responded."

"You're the closest one to campus," said Gavin to Brielle. Her family was from like an hour away from their college. So were Lilac's and Gavin's—in different directions. "She was a commuter, so she lives nearby, right?"

"You want me to drop by?" Brielle asked. She seemed unsure. "I don't know..."

"*Somebody* ought to," said Gavin. "If it was simply a matter of her wanting to be left alone or being busy, she should just send us a brief text saying as much."

Lilac shook her head. *Talk about being overprotective.* "Give the girl some space. We just saw her less than a week ago. Maybe she's not even the type to care to stay in touch after graduation."

"We promised we all would," said Gavin.

"Yeah, just like every other group of college classmates in the universe." Sighing, Lilac nodded at the camera. "How long do you think we'll even stay in touch? We'll get even busier with jobs, maybe husbands, maybe kids..."

"You're starting to sound like my grandma," said Gavin.

Their conversation lulled into silence for a moment and Lilac thought grimly of a future without her friends. She couldn't let that be.

Brielle broke the silence first with an exhausted sigh. "I should get going."

"Yeah, where are you?" asked Lilac. "Looks like a park." Since when was Brielle the "great outdoors" type?

Brielle seemed to get the implication and shrugged. "Just getting some fresh air."

"Wow, pigs must fly these days," said Lilac.

"Check in with me next week about Broke," said Gavin. "And sweep that comic book artist off his feet!"

"Look up how you have sex in a wheelchair—" started Lilac, but Brielle quickly and pointedly ended her end of the call.

"*Li*," said Gavin. "You're drunk. Go home."

"I *am* home," said Lilac. "Home for a while anyway." She blew him a kiss. "But you're right. I'm about to pass out."

"Good night," said Gavin. "Get out to the beach this weekend! Soak up some sun."

Lilac grabbed a bottle of sunscreen and shook it at the screen. "I'm missing my handsome single dad to apply this."

"*No*," said Gavin. "Just no."

Lilac wasn't sure if she turned off the call or if he ended it first. She woke up several hours later after falling fast asleep in her chair.

CHAPTER SIX

"Willow, please turn that down. I'm trying to work."

Nolan's dad rubbed his temples at the breakfast bar that functioned as his desk, the TV in the living room behind him blasting *Frozen* for the second time that day already.

Willow ignored him, singing along with Elsa as she twirled around the living room, a hairbrush in her hand acting like a microphone.

Nolan's dad looked up to face his eldest son, who was busy flipping two grilled cheese sandwiches in a frying pan. "Don't you get sick of hearing that at work?"

"Other theme park," said Nolan, scrambling to turn down the heat and turn on the overhead fan. He always managed to burn these.

"I want to go to Disney World!" whined Landon as he trotted into the kitchen. "I hate Tildy—ow!"

Nolan looked up to find that Willow had twirled right into Landon, knocking him over. Landon stared up in shock at the other three members of the family before remembering to turn on the water works—or at least screech and pretend tears were falling.

"Willow!" snapped their dad. "Stop that *right now* and say you're sorry."

Willow's face fell as she stopped spinning and Elsa kept singing her power ballad behind her.

Sighing, Nolan's dad got off his stool, bending down to pick up Landon and pat his back. *You're just going to make him want to cry all the more*, thought Nolan as he flipped the first and then the second sandwich over once again. *It's the only way he manages to get any attention from you.*

"*Willow*," said their dad sternly, staring down at her over Landon's shoulder. "What did I say?"

"Sorry," mumbled Willow quietly. She clutched the hairbrush she was supposed to be using to brush her still half-wild hair tightly at her side. "*He* walked right in front of me."

Landon screeched louder and Nolan turned up the fan as the sandwiches began to smoke heavily before he flicked the stove off entirely.

"I don't care," said their dad. "Turn off that TV and sit down at the table. *Now*."

Glaring up at their dad, Willow's bottom lip trembled, but she didn't say anything. Their dad brought Landon over to the table and plopped him into his chair as Nolan plated the sandwiches, scooping some of the canned tomato soup he'd heated up on the stovetop into two bowls for the kids.

"No!" screamed Landon, clutching their dad's shirt tightly. "No! I'm not hungry!"

"*Landon*," said their dad, "it's time to eat. Now let go—Ow! Fuck!"

Nolan felt his insides go cold as their dad spun around to see Willow gleefully staring up at him, the hairbrush raised in her hand. From the way their dad cradled the back of his head, Nolan could only guess she'd smacked him with it.

"Daddy said a bad word," she sing-songed.

"Give me that," said their dad, snatching the hairbrush away from her. "Timeout! I thought you'd be too old for that by now, but no." He snatched her by the hand and she tugged away, screeching. "I have *had* it with your misbehavior, young lady!"

Nolan turned off the fan and crossed the kitchen, trying to head off this family disaster as their dad tossed the hairbrush on the table, making Landon's eyes go wide as he jumped in his seat.

"Let me go!" screamed Willow, kicking vainly toward her dad. "You meanie poopy brain!"

"Stop!" said their dad, tugging on her arm but trying not to rip it right out of its socket. With her acrobatic twists and turns, she wasn't making it easy for him. "The more you misbehave, the longer your timeout will be!" He closed his eyes and snapped to no one in particular as the TV boomed. "Can someone please turn that off?"

Nolan did as asked and the room fell into a strange, uncanny silence, the likes of which his house almost never knew during the day when one or both kids were awake.

Willow sniffled and Nolan was sure the tear that fell down her cheek was real, even if she'd known exactly what she'd been doing when she'd smacked their dad on the head.

She'd been getting his attention, just about the only way she knew how.

Picking up where he'd left off, their dad tugged her toward the room she shared with Landon. "Inside!" he said, loud enough for it to carry down the hall to the kitchen. Noticing his brother in distress, Nolan stepped behind Landon, who was really crying now —but quietly. That's how Nolan knew it was real. Landon was pretty quiet when he was actually sad. Nolan ruffled his hair and brought him his lunch.

Their dad slammed the door and Willow shrieked, a pounding coming from inside the room, probably from her punching or kicking it.

"Stop that!" said their dad sternly. "If you don't stop that *right now*, you are *never* getting out of that room!"

"*Dad,*" said Nolan, trudging down the hall. He froze.

His dad was holding tightly on to the door knob with one hand, leaning against the wall with the other, his head pointed down and the redness in his face streaked with tears. Willow continued to shriek and holler.

"I can't do this," he said quietly, under his breath. "I can't do this without you."

She can't hear you, thought Nolan. *She's dead.*

He let go of the knob and walked down the hall, stopping in front of Nolan. The door opened almost immediately after he'd let go, Willow stumbling outside into the hallway, her face scrunched and her fists clenched at her sides.

Their dad looked about to say something to Nolan, but he closed his mouth and patted his shoulder instead. "I need to work today," he said at last. "I'm going out while they eat—and please get them out of here this afternoon."

"Dad, I have schoolwork to do—" started Nolan.

"No!" Willow pounded her feet on a worn patch of the carpet. "We all go out together on Saturdays! It's Saturday dinner day!"

"They *have* been looking forward to this all week, Dad," said Nolan. "You know that."

His dad shut his eyes and lifted a hand to cut him off as Willow shrieked behind them. "I can't," he said and he went into the kitchen long enough to grab his keys and pat Landon on the back before exiting out to the driveway.

"Nooo!" shrieked Willow again. "Liar, liar! You promised!"

"Back into your room!" said Nolan sternly, pointing down the hallway.

Trudging back down the hall, Willow slammed the door behind her.

Leaning on the wall, Nolan thumped the back of his head against it several times over. The house went eerily quiet again until he heard the scraping of a spoon on a bowl and he snapped back into the moment, returning to the kitchen to make sure Landon didn't spill any soup on his clothes.

————

Nolan looked up from his laptop every few seconds to make sure Willow and Landon were still doing all right in the playpen in the mall's Kidz Cool School center. (The irony of the business having both "kidz" and "school" in its name was never lost on Nolan.) He hated to "reward" Willow especially and even Landon for their temper tantrums that he'd known had just been to get their dad's attention and he didn't like to spend the money on yet more daycare, but the Cool School was more like a playground anyway. If it allowed him some sanity and relative quiet—beside the background buzz of the people talking throughout the mall and the endless trickle of the nearby fountain—then so be it. He didn't dare leave the mall behind entirely and find a quiet park or corner of the library because Willow was already on probation at the Cool School and if she got into one more physical fight, she was going to be banned entirely. Nolan knew she was more likely to behave if she saw him through the glass front wall of the daycare sitting there with the other moms. Of course, he kept to himself. He had no energy to organize playdates and discuss sales on kids' clothes with moms and dads a decade or two older than him. Besides, with playdates, they usually expected you to reciprocate at some point, and he didn't know how they'd fit even one more screaming child into their small three-bedroom ranch.

"I'm supposed to have your room by now," snapped Willow once earlier this week. *"I'm tired of sharing!"*

Yeah, and I was supposed to be in a dorm room so you could have my room, thought Nolan, although he hadn't said it aloud. He slapped his cheeks to wake himself up and focused on his assignment on the screen. It was going to take a few more years than planned, but he hoped to have a degree in computer science eventually.

He wondered if an IT job would offer free daycare to his brother and sister, though. But then he wondered if at this rate they'd be teenagers by the time he got out of Tildy World and into a "real" job anyway. He sighed and saved his work, closing his laptop lid and staring off at the Starbucks at the edge of the nearby food court. He glanced over his shoulder. It took him a moment, but he spotted both Willow and Landon, each with their own little friends. They were smiling. He hoped they'd stay that way.

He thought about asking the other people at the table to watch his stuff, but they were engrossed in their conversation and even if they had been willing, he doubted he could count on them to actually keep an eye on it. As he slipped his laptop into his backpack and slid his arms through the straps, he stared at one woman in particular, a sandy-haired woman in her forties wearing a colorful wrap over her white tank top and white pants. She reminded Nolan of his mom. Their faces were different, but the way she carried herself. He remembered being in Kidz Cool School himself over a decade ago—back when he'd been an only child, long before his mom had convinced his dad that they were financially stable enough to have more, that she'd always wanted a house full of children—and she'd be sitting here with her friends, talking. Every time he'd looked through that glass wall, she'd been here, just steps away.

Now... She was out of reach. Forever.

His heart ached at the thought and he shook his head, dragging his feet toward the Starbucks line. It wrapped around the corner, but he knew they moved fast. Besides, he had nowhere he needed to be. His dad had never texted to say he'd meet them for dinner after all. He probably thought it "bad" enough he'd be stuck with the kids on his own the next day. Heaven forbid he actually care about spending time with all three of his children and not just with the little two. Nolan was good for cash flow and taking screaming kids off their dad's hands. He knew what his dad thought of him well enough.

His breath caught painfully at the thought as he reached the end of the line and stepped in place behind two bubbly women who were mid-conversation.

"I should have you drive us both to the beach tomorrow," said the older woman, a redhead with short hair. With her sandals and a sunhat worn even inside, she looked about ready to head to the beach now.

"I want to practice the route to Tildy World first," said the other woman—and at those familiar two words, Nolan snapped to attention just as she happened to look around and catch his gaze. It was Lilac, the pretty new assistant manager at the resort.

"Oh, it's you! Hi!" Lilac positively beamed and Nolan looked over his shoulder for the person she must have recognized.

Laughing, Lilac grazed her fingers against his upper arm to get his attention. "You! Nolan, right?"

Nolan stared blankly for a second. *How did she remember me? We only met the one time out of costume.* "Yeah," he croaked out eventually. "Hi. Lilac." He nodded as if confirming her own name to her.

Stupid, stupid...

Cocking her head, Lilac chuckled. "You almost made me think I'd just acted like an idiot with a complete stranger," she said. "But I guess it's hard to forget a face after you nearly slam into it." She pointed to the woman beside her. "This is my aunt, Frankie."

"Hi," said Nolan, taking hold of both of his backpack straps. Then he thought better and extended his hand toward the woman —she didn't really look old enough to be this beautiful young woman's aunt, but she had a funky "eccentric aunt" vibe about her regardless. "Nolan Gregosky."

"He works at Tildy World, too," said Lilac. She chewed her bottom lip and Nolan had to drop her aunt's hand like a hot potato to stare down at his feet. It seemed necessary to stifle the unexpected raging fire that shot up from his groin at the sight of Lilac looking contemplative. "You're Silly Sandgrouse, right? I never did ask for sure. Well, I don't think I saw you again after that disaster in the hallway—"

"Disaster in the hallway?" asked Frankie. "Intriguing. The mysteries of the corporate world, I tell you..."

Nolan snapped his eyes back up to find Lilac's aunt sizing him up and down, almost like she knew what was going on in his mind right then and there and she found it amusing. Or even... attractive. She was plenty attractive herself and could make a good cougar—he had always been drawn to women just a bit older than himself, but just a *bit* older than himself. He hated to imagine what people would think if he started dating someone the age his mom would have been. Like he had mother issues buried deep down inside him.

He shuddered. No, he liked sophisticated and slightly more world-weary *young* women like... Like the gorgeous blonde in front of him. Just standing there, doing nothing in particular, she left his high school girlfriends in the dust.

Lilac's face seemed puzzled. "Sorry, is that some secret the Tildy Scouts are sworn not to tell? Oh my god, I just realized I might have been asking you to break a cardinal Tildy World rule."

Nolan laughed as he snapped back to the present. "No, sorry, I just... I didn't get much sleep." He yawned and stretched, as if to prove his point. Really, he was trying to still his rapidly-beating heart. "I'm usually Tent Tildy Silly, yeah. At least during the day Sundays through Thursdays." He scratched the back of his neck as they all moved forward a couple of steps and a few more people got in line behind him. This was him trying to remain casual, trying to remind his treacherous organ that he had no time for dating and little chance with a girl as hot as her. Maybe pre-accident Nolan would have been up to the challenge. Pre-accident Nolan had had game, if he did say so himself.

"I thought my kid brother and sister already spilled the beans on that one anyway," he said, shrugging. "You're not supposed to talk while in character, you're not supposed to go on social media telling the world there are actually people inside of those fluffy mascot suits, as if no one on Earth could have figured that out for themselves, but no, there are no Queen Animaliao's guards who sweep in at malls miles from the park to arrest me for leaking that info. Although if anyone asks, my official position is that I'm Silly Sandgrouse's 'friend.'" He winked, rubbing both hands up and down his backpack straps.

The aunt laughed and nudged Lilac, who'd gone scarlet and stared down at her feet, clutching her hands in front of her. "Lilac believed they were real long after she got the memo about Santa Claus being fictitious."

Nolan guffawed, loud enough that the people in front of Lilac and Frankie turned to look at him.

When Lilac's face darkened even more, he realized Frankie hadn't been kidding.

"I-I knew," said Lilac, suddenly more childlike than he ever imagined her being. Even on her day off in casual clothes, she looked like a curvy fashion model made flesh. "I just... loved Tildy and I didn't want to believe the truth."

Nolan laughed, more gently this time. "Who can blame you there?"

That brought Lilac's head up from studying the decorative pattern on the linoleum tiles on the floor. She smiled and Nolan actually stumbled a little, leading him to turn around to apologize to the guy he'd banged with his backpack.

"Thank you," said Lilac quietly. "Most people tease me endlessly for that." She glowered at Frankie, who laughed.

Nolan suddenly wanted to be different than everyone else. He made a note to never tease her about Tildy. "Is that why you got a job at the resort?" asked Nolan, trying so hard to keep things casual. Even the presence of her aunt and the endless crowd around him wasn't doing much to quell his aching heart. *No*, he told himself. *Bad heart. Stop it.*

Lilac beamed. "Yup." She exchanged a knowing look with Frankie, who shook her head and then turned around as the barista called her up. Lilac studied Nolan then, staring him up and down. He could feel himself shrink under her eyes, but she wasn't looking at him hungrily, he was sure of it. More like... deciding what to make of him.

"Li," said her aunt over her shoulder, and she rushed over to add her order.

Nolan ordered after them and felt like an utter idiot when it came time to pay. Ever the smooth operator, he pulled his wallet out of his pocket and coins went everywhere, some rolling under the lip of the counter, others scattering to a stop at people's feet. Both Lilac and Frankie joined in the crowd of people who helped him gather it all, and he thanked them as his heart beat wildly and he rushed to pay the barista to put the whole stupid stunt behind him.

He shuffled over to the pick-up counter beside Lilac and Frankie and clutched his backpack straps tightly, willing the eyes around him to stop staring at him. Eventually, they did—except Lilac's.

Nolan cleared his throat. "So, tourist or native?"

"Huh?" asked Lilac.

He exchanged a nod with Frankie then, like she got it. *Native?* he wondered about the aunt. "You loved Tildy World as a kid, right? Were you a tourist or did you grow up around here?"

"We both grew up in the Midwest," said Frankie then, reaching across them both to grab her drink and a cardboard cup sleeve. "A few hours from Chicago."

Lilac glared at Frankie then, like she'd betrayed her somehow by sharing that information. Frankie must have at least been a long-time resident, though.

"Thanks," said Lilac to the barista as she grabbed her own drink. A bright pink tea. She'd waited that long in line at Starbucks for a tea?

He was surprised that they both lingered even after getting their drinks.

"But I went to Tildy World *all the time*," said Lilac quickly, as if eager to "defend" herself, from what, Nolan didn't know. His own triple-shot espresso came up and he thanked the barista before stepping away. "We visited Aunt Frankie a lot," said Lilac, falling in step beside Nolan.

"That was just an excuse," said Frankie. She peered at them over her coffee cup. "She *really* wanted to visit Tildy."

Nolan made his way back to the table overlooking Kidz Cool School and to his amazement, Lilac and Frankie came with him. He put his bag down by his feet as he sat down and they both sat across from him.

He didn't know what to think. Lilac clearly wasn't hitting on him with her aunt there—or maybe the aunt *was* hitting on him and using her niece as a wingwoman? She *did* keep staring at him, a mischievous smile on her face. He cleared his throat as he sipped his drink, a jolt of caffeine shooting straight down to his toes.

"We got season passes," said Lilac proudly. She actually seemed *proud*.

"Despite living in Chicago?"

"*Near* Chicago," said Lilac before sucking on her straw. "You've never heard of it," she said through muffled lips before he could ask more. The scarlet of those lips popped against the green of the straw, the sensuous curve of them as she puckered and sucked demanding his attention.

Okay! Okay, calm down, boy. Mall. Aunt. Kids over there. Nolan stuffed down his feelings until he felt they might burst. But at last they were down, good and down, and they wouldn't jump back up to the surface to bother him again. Nope. He took a jittery sip of his drink.

"But a season pass is only worthwhile if you go at least five times a year," said Nolan. He remembered the days when he'd begged for a pass from Tildy World—from all the parks. But his parents had insisted he'd get tired of the parks if he went that often. He'd applied to work there part-time as a teen almost to prove them wrong. But sure enough, seeing one of them daily had certainly made the place lose its luster.

"We usually went that often," said Lilac.

"*Each year?*" Nolan hadn't meant to sound so accusatory.

Lilac shrugged, but something flashed over her eyes and Nolan wondered if she felt he was attacking her for it.

"That's awesome," he said quickly, although he was still

shocked he was sitting across from someone who could afford to fly there that often.

But it had been the right thing to say. Lilac brightened immediately and put her cup back down in front of her.

"So are you staying with your aunt?" asked Nolan.

She nodded and Frankie beamed, reaching into the small purse Lilac had strapped across her shoulders to pull out a set of keys. "And starting next week, I'll only be her host, not her chauffeur," she said. "We just got Lilac her own car today. A beautiful, brand-new hybrid."

"Wow," said Nolan, and he genuinely meant it—on so many levels. He was envious to be sure, but something unexpected also jumped up from inside him. Five vacations a year—and that was just the ones he knew of, to Tildy World of all places. A brand new car. He knew Lilac probably had a decent salary at her job—if she lasted, as Earl's assistant managers almost never did—but he doubted that was the reason behind the shiny new car.

Cradling his cup, he thought of the fifteen-year-old clunker with its rust spots and shoddy transmission that awaited him and the kids outside. Of course his dad had taken the new car. And by "new," he meant bought five years ago and used even then.

There was no way anything was happening with this girl. No way on so many levels.

He took another sip.

"Landon!" screamed a high-pitched voice, followed by a quick, "Hey! Stay inside! You can't—"

But Nolan turned around to see Landon outmaneuvering one of the Cool School workers to slip under the velvet rope they had to keep kids inside.

"Landon, you know you can't leave until playtime is over—" started Nolan, but the little boy made a beeline for Lilac instead, hugging her and nuzzling his face against her breasts.

Lucky kid, thought Nolan sheepishly. "Landon, don't hug people without asking."

"It's all right," said Lilac. The slightest smile made her lips curl as she looked down at him and began stroking his head. She looked like a diva in a painting. Beauty personified. Nolan had to look away—*fast*.

"Sorry," Nolan said to the Cool School worker who'd followed Landon. "He can be slippery." He looked at the clock posted atop a pole in the middle of the food court. "But it's about time we get going anyway."

The Cool School worker stared at him wearily and grabbed Landon's hand. "We have to check him out there," she said. "Protocol."

Nolan understood. The place took photos of the parent or guardian who'd brought a kid to the center to make sure that was the same person they sent the kid home with—unless other arrangements were agreed upon ahead of time. "I have to get my sister, too, anyway," said Nolan, standing and sliding his backpack back on. He watched as Lilac ruffled Landon's hair and smiled down at him. It struck him in that moment why Landon might have kept calling her "Mommy"—he'd heard about his behavior the day before at the Ballroom. She was maternal, this sexy fashionista who had the whole world in front of her. Way better suited for the job he'd been saddled with than he was.

"It was so nice to see you again," he said, his voice cracking halfway through. He glanced at Frankie. "And to meet you." He paused, thinking of what to say. "I... Come on, kiddo." As he grabbed for Landon's hand, the Cool School worker took the boy's other one, as if ready to engage in a tug-o-war for control of the kid if Nolan turned out to be less-than-savory. "Well, I'll see you at work," he added to Lilac.

Lilac locked her eyes with his and just about melted him into a puddle at her feet. "See you soon!" She waved at his brother. "Bye, Landon!"

Landon hesitated, clearly wavering between putting up a fight to stay near Lilac or just giving up before the battle began. Nolan squeezed his hand to remind him what would be the easier choice.

Just then a flurry of activity drew Nolan's attention. He looked up. Through the glass wall, he saw Willow standing there, practically smacked up against the glass, the long hair of a girl next to her threaded tightly around both hands as she yanked and pulled.

There goes Kidz Cool School as an option.

CHAPTER SEVEN

Lilac sipped on her tea and stared at Nolan through the glass wall of the oddly-named Kidz Cool School. It resembled a playground more than a school, though she could see a lot of interactive exhibits she imagined were intended to stimulate learning. But they looked more like games than anything.

Her hometown mall certainly had nothing of the sort—no daycare of any kind that she knew of, let alone one like a miniature theme park. She wondered if it was a metropolitan thing or more specifically a theme-park-town thing. She'd yet to uncover the non-touristy area of Orlando, assuming there was such a thing.

"He's cute," said Aunt Frankie, swirling her stirring stick, though she had to be finished with her coffee by now.

"Hmm..." Lilac's eyes flitted back to Nolan specifically. She struggled to remember why she'd found him so irritating when he'd bumped into her. She'd been frustrated after a tense first day. That had been the crux of it, really. At least it seemed he'd gotten over how bitchy she'd acted. His backpack looked heavy as he stood there, a sibling in each hand, a grim look on his face as the mother of the other girl seemed to be shouting at him while an employee of the Cool School tried to play referee. She mostly faced the irritated mother, who clutched her crying daughter to her side, but every few minutes she looked over her shoulder at Nolan, eventually guiding him toward the exit.

"He could probably use your help," said Frankie. "Rodney said you're a wonder with kids. I always thought you'd make a good teacher..."

Lilac pinched her lips into a straight line. *No. You're not thinking about that now. This is what you wanted. This is a good thing.*

"Oh, sorry," said Frankie. "I almost forgot—it's just... You always used to ask me if there were any good jobs at Tildy World. I'm surprised you didn't do one of those educational programs where you work at the park while taking classes and get some college credit."

"That's Disney," said Lilac. "And I didn't have time. I was too busy getting accreditation... Spain was the only semester I could afford to take off."

"Well, as much as I love Orlando, if the choice was between here and Spain, you made the right one." Frankie brought her phone out of her purse and scrolled through the screen.

"Why did you settle here?" asked Lilac. "I don't think I ever knew."

Frankie looked up from her phone and gazed off dreamily. "The heat," she said. She cocked an eyebrow. "That and the distance from your grandmother."

"But there are plenty of warm places far from Grandma Violet," said Lilac. "Spain has a pretty nice climate, for one."

"Yes, but your grandmother would love to visit Spain. She'd love to visit just about anywhere. Except Orlando. She finds it touristy and gauche." She laughed and set her phone down, standing before grabbing her coffee. "You done?" She motioned toward Lilac's empty cup.

Lilac nodded and Frankie took both their cups, looking around for the recycling, which was way back by where they'd gotten their drinks.

Turning back to Nolan, Lilac watched him as he left the Cool School, bowing slightly in apology, and dragged his little brother along with his stomping sister over to a corner. He bent down to her level and looked her in the eye, but she refused to look at him. He dropped Landon's hand to gently place a finger and thumb alongside Willow's face to push it back toward him.

Lilac had no idea when in life she'd get around to having kids—as much fun as somebody else's could be—but man, if her insides didn't melt seeing him like that. True, he still looked a bit like a kid in her eyes—albeit an older teen kid—but he would make a gorgeous, loving father one day. She was sure of it.

And she didn't realize how fast that would make her heart beat.

What about the worldly traveler you have your heart set on? she reminded herself. *How would you travel that much with kids?*

Lilac shook her head. So he was cute. And responsible. And fatherly. He still looked like a frat boy and frat boys weren't good for much beyond a few weeks' worth of fun.

Then again, she could do right now with a few weeks' worth of fun.

She dove into her purse for her mirror, checking her flyaways and quickly letting down her hair to redo it into a bun again. She had some pretty crummy granny panties on and her bra had seen better days—her stuff had arrived a couple of days before and she had more to fill Frankie's guest room closet with—but she wasn't about to do anything wild before they even had an official date. Besides, he had his brother and sister with him. Even on the weekend. Lilac wondered how busy his parents could possibly be.

She stood as Aunt Frankie approached the table again. "Maybe I *will*—" Lilac started, her eyes flicking toward Nolan, who now stood, grabbing both kids' hands again and leading them away.

"You'll what?" Frankie nudged her, a knowing look on her face. "Go after him. Quick!"

Lilac opened her mouth just as her phone buzzed. *Gavin has another date today*, she remembered, and thought of how she'd asked him to keep her up to date. If Gavin needed her, that was more important than this frat boy—and besides, he was clearly busy.

"Oh," she said, her face falling as she saw the screen. It was a call. From Earl.

Frankie frowned. "What's he want? It's your day off."

"I better see." She took a deep breath. *He's your boss. Be professional.* "Yes? Lilac speaking," she said. Nolan and the kids were gone now, lost to the crowd.

"Oh, good, you answered!" said Earl. Even just the sound of his voice was enough to send her impulse to gag into overdrive. "Night shifts and weekend shifts are all here," he said, referring to the other managerial crews that reported to him but took over when he had time off. "I thought I'd introduce you."

"Now?" asked Lilac. She regretted it almost instantly.

"*Yes,*" said Earl, clearly disappointed. "Unless you're too busy to come in. I can't offer you overtime, but this is a casual gathering, and everyone else managed to be here."

Then why didn't you warn me earlier instead of springing this on me at the last minute? He *had* mentioned wanting to introduce her to everyone else, but he hadn't said when. "No, it's fine. It's just that I'm not dressed for work—"

"*Casual,*" repeated Earl. "I'm sure whatever your pretty little self has on right now will do just fine."

Lilac swallowed as she looked down at her tank top and Capri pants. They weren't exactly cheaply made, but even so. She'd have worn it to Tent Tildy as a "camper," but not on the "Tildy Scout" side of things. Frankie studied her quizzically as she grabbed her own phone off the table.

"All right," said Lilac, taking a deep breath. "I can be there in thirty."

"Great! We're meeting at Tildy's Campfire," he said, referring to the resort sit-down restaurant. Lilac felt immediately better, knowing she wouldn't be headed back to that office with him.

It didn't bode well for her job if she couldn't stand to be in that office with him, but he just kept walking that line.

"See you there," said Lilac as she ended the call. She explained the situation to her aunt.

Frankie shook her head. "This sets a bad precedent," she said. "What if he wants you to come in on your days off all the time?"

Says the woman who's never worked an 8-5 in her life, as far as I recall, thought Lilac. She swapped her phone for her new set of keys in her purse. Her aunt had met her at the mall after the car lot, so they each had their own ride now. "Then that's what I'll have to do," said Lilac. "I'm here because I want to work here." She pushed visions of Minnesota and all her teaching degree work out of her head. "This is what I need to do."

"Okay," said Frankie, but she didn't sound sure. "Let me know if you're going to be very late. I don't want to worry about you getting lost in the dark on the way back."

Lilac grimaced. That, unfortunately, was the least of her worries.

———

Dinner went well enough. Earl and the weekend day guy, Christian, talked a lot—*a lot*—and that left the rest of the table rather quiet. But everyone else seemed nice enough. The one awkward moment had been when she'd sat down and shaken everyone's hands. When she'd finished, Earl had elbowed Christian, who, like Earl, had a wedding ring on his finger, and said, "I told you she was cute, didn't I?" Christian hadn't said anything, just chuckled, but she could feel his leer on her after that. Both their leers. The only other woman there, Jillian, one of the two night managers, had glared at Lilac then, as if it had been her fault and not the men's.

So Lilac had mostly just listened instead of talking. She knew Brielle especially thought of her as a talker, but that was only when she was comfortable around everyone around her. She was so completely uncomfortable at this table, the most she'd done was place her order. She hadn't drunk alcohol, though everyone else at the table had. Her head still ached a bit from the mini-bender she'd gone on the night before.

Earl had had several drinks. The longer the dinner went on, the louder and more talkative he became.

"Well, I suppose I've been away from the desk for long enough," said Christian. He and the other shift managers shared a single desk around the corner from Earl's office and he was supposed to be on duty. "Unless, Jillian, you want to get your shift started early?"

Sipping her water, Jillian raised her eyebrows. She'd stopped at just one cocktail.

"I'll take that as a 'no,'" said Christian. He stood. "Nice to meet you, Lilac. Welcome to the team." He winked as he grabbed his suit coat and Lilac tried to smile.

"Let's see if you last longer than any of Earl's other girls," mumbled Jillian from behind her cup. Lilac looked at her, but no one else seemed to have heard it and everyone else got ready to go their separate ways.

Lilac fished her phone out of her purse in an effort to look busy and unconcerned, despite how nauseous she was starting to feel. She was ready to make her own excuses, make up a fake message if need be, when she saw a text Gavin had sent a couple of hours before, probably right after Earl had called.

Call me? it asked. *I had a shitty day. A shitty date.*

Lilac felt guilty. She quickly texted her apologies and excuses, promising to call him when she got back home.

It took just a bit for Gavin's text to arrive. *It's okay*, he wrote. *I'm feeling better. But do call me. Brielle bumped into Pembroke and some shit is going down!* He stopped typing.

She'd almost forgotten about Pembroke. She was actually *fighting* with Brielle? Was Pembroke capable of fighting with anyone?

"No, it's on Tildy," said Earl to the dispersing group. He grabbed the server's arm as she passed and Lilac saw the way the young woman's face soured at the touch. "Charge it to my account," he said. "Add fifteen percent for yourself." He didn't let go of her arm. "Give me a smile and you can make it twenty percent."

She smiled then. Like a serial killer about to commit her first murder.

But it did for Earl and he laughed, letting go of her arm. She hustled away.

"Nice meeting you, everyone," said Lilac as she stood and pushed in her chair. She clutched her phone in her hand as she picked up her purse and slid it over her shoulder. "I have to go." She shook the phone, as if it would explain her need to depart.

"Wait, wait," said Earl, dabbing his lips with his napkin. "We have to discuss what you did yesterday—sorry I had to duck out early."

Lilac looked between Earl and Jillian, almost as if hoping Jillian might help her figure out what to say. Jillian just rolled her eyes and stared across the room at a screen playing Tildy Tapir cartoons.

Thanks, thought Lilac. "I'll tell you everything Monday," said Lilac, dropping her phone in the purse and fishing out her keys.

"I thought your aunt gave you rides," said Earl. "That's what Tara told me anyway."

Wow, so you do remember you have a wife? thought Lilac bitterly. "New car," she said, quietly.

"Nice! Hope she's a beaut." He stood, chortling as Lilac nodded and turned to go. "But since no one's here to pick you up, you can stay a bit. It won't take us long. Just twenty minutes or so."

Lilac caught herself about to sigh. *In and out*, she told herself. *Just update him on the event and get in and out.* "Okay," she said, trying hard to keep the reluctance out of her voice.

"I'll be at my desk in an hour if you need me," said Jillian then, and Lilac wasn't sure if she was speaking to Earl or Lilac herself. Earl answered, saying his goodbyes, but Jillian's eyes caught Lilac's knowingly, and Lilac felt something deep in the pit of her stomach warning her it wasn't too late yet.

———

Earl usually hung his suit jacket up on a coat rack the minute he walked through the office door, but today he had on a polo shirt and khakis. His arms were quite hairy—the grays and blacks poking out even more among the tanned, leather-like skin. She usually liked gray hair, but on *Earl*...

"Have a seat," said Earl as he closed the door behind them. He gestured toward the visitor's chair across from his, but Lilac purposely misconstrued his gesture and went to her own desk, booting up the computer and gathering what notes she had from the file in her desk. She wanted to get this over with quickly.

"Gyu-ri was really enthusiastic," said Lilac. She felt a flutter of actual excitement despite the warning bells going off in her head. The office was so empty. They'd passed Christian on the way—he'd been on the phone—and there was one secretary back near the door that separated the office from the showier camp-themed hallways of the resort—but it was so quiet here without most of the staff. "But she was realistic about the parts that had been less popular with the guests, and I thought if we operate on a smaller budget this time—"

"Whoa, whoa, slow down," said Earl, chuckling. Instead of sitting down at his desk, he strode over toward Lilac's, hovering behind her. Lilac felt an iciness down her spine, and it wasn't from the air vent above them. "I appreciate your enthusiasm—that's one of the reasons why I hired you—but there's a time and a place for work."

Lilac stared blankly up at him. *Was this not exactly the time and place for work?* True, he'd called her in when it wasn't her shift, but... "You said you wanted to talk about what I did yesterday," she said. "And that it wouldn't take long."

Grinning, Earl put both his hands on her shoulders. He hunched over and his hands began to rub and squeeze her muscles. His breath reeked of alcohol and his hands were rough and as cold as ice on her mostly-bare skin. "Relax first," he said. "All work and no play..." His right hand slipped under her tank top strap, under her bra, down to the skin of her breast.

For a second, Lilac froze.

Then she exploded.

"What the *hell* are you doing?" she screamed, slapping his arm hard. When he didn't let go, simply staring at her, shock clear as day on his face, she wheeled her chair back and slammed it into his abdomen.

He grunted, his hands falling to his stomach as he backed away.

Lilac snatched her purse where she'd left it on her desk. She could feel tears forming beneath the hot burn of the anger that burst through her brain, but she swallowed and gritted her teeth, determined not to let him find any tears on her face.

"Where are you going?" Earl snapped, all playfulness out of his voice at once.

She didn't answer as she made her way to the door.

Earl jumped in between her and the door, blocking her from the door knob.

"*Move*," said Lilac with a strength she didn't really feel.

"Okay, okay, message received," he said, as if he were the reasonable one in the room. "I'll leave you be, but I'll remind you that *I'm* the boss here and we've let girls go for far less than this—"

"Less than *what*?" demanded Lilac, crossing her arms. "All I did was tell you to fuck off."

"In not so many words," said Earl, grimacing and cradling his stomach.

Aw, poor baby. She wanted to gag.

"*Move*," said Lilac again.

"If you want a job here, you'll watch your tone with me," said Earl, straightening. "Do you think you're the first one who's led me on like this?" Something flit across his face then, something more sinister.

Lilac actually backed away a few steps, more from an instinct to put distance between them than a conscious thought.

"*Led you on?*" Her molars ground together. "If you—If you think I care about this job now," she said, but tears began falling then. She *had* cared about this job. It had been all she'd ever wanted. She'd thrown away everything she'd worked for for this job.

"Oh, I think you care. Your aunt made it very clear to my wife how much you care."

Asshole. Someone needed to tell that wife to divorce his sorry ass. Someone needed to tell the police, HR, the—

Lilac froze. Could she go through all that? For creepy innuendos and one touch too far? Could she talk to Frankie about it, her parents...? Could she admit to everyone what a colossal fuckup she'd made, letting him corner her alone despite the warning bells going off in her head?

Would the police even believe her? She looked down at her outfit and all the skin showing, the way her too-big boobs popped tightly against the too-small tank top. She'd heard horror stories about "police help" before.

And if she wasn't the first... How the hell hadn't this asshole been fired?

What was *her* testimony going to do to change things?

"Please let me go," said Lilac, staring at the floor. Her voice was quieter now.

He didn't say anything for a minute and then she heard him turn the handle and open the door. "Okay," he said, but he grabbed her arm as she passed. "This was just a miscommunication," he said. "I thought this was something you wanted and now you made it clear you don't. Okay? That's all this was."

Lilac would have laughed if she didn't feel like vomiting. *How the hell could you have thought this was something I wanted?* She shrugged her arm away and he let her go.

"I'm married, okay?" he said. "You know that. I wasn't asking for anything serious. This is nothing. Nothing serious."

She started walking away.

"I'll see you Monday," he called. "Have a nice weekend!"

As she passed Christian, still on his phone, Lilac felt the tears fall in earnest. She flung a hand to her mouth as a sob escaped her lips and she ran—actually *ran*—around the corner.

Lilac told her aunt she'd gotten food poisoning at dinner, ignored Frankie's joke about how Tildy Tapir's promise to make dreams come true had never included vomiting—and spent much of the evening vomiting for a different reason entirely.

She hadn't been raped. Not even close. Hell, Nana Abigail had told her about the men who'd slapped her ass at Papa's company and she'd laughed it off like it that was simply how childish men were, like they were just little boys reaching into the cookie jar for one more cookie their moms said they couldn't have. Nana had faced this type of behavior and then some. Sure, that had been ages ago, but...

Who could she tell? Who would believe her?

Gavin. She stared across the open bathroom door toward her purse, which she'd left on her bed. *He'd want to fly here and kill Earl. He... He'd be a knight in shining armor, but he has his own problems and he could put both his job and mine in jeopardy.* No, she didn't feel like telling him.

Her parents were in the Caribbean, but her daddy would want to kill the guy, too.

Frankie would probably insist they call the police...

No matter who she told, her job would be over. The whole reason she'd thrown everything away would be over. Her dreams would be over.

He'd promised he'd leave her alone now...

For an irrational moment, her eyes fell on the worn Tildy Tapir plush by the pillows on her bed. She'd been in the box with her things along with a note from Grandma Violet that she hoped "Tildy Tapir makes your dreams come true."

Lilac vomited again, all joy lost and all dreams broken.

When Lilac got on Skype the next morning, she wanted to ask

Gavin to tell her about his bad date, to offer support where she could. She wanted to keep him distracted—keep herself distracted—with whatever tale he had to tell about Brielle and Pembroke going at it—squabbling while she'd had that filth's hand down her bra—but she'd started crying almost the second she, Gavin, and Brielle had all exchanged their hellos.

"Whoa," said Brielle. "What's wrong, Li? Are you okay?"

"I'm... I'm sick," said Lilac, brushing tears from her eyes. "I... I got food poisoning last night."

"Aw," said Gavin, and he seemed genuinely concerned.

"That sucks," said Brielle. She didn't seem dismissive, but she seemed distracted. Her eyes kept gazing off to the side of her bed, where there was a stack of thin books.

"What are those?" asked Lilac, grabbing a tissue and wiping her nose with it.

"Graphic novels," said Brielle.

"*Somebody* got to go on a date with her hot comic artist client last night," said Gavin. He winked at the screen.

"It wasn't a date, really." Brielle laughed and tucked a bit of hair behind her ear. "Or it sort of was, but it was *not* just the two of us and oh my god, Lilac, did Gavin tell you about Pembroke?"

Lilac ought to have cared about Pembroke. Part of her really did want to know what had gone on and why she was the only one out of the loop. But then the thought struck her that she knew *exactly* why she was out of the loop because she remembered what she had been up to while this had all gone on and so she started sobbing harder.

"Lilac!" said Gavin, all sweetness. "What's wrong, honey? This can't just be food poisoning, can it?"

"It is," said Lilac, choking a bit on her words.

"*Lilac*," said Brielle. "What's going on? Seriously."

Lilac dabbed her eyes, deciding part of the truth would suffice. "I shouldn't have come here. I shouldn't have blown away all the hard work I'd done to become a teacher, I shouldn't have thought I could be happy here—"

"Told you," snapped Brielle, entirely unhelpfully. "I could have told you you'd regret it even before you went off like that on a whim."

"Brielle, I know you mean well, but that's not really helpful," said Gavin.

Lilac could feel that bitter anger burning behind her eyes again. "So I was stupid? Does that make you happy? For me to say I was stupid to do this stupid thing?" Her breath hitched.

Brielle actually had the audacity to look concerned. "Whoa, okay, look, I'm sorry. Let's just... Take deep breaths. You've only been there a week. Give it time before you make another rash decision—"

Lilac wanted to throw the phone across the room and scream. Instead, she grit her teeth and smiled sweetly, saying, "Yup. That's me. Rash Lilac. Look, I have to go. Talk later. Bye," and then swiped the call off before they could respond. She settled for tossing the phone—hard—into her purse, grabbing her keys and heading toward the door.

At the entryway, she hesitated, not knowing where she was going. "I'm going for a walk!" she cried over her shoulder to Aunt Frankie, who was at the kitchen table, reading off her tablet. She was sure she could find a park or a beach or something. She didn't care that she was still in yoga pants, a tank top, and a sweatshirt. She didn't care about applying sunscreen or grabbing a sunhat.

"Are you sure you're feeling well enough?" asked Frankie. "Maybe you should rest today so you're ready for tomorrow."

"I'm fine," lied Lilac, slamming the door behind her.

CHAPTER EIGHT

Nolan had a tradition after work on Sundays, even though it was technically the first work day of the week for him.

He'd take his time after ending his shift and follow a routine: showering in the locker room, stopping by someplace to get dinner for himself, and then heading to a bar—usually alone—and just enjoying the last hour or two he'd have to himself for the rest of the week.

Not a bar at Tildy World, of course. He got as far away from there as he could for this moment of quiet.

There was a bar within a twenty-minute walk from his house. He'd often park the car at home and just walk there—his dad, if he knew what he did, certainly never called him on it. He seemed to realize that Sunday was the one day he needed to take charge of Willow and Landon, the one day he could manage to step up to the plate and give his eldest son some peace. They often weren't even home when Nolan dropped off the car after his shift. Their dad couldn't cook even if his life had depended on it, so he usually took the kids out, even if just for fast food.

Nolan thought about all the schoolwork he still had to complete—even with a part-time class load, he felt out of his depth on top of full-time work and the kids—and the kid who'd spilled grape juice on Silly Sandgrouse today. He often did that, thinking of Silly in the third person, separate from himself, as if he weren't the one inside experiencing it all. As if he went on some heat-induced hallucination and floated outside of himself. Or maybe that was just the Tildy World rules rubbing off, his classification as Silly Sandgrouse's "friend" stamped on everything from his badge to his paychecks.

"Being part of Tildy's human entourage really pays," Eddie had said *once recently, holding up his check. "To think the poor girl has to* buy *friends despite all the fans she has."*

Nolan had thought about inviting Eddie and Jo to come with him today, but they didn't work weekends and no doubt had something more romantic in mind for wiling away their Tildy-free hours.

He could have asked Cheryl or DeShawn or even Angie, who sure could have used it since she had still been freaking out about the grape juice when they'd parted ways, sure the dry cleaning would come out of her paycheck, but as was often the case Sundays, something inside him told him no, this was *his* hour. He needed to be alone today.

He'd only been twenty-one half a year, but he'd already gotten into a routine at Thommy's. It was a very different routine than sneaking into an older friend's place and sampling their home collection—less fun and more sobering. That was an odd description for drinking in a bar. Sobering.

But it was. Despite the chatter and the soft overhead music, it was the only time he could feel his mind empty, the only time he could think.

"The usual?" asked the cute bartender, Claire, as he walked in and sat on his usual stool.

"Yeah," he said, nodding and returning her smile. She'd slipped him her number once and he'd put it on his phone, but he hadn't called.

Man, he had no idea why he hadn't called. He hadn't been with a girl in... It was like a punch to the gut to think about it. Why hadn't he called? She popped the top off his Coors and parked it in front of him. *I should call her*, he thought as she stood in the glow of the neon sign behind the bar that highlighted her sharply dark eyes.

The only problem was the question "your place or mine?" always had to be answered with "yours." And then he had to get back in time to get breakfast for the kids, make sure Willow got on her bus, and take Landon to work with him.

Well, that was a mood killer. Just thinking about what he'd need to do put a damper on things. That was why he'd never bothered calling her. He could never focus his thoughts on one point, even when a cute girl like Claire stood right in front of him. Nolan thanked her and then purposely stared off to the side at a signed baseball encased in a three-dimensional frame. Claire stepped aside, picked up a cloth, and started wiping some glasses.

"Did I tell you I have a boyfriend now?" asked Claire nonchalantly. Nolan thought he caught something there, like she was trying to gauge his reaction.

"That's great," said Nolan, putting his beer down and cradling it. He smiled. He meant it. It was his fault for being too slow. And besides, he found it actually didn't bother him much.

"Yeah..." said Claire, almost lost in thought. She responded to a guy calling for a top off at the other end of the bar and then made her way back toward Nolan ever-so-casually. "He's a fireman," she said, as if he'd asked and there hadn't been a lull in the conversation. "What about you, hot stuff?"

"What about me?" Nolan ran his thumb over the condensation on his bottle. The coolness felt like a balm to his brain, one that let the tension flow out from his body.

She put her hands on her hips, cloth and all. "Are you seeing anyone yet?"

She *had* asked him if he'd been single that night she'd given him her number a few months back.

"No," said Nolan. He stared at the beer instead of the cute girl. "No time. No energy." He took another sip.

"Bullshit," said Claire. "A man your age can *make* the time." She picked up another glass. "You're an odd one, Nolan."

"You're not telling me something I don't already know."

Claire smirked. "Odd but nice, not like..." Her gaze drifted around the room and landed on several of her customers. Then she put her elbows on the counter and leaned toward Nolan, giving him such a prime view of her cleavage that he had to immediately and pointedly lock gazes with her eyes instead. She smiled, as if she knew exactly what she'd just done. "Can I ask you to help me out?" she purred.

Nolan nodded, slowly, not following her. She leaned back and pointed over her shoulder to a dark corner of the bar, where someone—a blonde woman—had her back to them. "She's been here almost since opening. She's not being belligerent, but I've had to ask her to slow down. Some of the guys have sat down with her and she's screamed at them to keep moving and... I just want to make sure she's okay." She straightened up again. "And *you* I trust to make sure she's okay."

Nolan cocked his head, trying to get his eyes to adjust to the dark gloom of that corner. His *need* to be alone was eradicated almost the instant he heard she was being harassed. "I can keep an eye on her," said Nolan, grabbing his beer and walking toward the other end of the bar. He hadn't meant to sit at her corner booth— just near it, to make sure she didn't pass out or try to drive away drunk and to leer at anyone trying his luck and heading toward the booth. He understood the need to be alone more than anyone.

Although as he caught sight of her profile and the shapely way she filled out her sweats, a tiny part of Nolan could see exactly why more than one man had tried his luck, all evidence pointing to her wanting to be alone or not.

"Lilac?" he said out loud before his brain even caught up with what he was seeing.

She whipped her head around, all fire and fury. Her brow was furrowed, her hair in a bun behind her neck but somehow still mussed, her eyes bloodshot and puffy.

"Go the fu—" started Lilac, somewhat wobbly even in her seat, but then her facial muscles relaxed. "I know you," she said.

All instincts to respect her need to be alone thrown out the window, Nolan slipped into her corner booth, sitting across from her. "It's Nolan," he said. "Lilac, are you okay?" It was a stupid question. She obviously wasn't.

"No," she spat. She didn't scream at him to go away, just wrapped her hands around her shot glass, which sat next to a half-empty martini. He gazed across the room at Claire. How many drinks had she let her have before she'd cut her off?

Watching them, Claire nodded and turned, seemingly satisfied that Nolan would do no harm and that Lilac didn't mind him being there.

Nolan slid around the corner booth to sit closer to Lilac but stopped the instant she flinched as he arrived right beside her. He scooched to give her some more space. "Is there anything I can do for you?"

She scoffed. "Nope." Then she stared at him. "You're cute," she said, leaning toward him and wagging a finger. "Too cute, damn you. And too damn relaxed all the time."

"Uh, thanks," said Nolan, simultaneously flattered, confused, and concerned. If she were sober, he'd tell her she was drop-dead gorgeous, but he had a feeling she already knew that anyway.

Lilac scooched closer toward him and tried to whisper, but her voice came out loud and harsh. "Will you have sex with me?"

That got the attention of half the bar, even Claire.

Just then Lilac wrapped her arms around Nolan's shoulders and he grabbed them, gently, pulling them down. "You can ask me that later," he said, not about to entirely dismiss her in case there was some part of her that actually meant it. He chuckled despite himself. He was actually considering it with her if asked properly. He'd actually *make time*, as Claire had said, to have sex with her.

Even if he knew nothing could ever come of it.

His chest ached at that thought.

"I want sex now," she whined, rolling her head back. "With a cute boy. A gentleman."

"I'm half that, baby," shouted some guy—a regular Nolan sort of recognized—from a few tables over. He lifted his mug to her as if to toast the statement.

"Fuck off," said Nolan as Lilac giggled.

"You're not Silly Sandgrouse," slurred Lilac in the general direction of the guy who'd offered. "I want to fuck Silly Sandgrouse."

Half the bar burst into laughter. Nolan supposed that made absolutely no sense to anyone there, as he hadn't gotten into the habit of discussing the particulars of his job with the Thommy's crowd, not even with Claire.

"Lilac, why don't we go for a walk?" asked Nolan, pulling out his wallet. He had a ten in there—that was usually enough for his beer and the tip and it was really all he could spare. He came to Thommy's mostly to think, not to get drunk. He stared at Lilac's empty glasses.

"I got it," said Lilac, swiping a hand at him and fumbling in her purse. She pulled out a hundred-dollar bill and tossed it down.

"*Whoa, whoa,*" said Nolan, snatching the bill after it landed, as if he could stop Claire from seeing it and expecting what had to be at least a fifty-dollar tip. "Don't you have anything smaller?" He slipped out of the booth. "Let me ask Claire for change."

Lilac caught his arm. "It's fine," she said. "Leave it."

Nolan stared down at the hundred. He didn't know Lilac's salary—he imagined it was far better than his—but that was almost a full day's work for him.

"Leave. It," said Lilac firmly but with a twinge of playfulness to her tone. "The bartender is nice. She's cute." She leaned toward his ear. "I'm not gay, but she's super cute." She giggled.

Nolan turned to watch Claire, who was pouring for another customer, and his thoughts went wildly to the image of adorable

Claire kissing gorgeous Lilac, Lilac's light hands running through Claire's thick, dark hair, Claire's dark ones undoing that blonde bun.

He felt himself blushing, and Lilac might have noticed because she started giggling. "I know what you're thinking," said Lilac.

"Okay," said Nolan, tossing the hundred on the table. He looked at his own wallet and considered pulling the ten out but wondered if Lilac's one hundred would no doubt cover both his beer and his tip and then some. It wasn't that he was cheap, but—

"It's for yours too," said Lilac, giving him permission.

Nolan cleared his throat. "Thanks." He stared at his still only half-drunk beer and slipped his wallet back into his pocket. He slid out the free side of the seat and once he'd walked around to Lilac's end of the booth, he reached a hand out toward her. She slid her purse strap up her arm more than once and grinned, taking his hand, standing before stumbling right into his arms. She buried her face against his chest. "Fuck me," she said quietly—almost sadly.

Damn, stop putting images in my head!

He took a deep breath. "Let's go for a walk, okay?" He nodded at Claire, who gave him a nod back.

Stepping away from him, Lilac started rummaging through her purse. "My car," she said. "I can't leave it here."

"Oh yes, you can," said Nolan, and he put his hand atop hers, lowering it back into the purse until she dropped the keys. "Let's just go walk, okay?"

"Okay," said Lilac, giggling. "Walk me to your car and your apartment."

Nolan struggled to get the door for her with one hand as she leaned into his other arm. One of the guys catcalled as they exited and Nolan fought the urge to go back and slug him.

Lilac got ahead of him and stumbled into the parking lot. "Which one is yours?" she asked, her voice shaky.

"No car," he said. When she didn't seem to respond, he leaned forward and grabbed her hand. "Let's go to the park, okay?"

"Okay," said Lilac, still clearly out of it. "Tildy Park, baby!"

"No, not Tildy World. The *park* park. It's down here."

She stumbled after him. "It's a little dark," she said, looking around them. They approached the edge of the park and Nolan made a beeline for a bench under a tree to the side of the entrance. There were still kids out—and sometimes his dad brought his own siblings here—and the last thing they needed was Lilac making a scene.

"What time is it?" asked Lilac as she sat down beside him.

Nolan pulled his phone out of his pocket and checked it. "9:30." Landon would already be in bed.

Again, thoughts of his siblings sobered him, forcing his head clear of all the images of this gorgeous blonde sans sweats flashing before his eyes.

He would never, not in this kind of situation, but *damn*, if she wasn't making it hard for him to think clearly.

Lilac gazed up at him conspiratorially. "Are we fucking in a park?" she asked, chuckling. "So brazen," she said. "I love it." She grabbed for her zipper on her hoodie.

"Whoa, whoa, whoa," said Nolan reaching for her hand. "Slow down."

Clutching his hand with both of hers, Lilac slammed it against one of her breasts. It was so large, it spilled out beyond his palm. He'd never cupped a breast that large before.

Her eyes looked so earnest, so hungry.

He recoiled, yanking his hand away.

"You don't want me?" she asked, sad. "I thought you all wanted me. My boobs. My big, big, heavy, annoying boobs."

"What? No," he said. She looked crushed. "No, I *do*!" he said without thinking. "I just don't want you like this."

Lilac leaned back against the bench, practically spread-eagling herself. "Fucking take me and make it all go away. That's what you all want, right? Well, maybe I want it, too. Maybe that's what I need. Fuck love, fuck commitment, just fuck me."

Nolan watched nervously around him to see if anyone had heard. The nearest people—a family—were some distance away at the playground, but he caught the dad's head turning toward them and the guy's gaze lingered. Nolan grunted in frustration. Even if he hadn't heard them, he saw her there, practically melting into the bench, her arms and legs spread open.

He grabbed for her arms and gently guided her to snap her appendages closer together. She mistook the gesture, craning her head up and pressing her lips to his.

Nolan actually stopped breathing. He didn't know for how long. That moment felt like an eternity—in the best possible sense. He hadn't felt that way since he'd watched *Cosmos* a few years back and it had really hit him—*really* hit him—just how small and insignificant his life on this tiny planet in this tiny corner of the galaxy was.

Lilac's lips on his was like that—a discovery of more. More beyond his insignificance. And it was here, all for the taking.

He knew he took too long to slide back out of her reach. He hadn't meant to—it was just that that moment had made time stop.

Sitting back in the bench beside her, he ran a hand through his hair in frustration.

This was bad on so many levels. Not least of which was she was going to sober up and forget this ever happened—or worse, regret it.

She leaned against his arm and he jumped in place.

"Look, can I call someone for you?" he asked. "Can I call your aunt Frankie?"

"*No*," said Lilac, a touch of anger in her tone.

Had they fought? But Nolan was undeterred. "Does she know where you are? Is she going to be worried about you?"

"No and no," said Lilac, smiling and bopping his nose with the tip of her delicate finger.

Nolan sat there in silence as Lilac wrapped her arm through his. "Can I see your phone?" he asked. He wouldn't go through her contacts to call Frankie—yet—but he wanted to make sure there were no texts or voice mails asking where she was.

Giggling, Lilac fished her phone out of her purse. It had a glittery fake white diamond case. "It's pretty," she said, plopping it on his lap. He flipped it over. There was a Tildy Tapir sticker at the bottom. The tapir that had seeped into his blood and even haunted his dreams after all these years was no longer that cute in his eyes, though the little cartoon starlet did her darndest in that pose winking up at him. "Can I see if your aunt called you?" he asked, nudging her and pointing to the screen.

"She didn't," said Lilac, sighing like he was the most annoying person she'd ever encountered. She unlocked the screen and there was a text there from someone named Gavin.

Nolan's heart sank. Was she in a relationship? Had she been fighting with *him*?

Where are you?? the text read.

"Lilac, someone named Gavin is asking where you are," said Nolan.

Lilac snorted and peered over at the screen, tapping the message and bringing up the full exchange. She scrolled up the exchange, laughing all the while. Nolan didn't want to pry too much, but he did anyway. There was a lot of concern in Gavin's messages, demanding to know what had happened, begging Lilac to reply. At one point, he said he had to run to the airport to help someone named Brielle with her sister, but Lilac had had no response. Then a few hours later, he'd checked in with her again and she'd replied with an emoji and *"I'm drunk---"* although earlier in the conversation, she'd insisted she was fine and to leave her be. Once she'd asked for him to stop poking his nose into her business all the damn time.

"You are nosy," said Lilac, and he looked down to find her staring up at him. Damn, she looked so innocent and beautiful. She leaned up, aiming her lips at his cheek and he slid out of her path, as much as he hated to.

"Can you send a message to this Gavin?" he asked. "The guy seems worried about you."

"You do it," said Lilac, pouting and crossing her arms. "Tell him I'm busy because I'm going to fuck Silly Sandgrouse."

Like I would ever send a stranger a message saying that, thought Nolan. He wondered if drunken consent to use someone's phone was still out of line, but perhaps this guy could help him make sense of what to do.

This is Nolan, he typed. *Lilac's coworker. I bumped into her at a bar and she's plastered.* He hit "send."

Gavin started typing almost immediately, then stopped suddenly, a message never sent. Then the phone started ringing and Nolan saw the name "Gavin" come up.

"He's calling you," said Nolan.

"Who?" asked Lilac dreamily.

"Gavin."

She shrugged.

"You have to answer," said Nolan. "He's probably going to call the police if you don't." He winced, wondering what the guy thought Nolan was doing with her.

Sighing, Lilac held her hand out. Nolan dropped the phone into it and she swiped to answer, holding it to her ear.

"Hell-o," she sang.

She giggled as Gavin spoke, but Nolan couldn't make out what he said to her.

"I'm fine. I'm *fine*. I know I sound drunk. I *am* drunk."

Lilac stared up at Nolan then. "He's my sandgrouse. Silly Sandgrouse. Yes, *that* one."

Nolan wondered then what she could mean. Gavin must have asked who he was, but... Had she ever spoken to this guy about him? Why?

Why on Earth would she have ever spared a second's thought for him?

"Yes, he's a gerfect pentleman," she said, slurring her words together. "He took me to a park. I told him to fuck me in the bar and he took me to the park." She giggled, and after a moment she held the phone in the air and shook it back and forth playfully. "He wants to speak to you," she loud-whispered again, bursting harder into laughter as Nolan took the phone from her.

"Hello?" asked Nolan.

"What the hell is going on?" asked Gavin abruptly.

Nolan felt as if he'd been smacked. He was only helping her. "I don't know," he admitted. "I ran into her at a bar and she had a few too many before I even got there." Lilac leaned against him then, rubbing her cheek against his shoulder and closing her eyes. "I don't know what to do. She doesn't want me to call her aunt, but I think I have to. I don't know where she lives."

Gavin sighed audibly, more in what was clearly relief than frustration. "So you two haven't—?"

"No!" said Nolan, perhaps almost too quickly. "I would never... She's *drunk* and... I barely know her."

"Like that would stop half the straight male population," said Gavin curtly. He let out another deep breath, resigned, and Nolan thought he heard the echo of a train or subway running through a tunnel. "Sorry. It's just... Lilac's my best friend and I worry about her."

The way he'd said "straight male" made Nolan wonder if Gavin was gay. If he was her best friend and not her boyfriend, there had to be few other explanations as to why. He looked down at Lilac, who was breathing audibly now, her mouth puckering into a small circle that sent wildfire down to Nolan's groin. He snapped his eyes forward. *Yup, no other way a guy is her best friend.*

"She's not usually like this," said Gavin. "She would never drink without me or Brielle or someone she trusts with her," he said. "She'd never put herself in danger like that."

Nolan swallowed, looking down. What would have happened to her if he hadn't come along? He supposed Claire wouldn't have let anything bad happen to her, would have gotten her a Lyft or something, but even so...

Nolan didn't know who he was talking about, but he wondered if they were the answers to his predicament. "Are you and this Brielle in Chicago?"

"I am," said Gavin. "Brielle's in a suburb near here."

"So you can't... That is, if she doesn't want her aunt to know, are there any local friends I can call?"

"Not that I know of." Gavin guffawed. "I was just at the airport. I should have jumped on a plane to Orlando." His voice shook a little then. "Fuck this job. We should have never separated."

Nolan wasn't sure what to say to that. Wasn't that what people did—separate and go on their way? He didn't know if Gavin meant his own job or Lilac's... And then suddenly something hit him, something that made him sick to his stomach. The connection got shaky with some static on the line.

"...Sorry... subway..." said Gavin.

Nolan looked down at Lilac. "Did Lilac say anything about her boss?" he asked. Lilac wasn't the first assistant manager this year— Earl seemed to go through them like water. Not that he could blame them. The guy creeped out anyone who had to breathe in the same airspace. How he'd managed to keep his job was beyond Nolan, but he supposed the guy was an expert at creeping women out without ever quite giving them enough cause to risk his job. That's why they probably all left quietly. Surely, if the asshole had ever crossed a line, *someone* would have said.

The call cut out then and Nolan didn't get his reply.

Nolan stared down at the sleeping beauty on his arm, wondering how she could be both mature and businesslike—an unapproachable wonder woman way out of his league—and an innocent princess equally beyond his reach, even if she cuddled beside him at that very moment. He found himself leaning his head toward her and gently, softly pecking the top of her head.

That was all he would allow himself in her state. It was more than he ought to have, but just for a moment, he wanted to imagine this princess—this queen—could actually be his.

Lilac's phone buzzed as a text came in from Gavin. *I'm going to call Frankie*, it read, *and explain everything. I'll have her call you and you two can arrange getting her home.*

Okay, typed Nolan. *Thanks for the help.*

Thank YOU, Gavin wrote back. *Tell Lilac the next time you see her sober that I was wrong. Gaston may be sexy, but it's the sandgrouses that are actually Prince Charming.*

Nolan barely knew what to make of that.

CHAPTER NINE

When Lilac's phone alarm began to buzz, it was like a chisel working its way directly into her brain.

"What the hell...?" she found herself muttering, the concept of getting up as foreign to her in that moment as the idea of sprouting wings.

Still, the beeping wouldn't stop. Surprised to find herself sleeping on her stomach, she rolled to her side and raised her head off the pillow before the sudden and pressing urge to vomit swooped over her. Her instinct to rush to the bathroom kicked in, but she knocked over a garbage can that was sitting out of place right beside her bed, stubbing her toe something fierce, and cried out.

"Lilac...?"

She turned to find her aunt curled up in one of the wicker chairs with the comfortable cushions.

"What happened?" asked Lilac, suddenly realizing she had no idea.

She really had no idea.

She remembered being angry and driving around Orlando, remembered how every kitschy place that used to bring her joy as a kid suddenly felt so wrong, remembered walking into a bar, just an indiscriminate dump, not wanting the glamour and glitz of a nightclub, figuring she'd have a drink or two and she was close enough to Aunt Frankie's place that she could do it alone...

Did she remember Nolan just now? There were images of Nolan bursting into her brain as she shut her eyes tightly, massaging her head.

She heard her aunt pound across the room as her phone's alarm continued to go off.

"I should have figured you'd have set it," said Aunt Frankie. "Sorry I didn't think to turn it off so you could sleep in."

"It's Monday," said Lilac, her throat dry and scratchy. "I have to get ready for work." She opened her eyes and started moving, but Aunt Frankie slid in beside her on the bed and put an arm around her shoulder.

"You're sick," she said. "I already spoke with Tara last night and she passed on the message to her husband. They already know you're not coming in today."

Husband. Why had that asshole even bothered to make those vows to some woman?

"I have to go in," said Lilac, swaying slightly. "I just started last week..." Her throat grew tight then and Frankie grabbed a half-drunk bottle of water from Lilac's nightstand and passed it to her. Lilac took it from her and sipped, not sure she could stomach more.

Frankie stared at her in silence for a bit and then took the bottle from her, screwing the cap back on. "It's already done," she said. "You already have a sick day. Earl's an understanding man, Tara tells me. You'll rest up today and head back stronger than ever tomorrow."

Understanding, my ass. Lilac sat there, thinking. She didn't *want* to go back in. She didn't want to see him again. But she didn't want him to think he'd scared her off, either.

The truth was, she hadn't decided what to do next—to give up and explain to everyone *why* or give up and simply have them all just laugh and think of her as a flighty failure or... to keep trying.

The job was hard, but if not for Earl, she wouldn't have any complaints. True, it was nothing like being a "camper" at the park, but it was still gratifying to play a small part in the behind-the-scenes magic.

And if she left, Earl would win and probably do it all over again to another woman. She wasn't the first, he'd said—and she wouldn't be the last.

Not unless he learned that his *Mad Men* attitudes didn't fly in this day and age and that he was delusional if he thought he was bringing any Jon Hamm charm to the table.

Aunt Frankie put a hand on her shoulder. "I told Tara it was food poisoning or maybe a light flu." She laid the back of her hand on Lilac's forehead then, as if to make sure her lie wasn't actually true. "Why did you drink so much when you just had food poisoning?"

Shrugging, Lilac stared at her knees. Her aunt had changed Lilac's clothes apparently, but she was still dressed like a slob.

"Lilac, you can talk to me," said Frankie. "If you don't want me to tell your parents or grandparents, I won't, but if you keep it all to yourself, I just might have to ask them what to do."

"Don't," said Lilac without even thinking. "Please don't." Her mom and daddy hadn't really checked in with her since she'd seen them last. They would still be in the Caribbean, lounging beachside. She'd seen some of her mom's pictures and her mom had "liked" a few of Lilac's, had wished her good luck... But they hadn't really talked. "I don't usually get drunk like that."

"Is it the stress of work?" asked Frankie. "You know, if it's too much for you, it's not too late to—"

"Yes, it is," said Lilac. "It's too late to undo this. But that's not it."

"Well," said Frankie, taking in an audible breath, "if you wanted to unwind, you could have just asked me. I'm almost never behind with fulfilling orders. I could have gone with you to someplace better than *that*, could have been your designated driver."

"I went there to be alone," said Lilac, sighing. She reached a hand out. "It's not you, it's just... I needed to be alone."

"I get it," said Frankie. "Believe me, I get that feeling. But next time, please don't mix your alone time with your drinking time, okay? Unless you just want to have a few drinks here and let me know to give you some peace. I won't even bother you. I can use the time to meditate."

Lilac smiled and threw her arms around her aunt. "Thank you for understanding," she said. "But I don't want that to happen again. I went too far..." As if to prove the point, she was hit with a blast of nausea again and Frankie handed her the garbage can. Lilac cradled it for a while but luckily didn't throw up again.

Again? She really wasn't sure that she had, but it sure felt like it.

"Well, I think it might be nice for you to go out with people your own age," said Frankie. "If you ask me, your parents and grandparents never made sure you got enough of that growing up, always dragging you from one cocktail party to the next."

Lilac chuckled despite herself. A lot of people had mistakenly thought of her as grownup, a "mini adult." But real adults didn't obsess over a cartoon tapir.

"Nolan's a nice guy," said Frankie, and Lilac's stomach fluttered at the mention of his name. "If he were a decade older and I were a decade younger..." Something twinkled in her eye. "Hell, I wouldn't mind the difference as is if he didn't, but I noticed his gaze pointed in a different direction." She winked.

Lilac bit her tongue to prevent herself from revealing to Frankie that her pointed interest in Lilac's love life made her more similar to her family than she might have wanted to believe. That was part of the reason why Lilac had never really had much of one.

"I can't date anyone right now," said Lilac, shaking her head. "I'm too... What?" she asked when she saw Frankie about to burst into laughter.

"You certainly wanted to date him last night. Or I believe your exact words were, 'I want to fuck Silly Sandgrouse.' You kept shouting that in the park as Nolan and I walked you to my car."

The blood in Lilac's body ran cold. "What?"

"Nolan called me last night. Or I guess, Gavin called me first and explained the situation, then I called Nolan on your phone—"

"What *situation?*" *Oh, my god, what the hell did I do?*

"Nolan ran into you at your dive and fended off your leering potential suitors while also fending off your rather aggressive pursuit of himself, I might add." The sparkle in her eyes was positively glimmering now. "I could tell he wanted to leave that part out, but he couldn't stop you from literally throwing yourself at him, puckering your lips and making smooching noises." She chuckled. "I'm sorry. I don't mean to tease you. It's actually quite worrisome. What if you'd thrown yourself at someone less... gentlemanly? Or what if—"

Lilac bolted upright then, headache and dizziness be damned. The garbage can—thankfully empty—rolled off her knees to the floor. "I can't... I don't..." She ran to the bathroom and shut the door behind her.

Breathing hard, she pushed her back against the door. She never would have drunk like that in front of Earl—she wasn't that clueless. But how many Earls were at that bar? How had she planned to get home? Her brain hurt thinking about it, but most of the day was gone from her memories.

She massaged her temples and saw brief glimpses of Nolan, Nolan's shoulder against her cheek, sweet, comforting Nolan...

A light knock resounded behind her. "Lilac?" said Frankie from the other side of the door. "Are you okay? Do you need anything?"

"I'm fine," lied Lilac. "I'm sorry. I just... really needed to pee."

"I imagine so after yesterday..."

Silence fell between them and Lilac actually did what she said she'd come in there to do, never mind that she'd really just run in there to hide.

After she washed her hands, she slowly turned the knob and peeked out the door.

"Feeling better?" asked Frankie, smiling slightly.

She nodded. A small part of her actually did.

"Okay," said Frankie. "You get yourself together and I'll make you breakfast. Text Gavin, okay? And I told Nolan I'd call him—"

"I'll call him," said Lilac, determined to set it all straight. She already had enough making her dread going back to work. Heaven forbid if things were awkward between her and him. She liked him. She *had* thought about fucking him. She just... couldn't imagine that right now. And besides, she'd probably totally screwed that up. "I don't have his number," she realized.

"I do," said Frankie with a sly smile. "We exchanged numbers last night. I wrote it down for you and left it next to your phone on your nightstand."

Lilac found the slip of paper in question and stared at it, as if it would twist itself into an origami sandgrouse, come to life, and peck her on the cheek.

The thought was bizarrely comforting.

"And once you've eaten and you're sure you're up for it, I'll take you to go get your car," she said. "Nolan said he was going back to the bar afterward and he'd clear it with the bartender to make sure it was okay to leave it. Still, I don't like the idea of leaving your nice new baby all alone in that junky gravel parking lot."

Sighing as she hit the bed, Lilac cradled her phone in one hand and the paper in the other. He'd be working now probably.

She entered the number into her contacts, brushing aside several messages from Gavin and many more notifications, and opened up a texting box. *I'm sorry*, she typed. *Frankie tells me I embarrassed myself yesterday. I'm so sorry and so thankful you were there to* —she let her fingers hover over her screen, trying to think of how to phrase it—*watch over me. I'm so, so sorry. I'm not usually like that, I swear. I hope I didn't make working in the same building awkward for you.*

She let out a breath and hit "send."

Then she puttered around with her other notifications, favoriting and liking pictures and posts with a numb, empty mind.

She liked Gavin's post about going back to work like a zombie on Mondays without thinking and less than a minute later, her phone rang. Gavin was actually *calling* her.

She sighed. She owed him this. "Hello?" she said, putting him on speaker and turning down the volume so his voice wouldn't carry through the hall and to the kitchen where her aunt would hear.

"*You...*" said Gavin, as if that said it all. There was actually a hint of anger in his voice.

"Me," said Lilac, her throat still scratchy. "Don't you have work right now?" she asked. "Should we talk later?"

"Nope," said Gavin. "I have work, but right now that work involves waiting on five different variations of a latte, which apparently passes for work at his place. And I don't care if I was in the office of the boss man himself, I'm not letting you wiggle out of this conversation."

Lilac doubted very much that Gavin would have this conversation in his boss' office, but she didn't dare call him on it. Not with the mood he was in.

The sounds of foam machines and chatter permeated the air from the speaker.

"What do you want to talk about?" she asked, still frightened to say more.

"If you've found out what kind of panties Tildy Tapir wears under her Ballroom dress," snapped Gavin. "What do you think I want to talk about?"

"I fucked up," said Lilac.

"Duh," said Gavin. "I'd give you half a dozen lectures on drinking safety until I was blue in the face, but I hope Frankie did that much for me already."

"Yeah..." said Lilac, although she wouldn't say that Frankie had been much gentler on her than Gavin might have been. Or heaven forbid Brielle.

"Did you tell Brielle?" she asked, suddenly sick at the thought.

"No," said Gavin carefully. "I said I was worried about you

yesterday, but she had her own crisis to deal with. And that was before I knew you were half-passed out in a park, begging your co-worker to fuck you."

Lilac winced. She'd never been that forward. Brielle was always the one who was, though you couldn't tell by looking at the two of them side-by-side. It wasn't fair. Brielle got away with being beautiful but seeming innocent—and she totally wasn't, the minx.

"What crisis of Brielle's?" asked Lilac, a little curious.

Gavin sighed dramatically on the other end of the phone. "Fine. I'll talk—you'll listen. Then we'll switch it up, okay? Oh, those are mine!" he said, quickly switching gears. Lilac heard him say *thank you* to someone and ask for a tray, but he immediately dove back into their conversation. "Brielle texted me yesterday, panicked that her kid sister, Nora, was running away from home. She thought she might be at O'Hare and asked me to try to get there first to stop her."

"What? Why? What could *you* do?"

"I don't know," said Gavin, and he mumbled another *thank you* as a door chimed and suddenly there was honking and the distant racket of a jackhammer as well as Gavin's brisk footsteps. "I was closer and okay, I couldn't really do anything until Brielle arrived, but I like to think *some* of my friends find me a comforting presence."

"Gavvy," started Lilac.

"*Li*," he echoed back, his footsteps suddenly grinding to a halt. "So... We found her, I let the poor girl pour her little heart out to me, their mom came and all was well in the end. I even got to meet Brielle's hot new lay."

"Oh," said Lilac, unexpectedly hit with something like envy. "She and that comic guy?"

"Yeah," said Gavin. His voice lowered like he was about to whisper a national secret. "And oh my god, Li, he's *so* hot, I had to fan myself half the way home."

Lilac was glad to know that Gavin wasn't too broken up about his disastrous date Saturday at least. *Saturday...*

Lilac wasn't sure what Gavin was talking about for a little bit as her thoughts drifted, but then she snapped back to attention at what he said next. "But I didn't even tell you what happened between Brielle and Pembroke Saturday!"

Oh, yeah. Their fight. "What?" asked Lilac, glad for another excuse not to talk about herself again.

"Pembroke was dating Daniel fucking-whatever-his-last-name-is!"

"Who...?" asked Lilac, confused on more than one count.

"Brielle's ex! That scumbag."

"Oh," said Lilac, and an image of Earl flashed through her head. She found herself crying quietly without even meaning to. This was about Daniel and Brielle, not...

"I've been trying to reach her since then," said Gavin. "But she hasn't responded. Brielle said Pembroke pretty clearly broke the hell up with Daniel in front of her, but what the hell drove her to date *him* of all people in the first place? Oh my god, you women are going to kill me, you know that?"

Lilac felt immensely guilty then. They were supposed to be moving on. Gavin had his own life to worry about, his own problems. She listened as Gavin's footsteps suddenly became hollower, the sounds of construction abruptly cut out.

"How are you?" she asked, trying her best to stay outside of herself, to be the friend he deserved. She knew Gavin's other friends—most of whom were queer as well—teased him relentlessly for bothering with Lilac or the other two for that matter, but especially Lilac. The two of them were such a "trope," a "straight, white bitch and her gay best friend," she remembered one had said. To her face. Over drinks, but even so... She sighed.

"All right," answered Gavin, clearly busy. "Jenny, can you pass these out? I'm heading to the bathroom."

Lilac wasn't sure if that was where he was actually headed. "What about... your date?"

Gavin scoffed. "Old news. Over it."

She wasn't sure she could have been in his place. "But what happened?"

"Nothing," he snapped. Then a door slammed and all other sound died out. "Nothing he *wanted* to happen anyway..."

So his date had tried to pressure him into sleeping with him. Which Gavin never did on a first date.

"I'm sorry," said Lilac.

"Yeah, well, I'm not. Now I know he wasn't worth my time, tight ass or no tight ass."

Lilac laughed then and reached for a tissue to blow her nose.

"Lilac, I'm in a storage closet."

"That's a funny place to be."

"No funnier than hiding in my roommates' front closet to get a cotton-pickin' minute to myself," he said dryly. "But okay... I want to hear it."

"Frankie told me you already knew. I got drunk and—how *did* you know?"

"The Nolan-of-the-sexy-voice texted me and I called him and we chatted about it," he said. "He kept you safe for me."

"For *you?*" asked Lilac, laughing.

"For both of us. Lilac, I didn't mean the bender—I know about the bender. What I want to know is *why* you went on a bender. It's not like you."

"So I keep reminding myself," said Lilac. She blew a breath out and her lips vibrated. "I'm sorry I scared you. It won't happen again."

"Okay," said Gavin. "I'm glad to hear it. But, Li, you were upset yesterday morning and I... All day, I regretted not hearing you out."

"You had other crises to deal with apparently." Lilac was so jealous of Brielle in that moment. She had her hot new boyfriend and she had Gavvy a short drive away, and Gavin was *Lilac's* more than anyone's.

"What happened Saturday?" asked Gavin. "You texted me that

you were going to a dinner meeting..." Gavin paused. "I've been thinking and well, did... did your boss do something to you?"

It was a knife that stabbed into Lilac's chest—from hundreds of miles away. "Gavin, he..." She started crying. And fifteen minutes later, by the time her aunt knocked on her door telling her her breakfast was getting cold, Lilac had told him—and only him, her poor burdened best friend—everything.

CHAPTER TEN

Nolan put his Silly Sandgrouse suit on the same as anyone—one fluffy bird leg at a time.

But he was dawdling today.

"Clock's a ticking," said Angie, his Tildy Scout caretaker for the second week in a row. "We've got Tildy brunch at the buffet, then after lunch we're supposed to head out for photos in the B-area around the resort."

Of course, Nolan knew all this, but Angie had a habit of repeating their schedule aloud, as if to commit it to memory. "I've never had a character out there late before," she said, pacing in the break room, "and I'm not about to start now."

Nolan nodded and stuck one arm in his suit, staring across the room at Prince Beastly flirting with his Tildy Scout—Jo this week—and leaving poor Queen Animaliao—that would be Cheryl at the moment—off by her lonesome sipping tea from a straw beside a blowing fan. Her wig was rustling a tad off-center from the breeze, but he was sure Cheryl would fix it before she went out there.

"*And* the other arm, please," said Angie, grabbing Silly's empty wing from where it dragged on the floor.

"Just a second," said Nolan, and he used his free hand to dig his phone out from his pocket and tap the screen with his thumb.

No messages.

Usually that was a good thing. It meant his dad wasn't texting him to let him know Willow had gotten in trouble again and he was taking her home early.

But it'd been almost a day since Nolan had texted Lilac back—*Don't worry about it. I'm just glad we got you home. Feeling better?*—and the most he'd heard from her was, *I took a sick day. I'll be back tomorrow.* His *Maybe I'll see you then!* had only gotten an *Okay!* as a response.

He'd probably said all the wrong things. He couldn't help it. He was a bit rusty when it came to dating.

Dating. As if you're going to be dating this girl...

"Are you kidding me?" Angie snatched the phone out of his hand and Nolan was so taken aback, he practically lost his bearings for a moment. "Phones go in the locker room, you know that." She put it down on a nearby table gingerly with both hands as if handling a grenade. "You almost had me zip you up with a phone inside Silly. What if his thigh had started ringing? What was I supposed to say to campers then?"

"I wasn't going to take it out with me," said Nolan, but as he reached for the phone, Angie used the opportunity to slide Silly's vacant wing on his arm and flit around him in an instant to zip up the back of the costume. "Everything a-go?" she asked, picking up Silly's head and cradling it beneath her arm.

Sighing, Nolan stared for a moment at his phone longingly. "Yes. All clear," he said, finishing the Tildy Scout/mascot pre-deployment check.

Angie slid Silly's head over his and adjusted it so his long beak was centered at the front of his head. "I'll take care of it," she said into the small holes over one of his ears.

"Eddie!" she shouted.

Through Silly's eye mesh, Nolan could just barely make out Eddie's turn of the head.

"Lock up Nolan's phone in the locker room, will you?" asked Angie.

Eddie waved his hand dismissively at them but nodded before the prince locked lips with his commoner paramour.

Angie slid her arm through Silly's wing and they were off, Nolan's feet settling into Silly's slow shuffle automatically as he passed through the door Angie held open for him.

———

"I love you," said the little girl who clutched to one of Silly's wingtips. She had her other hand in her mouth, the tip of her thumb twirling between her front teeth as she stared up at him.

Nolan brought Silly's free wing up to his cheek as if in surprise and then twisted one foot and his head just slightly to convey Silly's embarrassment. Then he reached out for a hug.

"Aw," said Angie. "Silly loves you, too!"

"Give me a big smile, Carmen!" said the woman who was probably the little girl's mom. Nolan twisted their hug slightly to make sure Silly's and the girl's faces were turned toward the woman's phone and he closed his eyes just as the flash went off, his grim lips and his scrunched face probably resembling someone who'd just sat on forty tacks, but score one for animal mascot duty.

They, unlike the human characters, didn't have to actually smile or keep their eyes open for the pictures.

"What do you say?" said Carmen's mom as she took her hand in hers.

"Thank you!" said Carmen and Nolan put a wing to Silly's beak and then "blew a kiss" at her before waving. She was already scrambling over to the crowd gathered around Tildy. He forgot who was on resort Tildy duty today, but whoever it was was sure to need to take a load off by the time brunch ended.

There was another advantage Nolan had—Silly Sandgrouse was taller than Tildy Tapir and he was too tall to fit in the Tildy costume. On occasion, he had to sub for a Leah Llama, but he had his Silly mannerisms so perfected, DeShawn rarely bothered to rotate him off duty. If he slipped the man a few bags of Twizzlers when the end of the month approached, he might just get lucky and get a day or two as a Tildy Scout caretaker, but that was if Eddie hadn't gotten there first with the king-sized Twix.

"Let's see who's enjoying Tildy's yummy waffles over here," said Angie, slipping her arm around Silly's wing and guiding him toward a table. He could barely see beyond a few feet in front of him—let alone anywhere near his feet—so he counted on Angie to so much as move.

"Hi!" said Angie, as spunky as ever. Nolan wondered where she got her energy. "How are we enjoying Tildy's magical waffles today?"

Nolan couldn't make out everything the people at the table said, but he heard the scream and felt the double hug come at him from either side as two kids jumped out of their chairs to embrace him. A third was unmoved, carefully stacking several blueberries he'd picked off his waffle with his fingers on a single tine of his fork.

"Do we want a picture with Silly?" asked Angie.

"Yeah!" shouted one of the kids.

Just then, the blueberry-fork child looked up, locking eyes with Nolan's through Silly's mesh-covered cartoon eyeballs.

"Code Blue," whispered Angie into his ear.

Sure enough. Work at Tildy World long enough and you learn to spot them.

Blueberry-Fork Kid's eyes went wide and then he screamed— earth-shattering, monster-in-my-closet-like shrieking.

"What's the matter?" said one of the men at the table, who tossed down his cloth napkin like it was on fire and jumped up to lift Blueberry-Kid out of his booster seat.

The other man sighed so loud, even Nolan could hear him through those tiny airholes and all that plush. "Don't coddle him," he said and he stood as well, shepherding his other children around the table. "Let's go get our picture over here," he said. "Your brother is frightened."

Nolan stared at the crying boy, his dad patting his back and humming to him as Blueberry-Kid started quieting, his sobs softer and a longer pause between deep breaths. Nolan waited for Angie's signal, a tug backward to back off or a tug forward to turn on the charm. She slipped her arm though his and moved them forward.

Nolan put Silly's wingtip up to his cheek and flittered it just a little as if Silly had gone shy all of a sudden and just wanted to say *hello*.

Blueberry-Kid stopped his sobs then, staring at Silly Sand-grouse like he was a new breed of puppy who may or may not bite him—but he was clearly leaning toward for latter now.

"See?" said his dad. "It's Silly. You know Silly."

The boy reached his hand out and Nolan leaned in, letting the toddler's fingers graze the top of Silly's wings.

The kid grinned and Nolan put both wingtips on Silly's cheeks, turning on the "aw, shucks" charm.

"Let's get a picture," said Angie, pleased with the Code Blue turnaround. "With everyone!" She took Nolan by the wing and guided him to a spot against the wall. She grabbed a phone from one of the men and then the dads lined up their kids on either side of Silly, Blueberry-Kid still in one of his dads' arms but grinning all the same. His hand was on Silly's beak for the picture.

As the dads and older kids expressed their thanks and went back to their breakfasts, Nolan heard another voice. "...have a minute?"

Nolan couldn't hear clearly who had gotten Angie's attention, but he saw her turn and he waited. It was dangerous to fully turn around in a crowded environment like the buffet without his Tildy Scout caretaker to guide him. Kids and servers under his feet, tables where he didn't expect to find them—it was best to wait for Angie's guidance. He waved across the room when he heard a kid shout, "Silly!"

"Sure," said Angie, looping her arm through his wing. "You don't have to be eating here for a picture with Silly." She tugged

Nolan around completely. Before he could even take note of the kid, someone was clenching his side and saying, "Doo dee doo doo," which was one of Silly's catchphrases.

He patted Silly's wings against the kid's back as his eyes focused through the mesh.

There was a mom and dad standing there—next to Lilac.

Lilac. She wasn't wearing a blazer today—even through the mesh he could make out the long-sleeved, high-buttoned blouse and navy pants—and although her flawless face seemed strained, a little smile was dancing on her lips.

"I found him in the lobby," said Lilac, straight to Silly himself. "He's Silly's number one fan and I told him I knew right where he might find him today."

The boy grabbed Silly's wingtip in his hand and started swinging it. Nolan finally got a look at him and he was decked from head to toe in Silly-patterned gear, including a half-Silly head hat atop his head. Nolan made Silly do a little rocking dance and waved the wingtip held by the boy in the air like they were soccer champions together. The boy laughed. "Doo dee doo doo! Come on, Silly! Say it!"

"Oh, Silly can't speak," said Angie, stepping in to do her Code Purple routine. "He made a magical vow to Queen Animaliao that when he was in our realm, he wouldn't say a word—otherwise the spell keeping him here will be broken."

Nolan put Silly's free wingtip over his beak and shook his legs —frightened Silly, afraid the magic might break.

"Aw," said the boy. "I hate Queen Animaliao."

Nolan held Silly's free wingtip high up into the air. Shock.

The boy laughed.

"Now, now," said Angie. "Queen Animaliao is Silly's friend." The clock was running—all Tildy Scout caretakers reported how many groups the costumes took pictures with each shift, which DeShawn reported to Earl himself, and when the mood struck, Earl would come down to the break room and give some b.s. lecture about time and speed and customer service and the great impossible balance. No one wanted Earl in the break room. "Let's get that picture," said Angie, walking over to the boy's parents and taking a phone from one. She talked to them and the woman clearly hesitated, but she managed to get them both to step alongside Silly and their son.

"Doo dee doo doo!" said Angie—and the family repeated after them.

Because Lilac was standing right beside Angie, this time Nolan didn't close his eyes. In fact, he actually smiled. Not that anyone could tell that through the costume.

"Goodbye, Silly," said the boy as Angie returned the parents' phone.

Nolan patted the boy on the head and then the super fan ran off, following his parents back to the lobby.

Lilac lingered and Nolan stared at her, gorgeous even through his mesh eyes.

She stared back, then, seeing Angie slip in beside Nolan, she ran forward, tugging gently on Angie's sleeve. "Can I have a picture with him?" she asked.

Laughing, Angie cocked her head. "Sure." She knew she was Earl's new assistant manager—word got around fast and Earl had briefly brought her to the break room last week, Nolan heard tell from Eddie, who had turned his eyes away from Jo for long enough to catch sight of her "fine ass" apparently, so he said out of earshot of the girls in the guys' locker room. For better and for worse, Nolan had been in the bathroom at the time.

Lilac brought her hand up—she'd been clutching her phone the entire time and Nolan hadn't been able to tell through the suit—and swiped at the screen before handing it to Angie. She and Lilac switched places, Lilac slipping her arm around Silly's wing.

Even with the layers of sweat and plush between them, Nolan could feel his body flush at the touch.

She rested her cheek against Silly's shoulder and Nolan's mind raced to how she'd leaned all over him at the park.

"Say, 'doo dee doo do,'" said Angie, snapping Nolan back to reality.

If the camera had had x-ray functions and could have captured Nolan's face under Silly's head, it would have shown his head bent down slightly, gazing at the place he knew Lilac to be, his mouth turned up in a smile unlike any he'd worn in ages.

CHAPTER ELEVEN

Lilac had gotten through all of Tuesday morning with little incident. Walking to that office made her physically sick—she'd had to run to the bathroom to make sure she wasn't going to throw up—but she'd done it. Earl had been dismissive of her when she'd arrived, feigning being busy. Unlike during the previous week, he'd kept their office door open and was often either sending her out on errands or going himself—leaving them together as little as possible and never not within someone's earshot.

Good, thought Lilac. *I hope I scared you into decency.*

She didn't always feel as confident as that, though. She reached for paperwork with shaky hands, felt her throat dry up, always aware of who was to her side, aware of what had happened when she'd been in that seat.

Once she'd gone for a walk, her phone clenched in her hand, ready to text Gavin, and hadn't even told Earl what she was doing. He hadn't even looked up from his work to ask.

That was when she'd found the Silly Sandgrouse fanboy in the lobby and, remembering the shift schedule in the break room, had taken him over to see Nolan. He was their ice breaker, that eight-year-old.

They'd exchanged a few messages that night. Lilac had sent

him the photo she'd had taken of them together, along with the message: *Confession. I knew that was you.*

By lunch time Wednesday, she'd gotten the message: *I don't know what you're talking about. I'm Silly Sandgrouse's friend. When he's out of this break room, I cease to exist. He did tell me about this hot girl who was getting all cozy with him at the buffet. Girl has a thing for birds, I'd wager.*

She'd laughed then where she sat on the two-foot decorative concrete wall surrounding the bushes behind the Tent Tildy building, not caring that the few landscapers within earshot looked over to find her picking cilantro out of her sandwich and giggling to herself. She decided she liked being back there. No one bothered her back there. And it had given her plenty of time to text Gavin—and to think about what to say to Nolan next. Gavin had been determined to snap her out of her good mood, though.

If you don't report him, I will.

Lilac wiped her fingers on a tissue she'd commandeered as a napkin. *Don't you dare*, she typed. *Drop it, okay?*

DROP IT?? Are you crazy?

Thanks, typed Lilac as she said the word aloud wryly. The landscapers would really think she was nuts now, which only proved Gavin's point. *Look. I'm doing okay today. I appreciate you being here for me, but you pressing this issue is just going to undo all the work I've put in to reach this point. I'm okay. You've kept your promise and haven't told ANYONE, right?*

Yes! It's the wrong thing to do, but I've kept my word. And you're not okay—don't tell me otherwise—and someone deserves a big, fat lip, but... okay. I'll drop it... For now.

Thank you, wrote Lilac. She checked the time. She still had twenty minutes. Gavin was on lunch, too—apparently he could take it early. Hell, since they didn't pay him for his labor, they ought not to complain when he took his breaks.

Lilac decided to lighten the mood and sent him the picture of her and Silly. *Here's the hot guy you talked to on Sunday.*

Gavin sent an emoji of a laughing face. *He's more handsome than I imagined.*

Isn't he, though? He's so in demand that I worry he just wanted me there as some arm candy for his glamour shot.

Tonight's entertainment headline: Silly Sandgrouse, long-time friend and sidekick of Tildy Tapir, has a hot, blonde piece of ass on the side. What will Queen Animalia say?

Lilac laughed aloud again. *It's Queen AnimaLIAO. And she's not dating Silly Sandgrouse.*

Thank the gods, wrote Gavin. He paused for a moment. *Hey, isn't Silly Sandgrouse like sixty years old? And still a bachelor, eh? That's right in your wheelhouse.*

That deserved an emoji with its tongue stuck out. *I'll have you know that under all those feathers, he's a baby-faced boy whom I suppose must be at least 21 since he was in that bar. SO cute, I'll admit that. Not what I hoped for, but more than fuckable, believe you me.* A flash of Earl's hands on her shoulders, his hand traveling down her skin, shot through her. This, while he was married. If that's what older men had to offer her, then the hell with that anyway.

Happy to hear, wrote Gavin. *But I'm more concerned that when you skin a giant bird, he turns into a hot baby-faced boy.*

Lilac crumpled up her sandwich paper, shuddering at the sight of the cilantro as she squeezed it all into a ball in her fist.

Gavin sent a photo of a man with short, messy brown hair in a dark business suit in profile, his mouth in a thin line. At first glance, he seemed mature and he made Lilac's heart race just a little, but the closer she looked, the more she was certain he was no older than thirty or so. *How fuckable is he?* texted Gavin.

Laughing, Lilac let go of her trash. *Who is this??* she asked.

Answer the question first.

Lilac groaned. *Very, supremely fuckable. You happy? Now spill.*

That's Gabriel.

THAT's Gabriel??

I actually thought you might have recognized him.

How would I have recognized him??

I gave you his name. I said he was hot—you know where I work. Googling would have done the trick.

Lilac scoffed, although Gavin couldn't hear it. *Maybe I'm not that nosy.*

Since when?

She dodged the question. *So last week—before you said he was hot—and you were going on and on about him being a hardass, you didn't say anything about his fuckability then. Why now?*

Gavin waited a moment to answer. *I don't know. I doubt he's even gay—or with my luck, he is but he's not single. I'm just admiring.*

Lilac knew there was more to the story, but Gavin wasn't offering up any details. *So you're totally over disaster date.*

Oh my god, SO over disaster date. Gavin paused. *I should get going, but I'll have my phone on me. CALL ME if Earl does anything.*

Lilac hesitated a minute and settled on sending a *yuck* face, trying to make the situation lighter than it really felt. *But thank you. Love you!*

Love you, too, wrote Gavin. *Go pluck some feathers and find your happy, Li.*

Giggling like a madwoman, Lilac cradled her phone in both hands. She looked up, caught one of the landscaper's eyes, and grinned so widely, she actually scared him into taking a few steps backward to put more space between them.

———

By the time Thursday had rolled around, Lilac was in a much better mood. She still felt sick whenever she was in that office, which was why she might have literally jumped out of her desk when Earl told her he'd approved her Ballroom/Tent Tildy crossover project and that she was set to meet with Gyu-ri again about it.

She scrolled through her messages while in the shuttle that ran between the resort and the Ballroom. There was the usual silliness from Gavin along with a *Will you report him today?* question this morning she'd only written *Stop* to. Then there was the much smaller message string with Nolan. He'd sent a photo of himself with a bunch of people from the break room alongside an in-costume Queen Animaliao and Prince Beastly. *Costume crew says hi,* he'd written this morning. *Notice no Tildy, Silly, or Leah to be found here. You'll never find them and their "friends" in the same picture. Curious...*

"Last stop," said the shuttle driver. "Unless you're just going for a ride and you want a lift back to Tent Tildy." The man—kid really, probably like eighteen—winked at her and she rolled her eyes, stepping out to enter the Ballroom, her phone still clutched in her hand and a folder under her arm. Bypassing the footmen and women who offered to assist her down, she strutted through the procession with so much business on her mind, she almost forgot to take in all the magic. She almost forgot there *was* magic, like an enchanting royal dance that never, ever ended while the park was open was the most normal thing in the world.

The concealed employee door made her hesitate. She still didn't have her own badge and she hadn't even thought to ask Earl for his this time. Like she wanted anything that had hung around that slimy neck in her hands again.

She texted Gyu-ri, explaining her predicament, glad she'd exchanged numbers with her the week before. Within a few moments, the slightly-older woman was at the door, bursting through the mural of the palace garden to let her inside.

As they wove through the employee hallways, Gyu-ri talking all the while, they almost bumped into a Prince Beastly and his Tildy Scout caretaker, with whom he was locking lips and entwining limbs.

"Hey," said Gyu-ri. "You're on duty." She seemed nonplussed, though, as they wove their way around the lovers as well as a waiting Queen Animaliao and her Tildy Scout caretaker.

"Sorry," said the woman who'd been making out with Prince Beastly as she smoothed her clothing down.

"Apologies," said Prince Beastly, suddenly back in character. He put one hand across his chest and bowed to Gyu-ri before Queen Animaliao slipped in and took his arm.

Lilac recognized all of them from the photo. She opened her mouth to say something, but Gyu-ri was almost around the corner now and besides, the two Tildy Scout caretakers grabbed for the doors and the blast of music from the Ballroom ceased suddenly, a voice echoing over the loudspeaker. "Girls and boys, ladies and gentlemen, and people from all corners of the land—please welcome your rulers, Queen Animaliao and her consort, Prince Beastly!"

Lilac ducked behind them to catch up to Gyu-ri, who waited for her, grinning. "They do that several times a day," she said. "You get used to it. Eventually, it kind of loses its pomp and circumstance."

Lilac didn't realize it until that moment, but she'd been staring at the royal couple, practically drooling, just like she had as a kid.

She smiled sheepishly at that and stepped into Gyu-ri's office.

Opening up the folder, she laid out the spreadsheets and plan she'd written up, slipping her phone on the chair beside her. They talked about the plans and settled on a date—early fall. Right around the time Lilac would have been settling into her life as a teacher if she'd stuck to that path. She was hit with a sudden feeling of wistfulness, imagining the life she was supposed to have had—a life she'd figured on having just two weeks before. She'd have actually had most of the summer off. She could have traveled a bit—maybe even come to Tildy World for a few days as a "camper," as a guest. Her parents had talked about heading off to Europe for a week or two and had wanted to know if she'd like to come along and she definitely would have gone. Then she'd have moved to her Minnesota apartment in August. She wondered if that other educator she'd met online had ever found another roommate. Things had moved so crazily since then, it was almost like she'd been dreaming.

"Lilac?" asked Gyu-ri. "Are you all right?"

Lilac realized a tear had fallen down her cheek and she brushed it away. "Yes, sorry. Sorry about that."

She made a note in her phone about the event, brushing aside the notifications from Gavin. She hadn't spoken to Brielle since Sunday. "So what kind of weekly goals should we be setting until then?"

"Did Earl do something—something to you?"

Lilac's mouth fell open at that.

Gyu-ri immediately looked flustered. "I'm sorry. I shouldn't have pried—it's just, word gets around—"

"Word gets around?" asked Lilac. "People *know* something bad about him and he still works here without a care in the world?" Lilac thought angrily of Jillian then, her sly remarks, the way she'd stared Lilac down like she was in on the filth Earl perpetuated. She thought of Christian and how he hadn't said anything disgusting himself, but how he'd laughed at Earl crossing the line, how he'd let his eyes do some of the talking on their own.

Then there were the comments about Earl's assistant managers never lasting long and that fire that took turns coursing through her veins alongside ice and sadness burned her up from the inside.

Gyu-ri almost shirked back. "Just rumors," she said. "But the guy kind of... I don't know. I notice it more with the young women than the ones my age, but even with me, he can be belittling —sexist."

Lilac bit her lip. Was she talking about him being a general jerk or did she know he'd crossed the line from jerk to assaulter on at least one occasion?

"You're not the first girl to lead me on." It had to have been on more than one occasion.

"I..." Something caught in Lilac's throat. The fire died down and she didn't even know why. Her voice choked and she shook a little. Her phone buzzed then—just a notification that her mom had liked her Silly Sandgrouse mascot picture on Instagram—but she used it as an excuse. "I should get back," she said.

"I'm sorry if I said anything to worry you," said Gyu-ri. "I just...

wanted you to be on your guard around Earl." *Too late for that*, thought Lilac. Gyu-ri gave Lilac a faltering smile. "I'm sure it'll be fine."

Is that what everyone thought about all those other women in the job before me? Lilac raged then, both at people like Gyu-ri—as nice as she seemed to be trying to be—and even at the people in her own position before her. Why hadn't *they* said anything? Why was it up to Lilac? Didn't they know how scary it felt to face this alone, to not have anyone to back up her story—to go up against a man who'd been in a position of power at her employer for years, if not decades?

"I'm just saying you can talk to me if you need to," said Gyu-ri.

"Thanks," muttered Lilac. "I'll email you with my proposal for dates and goals to meet along the way." She shuffled all her papers together, not once meeting Gyu-ri's eyes as she made her way to the door.

She didn't know if she would have cried or screamed if she'd looked at her again just then.

CHAPTER TWELVE

Nolan spent almost all of his classes Friday with his mind focused elsewhere. He'd barely seen Lilac all week. Sure, she'd exchanged a few flirtatious texts with him over the past few days, but after that photo op on Tuesday, he hadn't seen her more often than when he'd caught her racing though the halls on occasion. He was usually in his Silly suit and couldn't say anything—though he made sure to wave when he did catch her eye—but he'd never gone to find her when on break or out of the suit. For one thing, she was sure to be in the proximity of Earl, with whom Nolan, like most anyone at Tent Tildy, preferred not to share the same air space. Even from their limited interactions, he knew he didn't like the guy, and he was in no mood to remind the man of what Nolan had said to him the week before. Besides that, she always seemed too busy and he hadn't wanted to get her in trouble. Assuming his well-intentioned confrontation with the boss hadn't already done just that.

Or maybe he'd just been chicken. But how do you flirt with a girl with your sleazy boss, potentially your little brother, and a bunch of cartoon animals around?

Today, though, he wasn't anywhere near that tapir. And one of his classes had been canceled—which meant that he'd have plenty of time to drive down to Cocoa Beach, have dinner, enjoy some sun, and drive the hour back home before his dad really missed him. A once-weekly babysitter picked up Landon from Tildy's Tots on Fridays after Willow got out of school and stayed with them until their dad got home.

It was now or fucking never and if she said *no*, so what? He'd still have the beach to look forward to. She couldn't be the only fish in the sea.

Still, as his sweaty palms reached for his phone—despite the lecture he was supposed to be paying attention to—he knew that was something he was just telling himself. He'd force himself to enjoy the beach regardless—it'd been too long since he'd last gone—but it just wasn't going to be the same without her.

Have plans for tonight? he typed. *What do you think about heading to the beach?*

———

Nolan paced back and forth on the spot he'd claimed with a beach towel from the back of his trunk that had seen better days. He regretted remembering to pack swim trunks this morning—he had a hankering to go swimming somewhere, even before he knew class was canceled—while forgetting to pack a better towel. There was no way he was going to stop home after class, though, in case he got caught up with the kids. He'd never leave in time.

He had a good view of the parking lot he'd told Lilac to use; he'd offered to pick her up but didn't blame her at all for wanting to take her own car. She didn't know him well, and they'd never been on an official date.

Before this evening.

If this even counted as an official date.

He'd have to clarify that at some point.

His nerves were getting the better of him now. Cocoa Beach was only an hour east of Orlando proper, pretty much straight down SR 528. Most people had GPS. There was no way she'd get lost, but if it was her first time driving there alone...

He stopped, gazing over the ocean, and took a deep breath. He wasn't her keeper. She was probably fine.

He still didn't know the full story behind last Sunday, but according to both Gavin and Frankie, it had been an oddity. Hell, he could understand feeling sad or angry enough to let loose like that. He had on occasion, before he'd turned twenty-one even— when the heartache of his mother's passing had been too much to bear. But he'd soon seen that he had people who relied on him and he didn't have time to dwell on heartache often. Not in such a potentially destructive way.

But he'd binged at friends' houses. Poor Lilac had done it alone. If she wasn't interested in dating him, he at least wanted her to know he would be her friend. She wouldn't need to get to that point again—do something like that without calling someone first —not here in Orlando.

If she wanted to get drunk and shirk off stress and heartache, she could call him and he'd be there for her.

He didn't care if his dad expected him at home.

Nolan realized that was the first time he'd allowed himself to think that since the accident. If his dad had asked him to give up his Sunday me-time, he would have.

But if he'd asked him to give up time with Lilac... Maybe he wouldn't have.

"Hi! So... Wow. This is nice."

Nolan spun around. Lost in his thoughts, Nolan hadn't even noticed Lilac approach him from behind.

She stood there and Nolan's eyes first darted to the golden bikini barely covering the most scandalous parts of her body before he snapped back into the moment and realized she was struggling with a tote bag on one arm and her other arm wrapped around an oversized umbrella. "I'm sorry I'm a little later than I expected. I stopped to get this."

Chuckling, Nolan scrambled forward to take the umbrella from her, pointing to the almost-setting sun. "You won't need that for long tonight."

"I know," said Lilac, pulling a bottle of sunscreen out of her tote, "but you can never be too careful." Nolan stuck the umbrella in the sand, struggling a little to open it as Lilac sat down on his pre-arranged beach towel. She squirted some of the lotion onto her delicate hand and started rubbing it on her arm. Nolan leaned on the umbrella stand and grinned. He knew sunscreen was important, but he hadn't bothered bringing any. It wasn't going to be sunny for much longer and a little tan wasn't too risky on occasion. Especially since he spent most of his day indoors and under several layers anyway.

Lilac moved on to her legs and Nolan found himself sliding down the umbrella stand, practically slipping into the sand. He recovered, whistling casually, sure Lilac hadn't seen.

She was staring right up at him and grinning, one pink-manicured hand resting on one of her thighs. She held the bottle out toward him. "Can you get my back?"

"Sure," said Nolan, stumbling forward to grab the bottle from her. She turned over and folded her arms to cradle her chin, revealing the most perfectly-shaped ass cheeks known to man and a long, slender arched back. *Down, boy*, he thought. Inhaling deeply, Nolan slathered his palms with sunscreen before diving into the space between her bikini top and her bikini bottom.

"Ah!" said Lilac, shuddering a bit. "Your hands are cold."

Nolan wondered if they were clammy because his heartbeat was drowning out all normal sensation. His hands tingled and his barely-covered nether regions throbbed.

He'd left his condoms in the car—and he was going to be sure to get them out before his brother or sister played around in the glove compartment and asked what kind of balloons those were. But he'd told himself to stash them there just as a backup because it was never going to happen.

But obviously, a small part of him hoped something was going to happen.

"You take sun care seriously," said Nolan, for want of anything else better to talk about. He finished on the small of her back and he went to move his hands up above her bikini top, but as he trailed his palms upward, she arched a little and let out a small moan.

He stopped.

"Sorry," said Lilac, grinning even with her eyes closed. "I'm just ticklish. Keep going." He did, applying pressure to her shoulders but going gentle on her neck, stopping only to refill his hands with the goo.

"My grandpa had melanoma," said Lilac, and Nolan's hands stopped moving.

"I'm sorry for your loss," he said. He removed his hands, his job done, though he ached when the touch between them severed.

"Oh, he's okay," she said. "They caught it in time, but he has to be extra careful and get checked every few months." She rolled her eyes as she turned over. "And yet the idiot still gets tanned. He hates how he looks pale, he says. Well, I'd hate how he'd look dead, I tell him."

Nolan snapped the cover back on the sunscreen, a smile faltering on his face. Any mention of death and his thoughts inevitably strayed toward his mom, even though it'd been just about three years.

"Are you okay?" asked Lilac as she sat up beside him. "I'm sorry, that was insensitive of me. Maybe you lost your grandfather—"

"I did," said Nolan, cradling his legs against his chest. "Both of them—so long ago, I don't even remember them. One of my grandmas, too. And the other one lives in Nevada, so I hardly ever see her."

"I'm sorry," said Lilac, all joy drained from her voice. Nolan hated that he was responsible for that in her. Her joy was so wonderful, so contagious.

But he decided it was time to lay it all on the table. That way, they could just remain friends if that was what she wanted, which was how he expected it to be. "It wasn't that, it's... My mom died. Three years ago."

"Oh," said Lilac, sitting straighter. "I... I'm sorry."

That's what everyone said when he told them. That's all he expected anyone to say. What could you say to someone who'd experienced loss? Words were never enough.

"She was our family's everything," he said, taking a deep breath. "She kept it all together. And then—bam—one night she was gone." He checked to see if he was totally bumming Lilac out, but she was gazing at him, concern etched on her features. "An idiot driving the wrong way down a highway."

Gasping slightly, Lilac rested a hand above her breast. "I don't know how you can drive after that." She shivered. "I—I'd keep thinking about it every time I got behind the wheel."

Nolan laughed dryly. "Orlando doesn't exactly have the greatest public transit system. It's drive or get nowhere—and if you opt for the latter, you can't even stay in your house for long because you can't get to a job and you run out of money and can no longer pay for it."

Lilac ran a finger in a circle in the sand just beyond the edge of the frayed towel. "You're right. I'm sorry I said that."

Nolan turned, laying a hand atop hers—hesitatingly at first to make sure she was okay with it. She didn't flinch. "Don't be. I just... Well, I apparently like to bum everyone out by talking about it." He tried to smile, but he could feel it didn't quite reach his lips right.

She locked her eyes with his. "You didn't bum me out. It's sad... I..." She sighed and shook her head. "I'm really messing up what to say."

"No," he said, sitting straighter but not letting go of her hand. "It's... I mean, how do you talk about it? Even if it's colored everything about my life since then, I can't... It's hard to talk about."

"You really step up with the kids," said Lilac. It was more an observation than a question.

Nolan's hand slipped off hers. "Dad isn't—he's not a bad dad. He's just easily overwhelmed. And he has his plate full working one full-time job and one part-time job to try to make ends meet.

We need my salary, too—it helps with the costs of raising two kids."

"But you're a kid, too!"

Nolan felt an invisible punch to the gut at that. Of course, this beautiful, mature woman thought he was a kid. "Well, I'm twenty-one now," he said, and sure enough, he saw something like disappointment flicker across her eyes. "I was eighteen when it happened. I was planning to go to college out of state and then... Well. I settled on community college for a computer science degree."

"But that's not right. I meant that you're *his* kid. You're a kid in the family. I'm sure that's not what your mom would have wanted!"

"I'm sure not," said Nolan, pushing back the bit of rage floating to the top of his brain. He knew it was unreasonable, but it wasn't the first time he'd felt like this. "But it doesn't matter."

"But can't your dad just hire someone?" she asked.

That elicited a double-take. Nolan actually stared at her to see if she was kidding, but she seemed nothing but earnest. He laughed. "With what? We needed Mom's income. She didn't have much of a life insurance policy—it paid for the funeral and that was about it—and the only reason we can even afford a babysitter for a few hours a week is because I can take Landon to Tildy's Tots for free since I work at Tildy World full-time. Willow usually has to *suffer* through after-school programs. We just have a sitter on Fridays when I'm busy with school. And then there was tuition. How were we going to afford that? And don't say loans—I wasn't saddling myself with over a hundred grand in loans."

Lilac bit her lip, then smiled, bringing up a handful of sand. "This is busy with school?"

Nolan grinned despite himself. "One class got canceled today, and okay, a couple of nights a week, I do stuff by myself." His scalp itched and he ran a hand through his hair. "Dad's home most evenings because he starts early. Like way early. And there's the babysitter on Fridays."

"I'm not blaming you," said Lilac, letting go of her sand and sliding in closer to him. He stiffened as she leaned across him, her beautiful, full lips less than an inch from his chest, but then she straightened, her bottle of sunscreen in one hand. "Did you put any on?"

Chuckling, he pointed toward the western sky and the parking lots and hotels and restaurants behind him. "It'll be twilight before too long."

Lilac popped the top and slathered her hands together. "But it's not nighttime yet." She nodded at him. "Turn around. I'll get your back."

Nolan wasn't going to object to that. He flinched but then relaxed as her small, soft hands worked up and down his bare back. "Thanks for coming," he said then, sure he wouldn't have her beside him for much longer.

"Thanks for inviting me." Lilac's fingers made their way up to his shoulders now, her digits doing little movements to melt the tension right out of his body. He was glad he'd clenched his legs to his chest to hide the stiffness in his trunks.

"I don't get to hang out with people much," said Nolan truthfully. "Outside work. Life is... kids at Tildy World and kids at home."

Lilac took a break then, filling her hands with more sunscreen. He didn't object when she started rubbing one of his arms, peeling it away from his knees.

He cleared his throat. "Tildy World seems like a place where dreams come true when you're a kid." Lilac's hands froze on his bicep. "But when you work there a while, it just becomes a stress-ful, hectic work day just like any other place—only glamoured a bit with fantasy and make-believe. I don't hate it there, but it's certainly lost its charm."

She didn't say anything to that, filling her hands again and going to work on the other arm. Nolan had to shift his legs just right so she wouldn't notice the bulge. He took a deep breath and tried to calm his mind as her soft touch went to work on his skin.

"How's it going?" he asked quietly, sure her bender on Sunday had something to do with the job. "How do you like Florida so far?"

"I love Florida," she said, almost too concisely. She stared at him then and poked his chest lightly. "Lie down. I'll get your chest and legs."

Nolan had never heard of anyone asking for help getting those easier-to-reach places, but he didn't object. He squeezed his legs together as his head hit the towel, fighting his hard-on, which had just been quieting down. She started down at his legs, filling her hands with sunscreen and then massaging his calf and working her way up to his thigh. Clenching his fists together, he tried to focus on what he'd been trying to do. *Get her to talk. Let her know she doesn't need to cope with stress in an unhealthy way.*

"A lot of people think it's too hot here," he said, knowing full well that Orlando weather wasn't what had set her on course to Thommy's.

Lilac snorted. "I guess the heat can be a bit brutal. Spanish summers and beaches probably have a leg up on Orlando ones, but after countless Midwestern winters, Orlando will do."

"You've been to Spain?" asked Nolan as Lilac crawled around him to start work on the other leg. The way her arms pressed against the bottom of her breasts as she crawled, hands and knees, up toward him framed her cleavage even more, like that needed more of a highlight. He squeezed his fists tight again and clenched his eyes for good measure this time, though he could feel his throbbing member down below.

She saw it, too, he was sure of it, because she chuckled, but still, she began work on his leg. "I spent a semester abroad," she said, "but I've been there for a few weeks in the summer, too. A few years back."

"Wow," said Nolan, genuinely impressed. He didn't even have a passport. He'd had no need. The most global traveling he'd done was to head over to Disney's Epcot Center and walk from one country's pavilion to the next. If seeing the world was anything like making your way through small, square plots of the country's most famous cultural icons and stereotypes, then he was sure to impress.

He laughed at his own joke.

"What?" asked Lilac, her hands digging soothingly into the muscles above his knee.

"I was just thinking that the most traveling I've done is at Epcot," he said.

Lilac's hands stopped moving. "We do not speak that name," she said, then she laughed. "Seriously, though, don't you get tired of everyone saying Disney is better than Tildy?"

"It *is* better," said Nolan without hesitating. "And Universal is, too. Tildy's just easier to get a job for." He scrunched his nose as he opened his eyes to look down at her. "Tildy's even more little-kid-y," he said, making up a word. But that was exactly how he felt about it.

Lilac's eyes narrowed and she crawled closer to his face, straddling one leg over his torso. All pretense of sunscreen forgotten, she put a hand on his chest and leaned her lips toward his. On instinct more than anything, Nolan raised himself up on his arm slightly and turned his head so his lips could meet hers.

She pulled back, though, just as he went in for the kiss. "Traitor," she whispered, and Nolan wasn't sure if it was on purpose, but she slid her butt down then, grinding gently but firmly against his hard-on.

Nolan actually groaned—she'd made him *groan*, on a public beach of all places—and lay back down against the sand. They'd shifted in all the movement, the towel lost somewhere to the side of them, their bodies catching the last of the day's sunbeams instead of being trapped beneath the stifling shadow of the umbrella.

He heard the slather and slap of Lilac's hands together and she started running sunscreen across his torso from where she still sat atop his body.

"The right answer was Tildy World is the best damn theme

park in the country," he said, teasing her. He opened one eye to catch her reaction. "Apparently?"

The smug turn of her lips was delectable as she squirted more sunscreen onto her palms. "Wrong again," she said, rubbing her palms together like she was about to devour him. "But I'll give partial credit." She put her hands on his chest and leaned forward again. "It's the best damn theme park in the *world*," she said, pressing her lips gently toward his.

"In the world," repeated Nolan once she'd let go. He couldn't believe how easily she'd maneuvered him into that one.

She finished rubbing on his chest and stood, reaching her hand out toward him. "Now show me this damn fine beach before the sun sets and we've wasted all this time applying sunscreen."

Chuckling, he put his hand in hers, letting her tug at him to get him up but relying more on his own power than hers to bring them both to standing. "Even if it were already completely dark outside, that was no waste, believe me."

Lilac's smile then was like sunlight itself.

CHAPTER THIRTEEN

Lilac held the hotel keycard between her teeth as she shifted her tote bag from one arm to the other and dug through the overnight bag she'd tossed in the backseat of her car.

"Are you sure you don't mind?" asked Nolan from behind her. He reached into his swim trunks to pull out a pair of keys. "I can get some cash from my wallet. These beachside hotels cost a bit much, but I can chip in forty or so dollars."

Lilac glanced over her shoulder to find him cringing. That was only a tiny portion of the hotel cost, but she didn't care. She'd offered to pay it all. She had her daddy's charge card for "things to treat herself," as he'd told her when he'd given it to her when she'd first gone off to college, and he'd never once questioned a charge or accused her of going overboard.

Besides, she wasn't stupid. She'd heard his story and knew the poor guy couldn't afford to spare much. She pulled the keycard out of her mouth and tossed it in the tote bag as she pulled her cover-up out of the bag. "Keep it," she said, pulling the long shirt over her head. She should have done that before she'd gone and gotten them a room because several heads had turned when she'd walked into the lobby in her golden bikini. "I offered. You accepted."

Nolan jingled his car keys in his hand absentmindedly. "I know, I just..."

"Will your family think it's weird if you don't show up tonight?"

"I'll text Dad," he said. Despite his clear nervousness, he cracked a smile. "I have condoms in my car."

Lilac grinned and rifled more through her bag, bringing out a variety. "You can get those or use one of mine," she said. "I didn't know what you'd like, so I came prepared."

Nolan's eyes widened staring at the rows in her hands. She *had* bought enough to bed the entire Miami Dolphins lineup, but she hoped he didn't think that meant she was the kind of girl to use them all. Not all at once anyway.

She slipped the condoms back into her bag and took out her sunglasses. The sun was almost gone by now, but the bright red orb glared harshly off the surrounding cars and glass structures. "And I'm on the pill," she said, "so no worries there."

"Right," said Nolan, swallowing. "I'll just grab my shirt—"

Lilac stepped forward and put a hand around his bicep. "The whole point of this is to take clothes *off*, not put more clothes on."

He stared pointedly at her cover-up.

"Touché," she said, letting him go. She pulled her phone out of her bag as he left to stop by his car—a decade-plus-old thing with rust stains near the tires and under the driver's side door.

Just letting you know I did wind up getting a room, she texted Aunt Frankie. *And no worries. I had exactly zero alcoholic drinks.*

She saw a message from Gavin, but she was too giddy to respond.

Nolan appeared again at her side and he looked even more handsome in a skin-tight, faded T-shirt than he had with his bare torso exposed, so apparently that was possible. "Shall we?" he asked, extending his arm. Lilac took it. *A gentleman. If only he weren't so damn young...*

But he'd do for the night and then some.

———

Nolan tried not to stare at the bottom of Lilac's golden bikini that poked out from beneath her oversized shirt as she put the keycard in the hotel room door. He realized she'd more than invited him to look—and she was clearly sober tonight, so it was nice to know all that talk last weekend hadn't *just* been the alcohol—but he still felt like a perv.

Tossing her bag on the floor inside, she turned around and his eyes snapped back up to her face, where her lips turned into a devious grin. "*You're* impatient." She wrapped her hands around his torso and pulled him into the room with her.

He didn't even look at the room as the door slid shut behind him. He put his arms around her waist, felt the softness of her lower back, and couldn't tear his gaze away from the picturesque depths of her crystal-blue eyes. As he leaned forward for a kiss, her finger went to his lips.

"First things first," she said. "I want to clarify a few things."

Nolan swallowed, his groin pulsating and threatening to tear a hole in his swim trunks if he waited a minute longer. He took a deep breath. Damn, he was rusty. He didn't want her to think he couldn't satisfy her.

He regretted more than ever that he hadn't made time for more tail over the past few months. He could have done with the practice when faced with the first girl for whom he really wanted to do it right.

"This is just fun," she said. "Right?"

A chill ran through Nolan's body then and his throat suddenly felt parched. The serpentine contents of his swim trunks cooled off somewhat then, which was ironic because his "other brain" down there should have given less of a shit than *he* did if there was any hope of a long-term relationship with the gorgeous woman in his arms. It was enough that there was a *gorgeous woman* in his arms.

"Su-Sure," he scrambled to say, clearing his throat and trying to appear casual. "I mean—if that's what you want."

Lilac let go of his waist and flipped the switch to turn on the light in the room. Usually, Nolan would say he'd prefer the dark, but there was no way he was letting a second of this evening with Lilac lurk beneath the shadows where he couldn't see her. She picked up her tote and strolled toward the bed—one king-sized bed, he noticed, which was, naturally, bigger than the twin XL he had at home. He'd never take a girl there, though, so that wasn't too much of an issue. The room was nice, he finally noticed—bright and cheery, sleek and modern like a beach cabana might be, and there was a view of Cocoa Beach and the ocean behind her that would have taken his breath away if Lilac wasn't already removing her shirt again.

She put her hands behind her back to reach the back of her bikini top, but she caught him staring. She turned around and undid her bun, letting her long, blonde hair unfurl down past the middle of her back. Lifting it up, she glanced over her shoulder. "Untie me?" she asked, slow and seductive.

Nolan didn't have to be asked twice. He strode the distance between them in four seconds flat, gently pulling at her string at the back of her neck and then the one lower down. The bikini top fell limply into his hands.

With slow, deliberate movements, she let go of her hair and turned around, letting him look at the biggest pair of breasts he'd ever had the privilege of seeing in person. They were well-shaped, too, and Nolan knew the flesh would spill from between his fingers if he laid his hands to rest there.

Before he could even realize he was doing more than just imagining that, Lilac grinned and grabbed hold of her bikini top, which he'd squished against one of her nipples in his eagerness. She slid it loose from his fingers and tossed it on the ground before leaning forward and whispering in his ear. "I've got sand in all of my cracks," she said. "I'm going to take a shower first."

A light bulb went off in Nolan's head just then. "I've never had sex in the shower."

Bursting out laughing, Lilac leaned back. "Sorry," she said suddenly, perhaps reading something on his face—some feeling of embarrassment he hadn't meant to convey—and catching her breath. "I wasn't laughing *at* you, I just—yes," she said. "Let's do it." She nodded. "It's been a while since I've done it in the shower."

She headed toward the bathroom door. "But do give me a moment to freshen up first. I'll call you when I'm ready." She paused and pointed toward her bag on the bed. "Grab a flavor."

As she shut the door behind her, Nolan strode over toward the bed.

Grape? Strawberry? Nolan hadn't figured the girl for having a penchant for candy.

———

Soaked, fresh and decidedly sand-free, Lilac let the warm barrage of the water from the showerhead help clear her head. She thanked God for the fact that there was a walk-in shower separate from the tub—she'd tried the traditional tub/shower combo before and had decided she wouldn't attempt it again unless she developed talent as a contortionist. No, the one time she'd gotten the shower thing right had been in Spain with a cute local in her global studies program. Spanish showers were just made better for such things compared to the ones crammed into tiny college apartments.

Stepping away from the showerhead, Lilac took a deep breath. She needed to focus. Focus on the now, push the niggling feelings of disgust away. Nolan was exactly what she needed right now. Adorable, sweet, and younger than her, if only by a year—a little fling and nothing too serious.

And she was going to enjoy the fuck out of this fling.

She wrapped a towel around her torso, opened the door, and peered out into the room. "You can come in now."

Nolan was pacing the room, a condom in his hand instead of on his dick. That hardly surprised Lilac. She knew a lot of guys liked her to be the one to put it on them.

"Can you hold this?" he asked. "Um, I need to take a piss."

Letting out a small chuckle, she stepped outside the room. She pinched the condom lightly between two fingers, her other hand struggling to keep the towel in place. "Those might be the most romantic words a man has ever uttered to me."

She liked the way his face went red when she teased him.

"Sorry," he said. "A bit off my game."

He didn't shut the door behind him entirely, but she gave him some space. A few minutes later, she heard his voice call out. "You can—you can come in."

She did. His clothes were on the floor in the corner and he was already standing there in the shower beneath the hot, steamy, steady stream of water.

Lilac took back what she'd thought earlier. He *did* look better naked. He was no bodybuilder, but he had definition and a pertness to his ab muscles that no one but college boys seemed capable of maintaining. His thighs were thick and defined, just how she liked him, and the way his hip bones jutted out made her want to run her fingers along them. She crossed the room and did just that, gently putting the condom between her teeth and staring at where her fingers went as they traced those sharp bones toward the flaccid penis that hung down there, just waiting for her.

"You're soaking your towel," he said then.

"Don't care," she replied, and she got on her knees, the dregs of the shower water that made its way over Nolan's shoulders and torso spraying like a gentle waterfall over her head. She repositioned the condom so she could use her fingers and teeth to slide his sword into its sheath.

It grew hard almost instantly, but Lilac just stretched her torso straighter, dug her free hand into his thick thigh and unfurled the rubber—gently, slowly, letting him savor every moment of it.

He stumbled a bit and leaned his back against the tiles as his hands found purchase on her shoulders.

Once the condom was fully on, Lilac took a deep breath and slipped the tip of his member in her mouth. Her towel slipped then, and his eyes were drawn instantly to the tops of her breasts and her erect nipples. She purposely pushed the tips of her breasts against his thighs, letting her nipples trace a pattern like feathers against his skin. Her tongue, meanwhile, worked its way around the strawberry-flavored condom, up his shaft, taking as much of him inside her mouth as she could, letting her throat relax.

Nolan groaned, letting his hands fling wildly to the back of her head and she moved her tongue around and around until he seemed about to burst.

"Stand," he gasped, surprisingly commandeering in the moment.

She let him slide out of her mouth and leaned back, collapsing onto her calves. She stared up. The water cascaded around the back of him and dripped down his hair, down his arms, down his torso and he looked amazingly like Tarzan beneath a waterfall in the jungle.

Shower sex had never made her feel as wild and raunchy as this.

"Come on," he said, his hand extended toward her. He smiled, invitingly—sweetly. "Stand, beautiful. Let me return the favor."

On shaking limbs, she did as bidden. Nolan locked his lips with hers immediately and she grabbed tightly to his hair, pulling him closer, needing to merge all of him with her. His hands cupped her breasts and slid down the sides of her, pausing at her hips and sliding to her buttocks, where they worked in massaging motions down and under her ass cheeks. He gripped them hard and somehow found a way to tug her even closer. His lips an inch from hers, the water pebbling down both of their foreheads, he asked, "Shall I reach inside you?"

She nodded breathlessly. "Hurry," she said, feeling a wave of need and *hunger* rise inside her.

One hand let go of her buttocks and his fingers traveled around the length of her flesh along her hips and to the front. Slipping between the lips of her labia, the fingers circled around and up to that most special of spots on her body. They danced lightly there and her knees buckled as she fell into him, clutching to his back for support. "More," she whispered.

And he gave her more, his fingers moving down and inside her, breaking through her defenses gently, expanding and sliding up, then down. Lilac clutched to his skin, trying not to let her nails dig in and hurt him but feeling as if she might collapse out of pleasure if he didn't anchor her.

"Can I come in?" he whispered in her ear and she wanted to laugh—she did laugh, but it was drowned out by the sound of the water falling and the groan that passed her lips as his thumb went to work in tandem with his fingers. "Yes," she gasped, and in a moment, his fingers were gone and she almost wanted to cry out to him to put them back, but he had flipped her around, slowly but firmly, taking care to make sure she didn't slip in the gathering water that sloshed over their toes. Her hands slammed against the tile to steady her legs. Before she could even make another sound, one of his hands reached up to gather her left breast, the other wrapped around and parked firmly on her clit, and then she felt his cock slide all the way up inside her.

She screamed, then—not in pain or fear, but a real, guttural, primal sound as she worked through the burst of pleasure unlike any she'd quite felt before.

He withdrew slightly—then went back in.

"Again," she said, her voice rough, but she didn't care. She didn't care that he utterly destroyed her in that moment. She didn't care about anything except feeling him inside her. "*Again*," she whispered.

And he did. They did. Again and again with her back to the wall and their own personal waterfall flushing down over them, washing all their dirtiness away. But she begged for it again and again, refusing to let the water cleanse them entirely. Again and again, after they shut the faucet off and toweled dry, only to find their lips locked and Lilac's ass on the bed and the whole dance begun anew.

CHAPTER FOURTEEN

Before Nolan opened his eyes, for the briefest of moments, he luxuriated in the feel of Lilac's cheek resting on his bare chest, her hand resting over his front, tucked against his hip.

Like a balm over the chapped and ragged thing that had been his heart the past few years, her touch had soothed and awoken him, even though a part of him still felt like there was the ghost of something there behind it even on her side—a touch of heartache.

He wished he could be the one to soothe her pain. He wanted to be.

In a jolt as his eyes fluttered open, he realized it was Saturday morning and he'd left his phone in his car's glove compartment. He'd texted his dad about being gone for a while after school, but despite assurances to Lilac that he would, he'd never texted to say he'd planned to spend the whole night away from home. Part of him hadn't wanted to see his dad tell him he couldn't stay because he was needed the next morning, and part of him honestly thought he'd be on his way before the sun rose. As if he could willingly walk away from her.

Once the jolt settled, he really didn't care. His dad didn't work most weekends. He could deal with the kids.

Right now, he just wanted to commit her touch to memory.

She stirred then, letting out a little groan that reminded him mischievously of her groans from the night before. "Good morning," she said, yawning. She shifted herself up and pressed her lips lightly to his.

"Morning," he replied. He rested one hand on her shoulder and laid his lips once lightly on her forehead.

She grinned and gently detangled herself from him, pushing aside the sheet that covered part of their legs. "Do you want breakfast?"

Grabbing for her elbow, Nolan missed but kept trying, holding on to nothing but air. "Stay," he said, and he felt his voice crack. It sounded pathetic, but in that moment he didn't care.

The pain he'd shoved down and shoved down as he moved forward through every day shot to the surface like a bolt of lightning as she stood beside the bed. She stared at him over her shoulder, something illegible on her face, but she gave him a faltering smile and slipped back in beside him. "Just for a bit," she said. "Checkout is at noon."

Nolan felt guilty then as she wrapped one arm back around him and snuggled against his side. He didn't want her to pity him, he just thought—well, this was part of it, too, wasn't it? The cuddling? Even if that was difficult to do when she was in the nude in his arms.

He took a deep breath. The surest way to settle his loins was to focus on something else—focus on the friend he wanted her to be, if she wasn't interested in letting them be any more. He could handle that. He'd expected that. Why would someone like *her* consider being his girlfriend?

"Tell me more about you," he said, staring at the ceiling and rubbing his fingers through her hair.

"What about me?" she asked, and although her tone wasn't entirely defensive, there was something there, something that was hidden behind a shield she kept guarded.

"Well, you're from near Chicago," he said. "You've spent a

semester in Spain… You love Tildy World. The *greatest theme park on the planet*," he added to make her laugh.

She *did* chuckle a bit. "That's about it."

"I doubt that," said Nolan. Giving her shoulder a squeeze, he started rubbing his hand up and down her upper arm, careful not to touch her breast and stop this conversation before it truly started.

"What do you want to know?" she asked.

"Did you always want to be a theme park resort assistant manager?"

She stiffened beneath his touch. "No. I never even considered it."

"Then how——?"

"I was set to become an elementary school teacher until a few weeks ago. In Minnesota of all places."

That caused Nolan to chuckle. "How do you go from snow to beaches?"

Shrugging, Lilac nuzzled her cheek against his chest again. "It just happened."

Nolan waited for her to continue, but she didn't. "I can see you as an elementary school teacher. Landon loves you. Even my bratty sister has nothing but good things to say about you—anyone who can make Landon smile is A+ in her book."

The little peal of laughter Lilac gave off then made Nolan's heart flutter, and it didn't help that she started running her fingertip across his stomach. "I like kids," she said. "So I decided to teach them. But I was never overly obsessed with becoming a teacher. It was a *lot* of work just graduating with an education degree and a proper license. I was so busy the whole time, I barely had time to second-guess my decision."

"How did Spain fit in to that?"

Her fingers stopped moving. "It didn't, really. I just wanted to go. Well, I turned it into a Spanish minor, which certainly doesn't hurt to pair with an education degree. But mostly, I just… Needed the break."

Nolan knew that feeling too well. He just didn't know how it felt to have the means and opportunity to take that break—although if this was his break, this certainly wasn't too shabby.

"My time in Spain was *amazing*," she continued. "And I just... I don't know. I started regretting thinking so small."

Nolan wasn't sure he'd consider teaching elementary "thinking small"—surely, it paid decently enough and it was definitely a more admirable job than putting on a silly plush suit and entertaining kids that way—but he didn't say anything. To a point, he knew what she meant. Living abroad was more glamorous than teaching. "My mom was going back to school to be a teacher," he said at last. "It was on her way back from a night class that she got into an accident."

"Oh, I... I'm sorry. I don't mean to demean the profession. I met a lot of women—and men, but mostly women—who'd make amazing teachers. It's just, I..."

"No offense taken," he said. He wanted to steer her back to herself. "If Mom could have lived in Spain, I'm sure she would have found that more appealing, too."

"I know," said Lilac. "And I feel stupid for complaining. I could... I could do almost anything. Mom and Daddy would make sure I had everything I needed, even if I'd just wanted to take a year or two off to travel."

Wow, thought Nolan. *A year or two off to travel? She lives in a different world than I do.*

"But no, I was determined to show them I would work. Determined to *do* something, to have a reason for my degree... I was all set to be a teacher and then Frankie told me about this job opening at Tildy World and—I knew I wasn't qualified, I *knew* that, but you have to understand how much Tildy World meant to be as a child. I just felt like... If I didn't at least try, I'd regret it the rest of my life. I didn't think I'd regret not taking the teaching job. Not..." Her voice cracked. "Well, I do now, but not for the reasons I would have thought."

A jolt of panic shot through Nolan's body. "You regret coming here?"

"I wish I didn't." There was that sadness again.

"I'm sorry," he said, trying hard not to take it personally. He knew for a fact that she'd been miserable last weekend before they'd begun their flirtation. It wasn't about him—but oh, how it hurt to know he hadn't been enough to make her feel better or to want to be here in his arms. "Is this... What happened last weekend?"

Lilac's voice caught. "I don't... It's nothing."

"It doesn't seem like *nothing*," he said. "Lilac, you were wasted last Sunday—"

She jolted upright and was off the side of the bed before he could even finish his sentence.

"Lilac." He raised himself up on one elbow and ran a hand through his hair. "I'm sorry, I didn't mean it like that."

"It's fine," she said through gritted teeth, giving Nolan one final view of her beautifully round ass as she bent over to grab something out of her tote bag. She put one leg and then the other through a pair of black-laced panties. She looked even hotter in them than out of them, which Nolan was surprised to discover was even possible. "I just... I don't want to talk about it."

"Then we won't talk about it," said Nolan, reaching a hand out toward her.

She was already clasping a matching black lace bra. Nolan knew that if he got up and she saw his erection, she might snap at him for the inappropriateness of his lust at this particular moment. He settled for clenching the bed sheets hard with one hand instead.

Before he could think of what else to do, she threw on a tank top, tossing a pair of jeans atop the nearby table. *Someone came better prepared than me*, he thought.

She'd *planned* to sleep with him—that much was clear. So didn't that mean something? "I just wanted—that is, can't we be friends?"

"I'd say we're a little more than that now," said Lilac, tugging one leg of her jeans up.

"Then talk to me, Lilac," said Nolan. Erection be damned, he sat up then, shifting the sheets slightly to hide what was going on down there.

"I *am* talking," grunted Lilac as she finished tugging the second leg of her pants up. She jiggled her butt so divinely just then, Nolan had to actually bite his lip and squeeze the sheet harder before he burst. "I'm trying to keep it casual, as we agreed."

"You mean, you *decided*." It slipped out before he could think better of it.

Lilac stared down at him, tears somehow bubbling from her eyes at the same time her brows furrowed and her lips trembled. "And you *agreed*." She threw her hands up. "Isn't this what you all want?" She gestured to her body, still so luscious even under those layers of clothes. "I let you have it. Doesn't mean I'm going to pledge myself to you."

"Whoa, whoa," said Nolan, swinging his legs over the side of the bed. "Who said anything about *dating* you? I asked you to the beach is all. You're the one who took it a step further. Not that I'm *complaining*, mind you..."

That seemed to be the wrong thing to say. Or maybe there was no right thing to say just then. "See?" Lilac snatched her tote bag up off the floor and slid it over her shoulder, digging through and tossing a keycard down on the bed. "Well, then, we're good. Just... Give that to the front desk before noon." She was clearly trying to seem cool and collected, but Nolan couldn't tell if it was anger or sadness that colored her every casual movement in that moment.

And—feeling lost in his own mixture of the two—he empathized. "Sure," he spat, grabbing for the key. "Casual, then. You've made it clear what you think of me. It's all on the table." *Everything except the feelings I thought I had—I still have, damn it—for you...* He was lying to himself. He still had feelings, fledgling though they may be, and his damn cock down below was currently raging at him, begging him to make this right—just for more access to that beautiful, curvy body. *I'm as bad as she thinks I am*, he thought.

Lilac took a step toward the door, but she hesitated. "No," she said. "I... I think better of you than that." She swallowed. "You're a good guy. That's why I felt safe coming to you for this."

"For *this*?" he asked, raising a hand in question. "I... I'm glad you think of me that way, Lilac, but I mean, I... I don't usually do this."

"Do what?"

"Sleep around. Keep it casual."

Lilac's lips pinched. "And I suppose you think there's something wrong with me for doing that?"

"No, that's not what I meant—"

"No, I get it. It's my fault. I shouldn't have..." She really started crying now, though she did her best to ignore the tears tumbling down her cheeks. "Just pretend this never happened. I don't know how much longer I'll be here anyway."

Jumping off the bed, Nolan stumbled toward her, carrying the sheet in front of him. "Lilac, please. I don't want things to end like—"

But she was gone, the door shut closed behind her.

Unless he wanted to waddle through the hotel hallways with the sheet over his member, he had to let her go.

Nolan stood there behind the closed door a while longer, trying and trying to convince himself it was all for the best.

———

After a shower and putting on his wrinkly, damp swim trunks along with his shirt, Nolan stared at his face for a long moment in the mirror before taking a deep breath and leaving the room behind. Lilac's bikini was missing—she'd gotten up to go to the bathroom after they'd finished his third or fourth climax the night before, he couldn't remember which—and she must have prepared to leave straightaway come morning. Just as she'd prepared to spend the night with him. All these plans and she hadn't even let him in on any of them until he'd felt tugged and pulled and led by the nose in whichever direction she'd desired him to go. And like a dog—or a silly, clueless sandgrouse—he'd let her lead the way.

She was the first girl he'd taken to a bedroom—or, more accurately, who'd taken him to a bedroom—who'd led him around like that. He thought he'd liked leading the way, but last night had been... Well, so much for that assumption. Still, he'd kind of had his way in the heat of the moment and he thought—if he wasn't just being a touch too full of himself—that she'd liked it.

The keycard given to the front desk, though they told him he could have left it in the room, and the whole night behind him, he sighed as he made his way to his car, pausing to confirm that sure enough, Lilac's shiny new vehicle was long gone, replaced by a minivan carrying a family that was working to unload the day's accessories from the trunk. Two little girls and a boy ran around the van, tripping up their parents, ignoring their cries to calm down.

He looked longingly at the beach, so beautiful in the rays of the early morning sun, but he knew he'd find no comfort there—not now anyway.

After getting inside his car, he fished out his phone. He'd missed half a dozen calls and there was a text message. He'd *known* his father wouldn't be happy, but was it too much to ask him to give him a break just once?

Then he saw the first text message that awaited him: *Where are you?* it asked. *Willow's in the ER.*

It was dated yesterday evening. Nolan felt as if his stomach had dropped out to the car floor.

CHAPTER FIFTEEN

Lilac didn't want to talk to Gavin. She didn't want to talk to anyone. The wind on her face did little to dry the tears that ran down her cheeks as she drove back to Aunt Frankie's, more than once tempted by a random turnoff leading to who-knew-where—anywhere. Anywhere but here. Anywhere but this mistake.

One call to her mom and daddy and she knew they'd tell her to just go home. If she explained why, her daddy might even show up in Florida himself and knock some sense into Earl.

Only it wasn't just Earl who tugged at her heart now—it was Nolan, too. For completely opposite reasons. Last night had been amazing and... That was more than a little scary.

Lilac knew this routine. Fuck the frat boy, have some fun, get over it, let a few months go by, hear the roar of her natural urges building up from below until they dominated her mind, fuck a new frat boy.

Cute, eager, not that into romance and commitment—they made perfect bed mates.

But Nolan wasn't a frat boy. He looked like one. With his goofy demeanor and A-game flirtations, he'd probably pass as one. But he was also kinder, more responsible. He had a baby face but a far more mature heart.

And she'd stupidly convinced herself that this was more of the same. That she'd still be able to see him around the park—go on dates on occasion—and there wouldn't be this awkward, lingering tension between them.

But the fact was it scared her, this tug in her heart. He was supposed to be a distraction. He wasn't supposed to make her think about what had happened, what her life had come to.

She'd embarrassed herself in front of Nolan again and again. Instead of proving the boost she needed to stuff that workplace nightmare down deep where she wanted it buried, he'd just opened her up to so much more.

Wiping her face with her palm, Lilac did take a random highway exit, pulling into a gas station and fueling up her hybrid. The nozzle in place and pumping, she grabbed her phone out of her bag and leaned against the driver's side door. It seemed as if everyone and their mothers had sent her messages or commented on the pictures of the beach she'd posted when she'd been in a better mood the evening before. Frankie's emoji-filled text cheering her on—she'd guessed it was Nolan and she knew what spending the night meant—only made her stomach sour now. There was even something from Pembroke of all people, an FB message just asking how she'd been and how she liked Florida. *Where to even begin?* She hadn't even told Brielle what had happened —she might have, had Brielle not been so dismissive last weekend —and she certainly couldn't tell Pembroke.

Gavin was the only one who knew. She'd begged him to stop harping on it all week, but he'd been there for her, trying to make her laugh, even if he was always circling back to the issue at hand.

She started up a text, but her heart almost caught in her throat. Looking around—no other car was at a pump nearby—she hit "call" for his number instead.

Gavin answered on the third ring. "Li?"

Lilac traced a finger over the top of her side view mirror. "Is this a good time?"

There was laughter and muffled conversation in the background. "Yeah," he said. "Just give me a minute." She heard footsteps and then a door open and close, more echoing footsteps, and then a static-like sound that could only be the winds of the windy city. "Sorry, the guys are having some friends over."

"I'll call back later." Lilac's voice trembled. The gas was finished pumping and she felt dumb for calling him from there, but she'd wanted to hear his voice.

"It's fine," said Gavin. "I'm on the roof. And before you ask, it's allowed. Sadly, there's no pool or anything up here, but smokers have to go somewhere in an apartment building, I guess, right? I tend to avoid it because smoke is impossible to get out of your clothes. It's too bad, though. The view is incredible from up here."

Lilac closed her eyes for a moment and pictured herself atop some Chicago building, the wind on her face and Gavin beside her. But it was so hot and sticky here. The only time she felt anything resembling a breeze was when she was driving.

"Gavin, I want to come home."

Gavin didn't say anything at first and Lilac wondered if maybe he hadn't heard her over the sounds of the whipping air all around him. "If that's what you need," he said. "Just let me know what you need from me. I'll meet you at the airport or drive down there to help you pack or—"

Snorting, Lilac wiped away more tears from her face. "I don't need you to come down here," she said. "Besides, if you drove, you wouldn't be able to get back in time for work on Monday. And since when do you have a car?"

"They're called rentals and details, details. It's not like this is a real job." He sighed.

"I'd pay for you to fly here if I needed it," she said. "But I don't."

"Okay," said Gavin. A moment of silence hung between them. "Then tell me what you need, Li. I'm here for you. And your other friends can be, too—"

"What other friends?" scoffed Lilac. She reached inside her tote bag to grab a tissue.

"Brielle and Pembroke for starters," said Gavin.

"They're more your friends than mine."

"You introduced me to Brielle!"

"And yet somehow, she's more your friend than mine." She took a deep breath and cradled her phone between her cheek and her shoulder to remove the fuel pump from her car. "Never mind—I know why. You're amazing. You're—you're—"

"What is it?" Gavin asked, his voice quieter. "What happened today?"

Hanging the pump back in place, Lilac found her voice wavering. "It's not… It's not what you're thinking. I—I actually had a great night last night."

"Well, that's great to hear. What happened? Please tell me it had something to do with that knight-in-shining-sandgrouse-suit."

Lilac's throat went dry. "It—It did."

"That's amazing, Li! I… Look, I wish you were near me as much as anything, but I also know this was your *dream*. You gave up something you worked very hard for because you love Florida. You love sun and beaches. You love Tildy World. You can fight for what you love—for what makes you happy. For what *you* deserve and what that asshole *actually* deserves…"

"I don't love it here anymore, Gavvy. I miss you. I miss home."

Silence. "Then come home, Li."

A car honked and Lilac jumped. Looking around her, she realized the station had grown more crowded and there was a line forming for free pumps. "I've got to go."

"Lilac, I wish you'd let me help more. I wish you'd let more people know."

"Tell whoever you want," said Lilac, opening her car door and flipping off the driver who kept honking at her. She pushed the ignition button and ran a finger tipped with hot pink nail polish under her eye to pick off an errant eyelash. "I don't care anymore." She put the phone down in her cup holder and put the car in drive. "I'll call later," she said, disconnecting.

After that, she didn't really remember the trip home. If it

weren't for her GPS talking to her along the way, she wasn't sure she would have even managed to get back to Aunt Frankie's bungalow.

———

Lilac wasn't going on a bender again. She'd learned her lesson there —though part of her wished she more clearly remembered the start of her little fling with Nolan. Gavin had spoken highly of him and apparently, no matter how crazy she'd gotten, it hadn't been enough to scare him away. Not until she'd stuck her foot in her mouth and completely ruined things the day before.

Instead, she settled for drinking iced tea and lounging on Aunt Frankie's covered patio on Sunday, collecting her thoughts and weighing what to do. She'd brought her worn stuffed Tildy Tapir with her, cradling it between her arms against her abdomen. She still wore her pajamas from the night before.

She could take those years off to go traveling. She wouldn't even have to explain to her family *why*—they'd all just assume it was simply *Lilac being Lilac*.

Gavin must have said something to Brielle and Pembroke, though—even to *Pembroke*, whom she couldn't ever remember exchanging a non-group message with—because both sent her messages saying they were there for her if she wanted to talk. Brielle even apologized for being so flippant the week before.

Lilac felt better reading that, but she still didn't feel like writing back.

Gavin must have said something vaguer to Frankie, too, because she'd gone from cheerful and chatty to silent and awkward about mid-morning. Finally, Sunday afternoon, after Lilac had refused both Frankie's homemade brunch and her lunch, Frankie took the lounge chair next to her, a glass of iced lemonade in hand. Even in the shade, she wore her sunglasses. The Florida sun was bright like that, the sun-coated parts of Frankie's yard almost blinding to take in, even from the shade of the patio.

"Gavin tells me I should ask you to tell me what's bothering you," said Frankie. "I... I know you were stressed last week, but if there's something more to it, you should tell me."

Lilac shrugged.

"Are you really thinking of going home?" asked Frankie. "It's your life, and you know your grandparents and parents won't mind, but... I thought, I don't know, I thought you were different from the rest of us."

That got Lilac stirring. "What do you mean by that?"

Frankie slid her sunglasses down her nose slightly to peer over at her niece. "You're as gorgeous as your mother and grandmothers, but you never treated college as a playground like they did. You worked hard, you got your degree—"

"And then totally blew the job path I'd created for myself."

The ice cubes jingled against the glass as Frankie waved her lemonade in the air. "Even so, you stuck with it and put in the work and only changed your mind when something more appealing came along." She took a sip from her glass. "You could have just coasted through college, then spent the rest of your life traveling, like the rest of the Townsends."

Lilac didn't point out the Etsy store Frankie managed or the jobs her daddy and Grandpa Matthew had had back in their youths. She knew that most of their wealth came from investments and inheritance and that she had those to fall back on, too.

"My point is," said Frankie, readjusting her glasses, "you work hard, kiddo. And I know that no matter where you land, you'll land on your feet, but I just want you to make sure you really want to give this up. If you leave, I doubt you can come back—not to the same theme park anyway."

Lilac cuddled her worn Tildy, not saying anything.

"You remember when you got that, don't you?" asked Frankie. "It was your first time visiting me since you could walk—you must have been three or four. Your parents wanted to bring you to Disney, but—"

"I wanted to go to Tildy World," said Lilac, the vaguest of memories popping into her head. "I liked her cartoons."

Frankie's lips tugged into a gentle smile. "Do you know why you liked them? At least, the reason you gave me when I asked?"

"'If you dream hard enough, I'll make your dreams come true,'" said Lilac, quoting Tildy Tapir herself.

Frankie put her glass down on a coaster on the small table between them, her jangly bracelets sliding down just past her wrist as she moved. "And yet you never once counted on Tildy making your dreams come true for you," said Frankie. "I admire that. You didn't get that from the Townsends, I assure you."

Lilac laughed and tucked her chin behind her plush. Its fur had started piling in patches. "You give me too much credit," she said. "I never would have gotten the job here if it weren't for you and your connections."

"Maybe." Frankie shrugged. "But you don't know what. You might have applied on your own."

And that asshole might have still seen my boobs and given me the job. She sighed. "But I... I felt safe taking risks, striving for my dreams," she admitted, thinking painfully all of a sudden of Brielle and how she'd teased her about not having much of a job after graduation. She wondered if she'd studied history and philosophy if her daddy would have just called some museum where he'd made a donation and given her a way in there. She wondered if she couldn't have asked her daddy to do the same for her friend—if she'd ever been cognizant of things outside of herself to think of it.

It was like a punch to the gut.

She thought of Nolan then, of how hard he worked while going to school, of the way he stepped up to take care of his siblings. How there had been something there when he'd offered her cash for the hotel, a reluctance he was trying to stifle—he probably really *needed* the money.

Lilac worked hard for her dreams, but there was no escaping the fact that she had a fairy godmother of sorts in the form of a trust fund and a family with connections.

It struck her then. She'd been considering turning tail and going home—stuffing it all down and putting it all behind her. She'd suspected women had been harassed by Earl before her and had lamented that none of them had stepped forward to stop it.

Maybe they couldn't have. Maybe they didn't have her resources and her fairy godmother.

But *she* could. And even if it meant the end of her time at Tildy World, that was exactly what she was contemplating regardless. Rather than let him get away with it, pave the way for him to assault another woman—she could raise a fuss, cause a stink.

"Frankie," she said, her lips cracking, "I might need a lawyer."

That actually got Aunt Frankie to remove her sunglasses from her face entirely.

CHAPTER SIXTEEN

The past week and a half were a blur in Nolan's mind. There was the work—that stayed consistent, and even if he was frowning and sweating inside Silly's head, he knew that Silly's grin and Nolan's own hand flourishes made it seem like he was Mr. Cheerful personified—but everything else was like ripping his foundations away. He could barely focus during class. He fell behind with a couple of projects, and though he got an extension, he hadn't been making the most of the extra time allowed him.

He was just a mess.

"How's the little bean doing?" asked DeShawn as they entered the break room and Nolan was finally able to take off Silly's head.

DeShawn called most kids "little beans." Not that he expected his shift manager to remember the names of his siblings.

"She's all right," said Nolan, aware that his coworkers knew all about Willow's broken wrist and leg. Nolan had felt his world narrow to a frightening tunnel he'd experienced before—that time when he'd gotten the message that his mom was in the ER—but before he'd taken off like a shot, he'd listened to the rest of the messages. They'd gotten progressively angrier until they'd turned resigned. Willow had fallen off a park jungle gym while trying to smack another kid and she'd broken some bones. But she had had them set and she was home the next morning.

His dad had seemed to want to explode at Nolan the moment he'd walked through the door, but both kids were napping after the late night they'd had and he'd settled for grabbing him by the arm and pulling him outside.

"Where were you?" he asked. As if they were the co-parents of these kids, as if his dad was looking at his partner in this journey instead of *another one of his kids*.

"At the beach," said Nolan, digging his hands into his swim trunk pockets. There was no hiding that.

"I thought you had class, but then—the *beach?*"

"Class let out early." Nolan shrugged. "I didn't know there'd be a crisis. Cut me some slack." He felt like a sullen teenager all over again.

His dad ran a hand over his face. "If you wanted to go to the beach, you could have come home and taken the kids with you."

Nolan snorted. "On a Friday night? Landon would fall asleep before we even got halfway there."

"You could have waited until the weekend, then!" His dad paced the porch stoop now, his hands flailing. "Maybe then I'd have had them in bed earlier and I wouldn't have brought them to the park and Willow wouldn't have..." His voice caught in his throat.

Drawing his hand out of his pocket, Nolan placed it on his dad's shoulder, as much to stop the man's pacing as anything. "She's okay, right? You can't blame yourself."

"I can," said his dad. "I—I was focused on an email from work and I wasn't paying attention. You would have... You know how to handle them better."

Sighing, Nolan sat down on the porch step at his dad's feet. "Keep talking like that and you'll never fully step up," he said, knowing those words were going to start something.

But his dad was quiet as he sat beside him. "I know it's been hard for you, too, son, since your mom—"

"*There*," said Nolan. "See? I'm your *son*. I'm not supposed to be in charge of these kids around the clock. It's not supposed to be a big deal that I head out to the beach for a night. I'm old enough to legally drink and gamble, Dad. Half the guys I knew my age are getting ready to start their own families and the other half are at least far away from home." Leaning forward, he rested his chin atop his knees. "I was the only one left behind."

His dad rested a hand on Nolan's back. "I'm sorry. I shouldn't have snapped at you. I really wouldn't have minded except that this happened and—I panicked." Nolan could hear him choking on his words, fighting back his tears. "I... I was going to tell you. I quit my second job."

"What?" said Nolan, snapping upright. His dad's hand fell limply from Nolan's back. "But, Dad, things are tight enough—"

Waving a hand, his dad cut him off. "No. It's a good thing. The reason I've been so caught up in work—my first job, at the office— is because I've been competing with a few others to pull off a good second quarter of sales. The quarter isn't even over yet, but the boss has already been impressed with what I can do and—well, he already offered me the promotion." His smile faltered. "More pay and, since I can quit my store shifts, more time to be at home." He nudged him. "Which means more time you don't have to worry about being at home."

"That's... That's great." It really was, but Nolan was still more in shock than anything. *That's* why his dad had been harried and distracted? Not because he'd been in over his head—although that was probably true, too—but because he'd had a goal in mind, a goal that would make things easier for them all?

But that still didn't solve the problem of daycare for Landon. Dad's office didn't offer any like Tildy World did.

"Landon's going to be in kindergarten in the fall," said his dad then, as if he knew the trajectory of Nolan's thoughts. "I enrolled him in the full-day program—half is just the school's version of daycare, I suppose, but whatever will keep him around his peers and learning." His lips curled up into a faltering smile. "And I can afford to add more babysitter hours for the rest of the times we need one. I guess, what I'm saying is... If you want to go to college this fall... Proper college... I can't offer much by way of tuition, but maybe you and I can co-sign a loan."

"No," said Nolan without thinking. "Loans are a bad idea." They already owed on one of the cars and the house, and he was sure his dad had maxed their credit cards.

"Son, most kids take out some loans for college."

"Well, not this one." Nolan reached beside him to grab hold of an overgrown weed that had snaked its way up through a crack in the pavement. The yard really needed a mow. "The thing is, I... Since Mom died, I've barely had time to stop. I've barely had time to think. But I know now how it feels to live paycheck to paycheck, for that to not even be enough. I never realized how hard you and Mom worked for me—"

"We didn't want you to worry about such things growing up," his dad said. "I wouldn't want you to worry about it now. Oh, lord, if Lorna knew I had resorted to saddling you with all this responsibility..."

Nolan let go of the weed and patted his dad on the back. "I was an adult by then. I wanted to help."

"Helping is one thing. Becoming my rock is another." He took Nolan into his arms then, not even bothering to wipe the tears from his eyes. "I'm sorry. And thank you. I love you."

After missing his sister's accident, this was the last thing Nolan had pictured coming home to. "Love you, too," said Nolan, clearing his throat and trying to brush off the wave of emotions hitting him hard right then, smack in the sternum. As they broke apart, Nolan grabbed hold of his weed again and this time, he yanked and tugged until he'd ripped it out by the roots. "Dad, last night, well... I wasn't just at the beach all night."

"I would hope not." His dad paused then, waiting for Nolan to continue, but he didn't. "You met someone...?"

"Yeah," said Nolan, more resigned than happy. He barely cracked a smile. "And I screwed it up already."

Wrapping an arm around him then, his dad patted his shoulder. "Son, welcome to the club. When you figure out how to not screw up with the ladies, let me know your secret." He winked. "Better yet, when you find the girl who overlooks your screwups—like your mom did for me—bring her over here to meet me sometime."

Now, a week and a half later, as hectic as things had been at home, they'd been... Okay. Not painful anyway. As noisy and as stressful as ever, but his dad had been there—really *been* there, in mind as well as body. Willow could walk with a crutch since it was her right leg that was broken and her left wrist, but she still struggled and their dad had even taken a couple of personal days to stay home with her while Nolan and Landon had gone off to Tildy World for Nolan's usual shifts. Willow, the little scamp, seemed to like all the special attention. Were it not for the fact that she spurted tears—actual tears—when she said her skin itched or her bones hurt, Nolan would have been sure she'd done it all on purpose to get her dad to pay attention.

She'd gone back to school the following Wednesday and Nolan's dad had spoken with the woman who usually watched Landon on Fridays and had managed to get her to pick her up and drop her off, so she wouldn't have to climb up the bus.

Willow had come home that first day with tons of drawings and signatures on both casts, exhausted from the extra effort of all the walking, but so thoroughly soaking up all the attention.

"She's a little celebrity at school now," said Nolan to DeShawn as DeShawn tugged on the zipper on the back of the suit. The rush of cool, air-conditioned air from the break room was like a sweet, icy kiss. "So I think all in all, she's more happy this happened than not."

DeShawn chuckled at that. "We should get her and Bev together again some time," he said, referring to his own little sister, who was a few years older than Willow. They'd played together at Tildy World before, though Nolan wasn't sure their friendship extended much beyond that. "Are your brother and sister planning on coming to the big Ballroom/Tent Tildy crossover event this fall?"

"Are they doing that again?" asked Jo, who cradled Tildy's head under her fur-covered arm. "I thought they stopped."

"Word is, Gyu-ri is starting it up again with..." DeShawn tapped a finger to his lips, thinking. "Well, with that fine new assistant manager, whatever her name is—"

"The one who's threatening to sue the company?" asked Tildy Scout caretaker Eddie then, taking Tildy's head from Jo and helping her out of the rest of her suit. "Yeah, that's not happening."

Nolan's stomach ached as if someone had kicked it. Lilac hadn't been seen around Tent Tildy in over a week—well, as far as most people knew. Rumors said she'd been in to speak to HR, a besuited lawyer and a middle-aged woman with a pixie cut marching alongside her. Nolan knew that had to have been her aunt, but Lilac had been cagey in the few texts they'd exchanged since then.

The rumors were Earl had done something to her and no one— absolutely *no one*—was surprised. But Earl was still working, his unearned sense of joviality fairly diminished. He was as liable to snap a person's head off as he was to make a crack about a woman's ass these days.

Nolan felt sick then. Why *had* Earl been allowed to do such things again? Why had Tildy World of all places been okay with that asshole walking around in a position of power? As long as he didn't bother the guests, then anything goes?

"Jillian says his wife kicked him out," said Cheryl just then, cackling, a carrot stick in her hand as she approached. She had a Tildy Scout caretaker outfit on, too, her Queen Animaliao for the day one of the new girls over in the corner across the room. "And he's not wearing his ring anymore." She grinned evilly, putting her hand over her mouth to stifle her laughter.

No one liked that guy.

Eddie frowned. "Seems premature to celebrate a guy's life

getting ruined, don't you think? I mean, we don't know what happened."

Her hand now free of Tildy's furry arm, Jo smacked him—*hard*—on the shoulder. "Oh, no, you don't. You don't get to be one of *those guys* and be my boyfriend."

Eddie rubbed his arm, his lips halfway between a smile and an expression of pain. "What?" he asked, seeming genuinely flummoxed. "Just because I dared think a man innocent until proven guilty?"

"It's *Earl*," snapped DeShawn then. "You know what he's like."

"I mean, I know he's not the greatest of guys..." started Eddie.

"And how would she *prove* anything anyway?" asked Cheryl. "If he didn't do... whatever he did... where there's a camera, how is she supposed to *prove* things to your satisfaction?"

Eddie looked a bit put on the spot then. "Well, yeah, but I mean, can't a girl just make something up then? Why does everyone automatically assume—"

"*Oh, my god!*" Jo threw her hands up and started shuffling away, her legs still in the Tildy suit. "I'm not hearing this. I'm not hearing this from *my boyfriend*." She couldn't get far quickly at her Tildy-hindered pace.

"Babe," said Eddie, bending down to grab her legs and help her out. "I'm sorry. I bet you're right. I bet he's scum. I mean, he *is* grating. It's just, look, he's still working here—"

"While the investigation is pending," said Jo.

"And *she's* not—"

"Like *you'd* want to work around some grabby asshole?" shot Cheryl.

"She *is* still working," said Nolan, then, his throat dry as he finally opened his mouth.

Everyone looked at him. Lilac hadn't told him what had happened—she'd barely explained any of it to him, but she had said that she had an investigation pending and that she and HR had agreed she'd work down in Gyu-ri's office and focus on that big crossover event until the investigation was over.

Brad in HR had even asked her if *she'd* wanted to quit instead, but her lawyer had apparently jumped all over them for that and they'd gone out of their way to accommodate her wishes.

"She's in Gyu-ri's office," said Nolan. "At the Ballroom."

Everyone grew thoughtful then, quiet a moment, until Eddie opened his big mouth again. "Okay, he's a creep. But I've never seen him do anything *illegal*."

"Like he's going to hit on someone in front of you," said Cheryl, shaking her head.

Nolan stepped out of his costume fully then. "I saw him do something," he said. "Lilac was on the ground, picking up some things that had fallen, and he was brazenly checking out her ass—"

"Like *you* wouldn't," said Eddie then, just as he freed one of Jo's legs. She kicked his shoulder with it, causing him to rub his other arm.

Nolan ignored that—it was more true than Eddie could know. Because he sure as shit hadn't told any of them about his night with Lilac. "He also made a comment. Something about having her on her hands and knees as he stared right at her butt—and she saw it. We both did."

Cheryl frowned. "Did you tell HR?"

"No..." It was like she'd slapped him. Why hadn't he? Why had he let that asshole get away with it? "Lilac didn't seem to want me to."

"See?" said Eddie. "It was no big deal then."

Free of her costume, Jo finally walked away and Eddie ran after her, calling out multiple terms of affection, but Jo's lips were pinched and she stomped right into the women's bathroom.

DeShawn snickered. "Boy's about to get an education or lose some tail," he said. Cheryl glowered at him then and he chuckled nervously, almost as if he'd forgotten she was there. There was an "off button" to most guys' dirty talk when women were around, something Earl never seemed to grasp. "Anyway, I should, um, check those... Half an hour left," he said to Nolan, referring to when their lunch break would be over.

Cheryl watched him go and shook her head. "DeShawn's so sweet," she said. "But even he can't get his mind out of the gutter." She turned back to Nolan. "Whenever Lilac told you not to bother reporting Earl? That was then. Maybe she was still struggling to hold on to her composure, to ignore it all. Maybe he hadn't done whatever it was he did yet." She jutted her chin forward as if to study him and then nodded. "I bet she'd want you to come forward now. It would certainly help her case."

Nolan stood there thinking and for the briefest of selfish but practical moments, he thought of what would happen if HR sided with Earl. Would they accuse Nolan of lying—or would Earl settle for making his life hell? Either way, he couldn't afford to lose this job.

Fuck the job. Landon would be in school in a few months and there were other jobs, other places to work if need be.

Lilac hadn't told him what had happened, but he remembered her sorrow the day he'd found her at Thommy's. He remembered the pain that seemed to exist there just below the surface during their night together.

"Okay," he said. "But maybe I should ask her first."

He headed to the locker room to grab his phone and bring it back into the fan-cooled break room to do just that.

CHAPTER SEVENTEEN

"Are you sure you don't mind? I can ask Tanya to stop by later—or take it over myself." Cradling her office phone between her cheek and shoulder, Gyu-ri looked up at Lilac, who stood in the office doorway and used her knee to shift up the big box of pamphlets she carried.

"I'm fine," she said. "Tildy's Tots isn't that near the management offices and whatever they think, HR at least ordered both of us to walk the other direction should we bump into each other."

"And you expect *Earl* to do that?" asked Gyu-ri, the skepticism clear as day on her face.

"I expect tail-between-his-legs, scared-shitless Earl to do that, yeah," said Lilac, grinning. She couldn't help it. None of this was funny, but it sure was less scary these days.

"Well, if you're sure—hi, this is the Ballroom management office," Gyu-ri said, obviously getting off hold and beginning her call.

Lilac squared her shoulders back and headed toward the Ballroom entryway. The door out to the area where guests arrived was like a delineation in the sand. On one side of the colorful door were the plain, compact offices—the most decorative bit of design an occasional framed cel of Tildy or one of her animated friends on the wall. On the other side was light and color and magic, but Lilac knew it'd ruin the illusion to have a businesswoman with a box just stand there gaping, so she passed through quickly, smiling to herself when a little girl shrieked in delight and started twirling right there in the entryway.

She remembered feeling like that once. And truth be told, a tiny part of her was rekindling, reminding her that she *could* feel that way again.

It had been scary telling her aunt and asking for the lawyer. First and foremost because that meant she'd had to tell her parents —and of course that meant they'd tell her grandparents—and Grandma Violet had flown in for a few days to help her and Frankie get it all sorted.

Even though Grandma Violet had stayed in a hotel, the two women had hardly been able to spend more than a minute together without sniping at one another. But they'd put their differences aside when it came to helping Lilac.

"I don't know why you just don't leave this dreadful place," said Grandma Violet as she kissed Lilac's cheek goodbye at the airport the previous Friday. "The lawyer will let you know when or if you need to come in to testify or interview or whatever it is they might need you for—"

"I'm fine, Grandma Violet. I can do this." Lilac took a deep breath, as much to convince herself as her grandma. They'd begun the complaint to HR before Grandma Violet had arrived. She'd been great as some emotional support, but Lilac could stand on her own two feet without her.

"Well, at the very least you could quit that job," said Grandma Violet. "And just wait here in Orlando until it's all over."

"And let that slimeball win?" said Aunt Frankie, folding her arms over her chest. "I think not." She'd been happy to report that Tara had kicked Earl out of their house after this had all come to light—that he'd denied it, of course, but that Tara had said it was just confirmation of all the suspicions she'd kept buried deep inside her.

"If you're sure," said Grandma Violet, taking Lilac by both shoulders.

"I am," said Lilac, embracing her. "Thank you for being here for me."

True, she'd told her parents not to cancel their trip—they'd moved on to Japan now, and Lilac had made poor Pembroke a bit jealous by showing her her parents' vacation photos, though it wasn't like Lilac herself was there—but it had still felt weird to just talk to them over the phone about it. Her daddy had seemed indignant, pacing back and forth in a hotel room and rambling about the disgusting "P.O.S." who'd done that to his "baby girl," but neither had fought that hard about not canceling their trip to be there for her. Her daddy had quickly shifted gears to tell her all about the Shinto ritual they'd witnessed.

It was just as well. Lilac would have felt more self-conscious about it all with a house full of relations. Heaven forbid Nana Abigail had found her way down here—she'd told Lilac it hadn't sounded like that big a deal to her. "Just pinch those fingers," she'd said. "That'll get them thinking twice."

She'd just wanted to know if the boss had been handsome. She'd been *a touch* more sympathetic when Lilac had said he wasn't. As if him being handsome would have made that all right.

But Lilac was happy now—she felt like she could breathe. She knew she had her family and her family's money to thank. Without that lawyer, she probably would have just done what HR had suggested and taken a leave of absence while it was all "sorted," but the lawyer had threatened legal action so fast, they'd scrambled to accommodate her wishes. Even so, she still felt a bit proud of herself, too. If all this could stop Earl from doing this to someone else—someone without Lilac's resources—then it would all be worthwhile. And she'd actually looked forward to coming to work each day.

"I haven't seen you here in a while," said the shuttle driver as she slid in toward the back, her big box on her lap. She smiled and nodded, quickly turning away from the young man's mischievous grin, thankful for the wave of "campers" who filed into the shuttle and filled the space between them.

Gyu-ri had told Lilac that her accusation was all the talk among staff back at Tent Tildy—even as far as the Ballroom. People were probably talking about it all across Tildy World beneath those smiles and between those cheerful, rehearsed lines that they used for guests.

When they arrived at Tent Tildy, Lilac was the first one off, keen not to be left alone with the driver, who might ask her more about the situation that had rocked Tildy World behind the curtain. She walked briskly through the resort lobby, heading straight for Tildy's Tots, which she got to without incident.

She bypassed the line of parents and kids about to check in, turning to the woman at the desk. "Gyu-ri sent me to give these to Tanya."

The woman looked up and Lilac was certain her bored expression grew alarmed when she took in whom she was talking to. She nodded. "Go ahead," she said, clicking a button on the desk to unlock the hidden door.

Lilac took in the room around her, the laughing kids, the brightly-colored screens flashing games and cartoons.

"No running!" called one Tildy Scout, and Lilac chuckled at the fact that that seemed to be a refrain of all people who worked with small kids. She'd said it more than a few times herself during her licensure.

"Lilac!" It had taken approximately half a minute for little Landon to zoom in on her. Lilac hadn't even seen him coming. She just felt him slide in under the box she was carrying and squeeze her legs tightly.

"Oof," said Lilac. "You're going to grip the air out of me, buddy."

He laughed and she shifted the box higher so she could see his face, though it strained her arms to do so. He grinned up at her, a tooth conspicuously absent from his line of pearly whites.

Concerned, Lilac put the box atop a squishy rubber chair made to look like a tree stump. "Did you lose a tooth?"

Landon let go of her legs to run his fingers over the gaping hole, as if just discovering it was missing. Then he grinned some more. "I fell," he said. "Off the jungle gym at the park. With Willow."

"You fell *with* Willow?"

"A meanie boy said I was too slow and he pushed me," he said. "Willow hit him and he grabbed her hair and I fell, but Willow grabbed me." He looked almost proud then. "She has casts," he said, pointing to his leg and to his wrist.

Lilac knelt down to his level and put her hands on his shoulders. "Your sister broke her arm and leg?"

Landon nodded, chewing on his thumb.

She hugged him then, her mind racing over the texts she'd exchanged with Nolan since... Since the day they'd last spent time together. He mentioned it being hectic by him, a "mini family emergency," but he hadn't said... Then again, she'd hardly told him what had been going on with her. But her lawyer had advised her not to share it with anyone. She'd only told Gavin, Brielle, and Pembroke that she was filing a complaint with HR about what had happened and she hadn't gone into more details—though Gavin already knew. He was so proud of her, like her reporting a creep was equal to saving someone from a burning building or something. Fortunately for Lilac, who'd just wanted to be happy, to do things that made her happy, he'd spent most of the week telling her all about work. And Gabriel.

Hoping it all worked out for the best for him, she'd invited him and a "guest" to come stay with her and Frankie and hit the parks —even Disney, if she must, so he could find his Gaston. But they'd agreed to wait until they knew how things were going with Lilac and after Gavin's internship was over.

"Is she okay?" asked Lilac, a dumb think to ask about someone who'd broken two limbs.

Landon nodded, though. "She went back to school," he said.

Lilac let out a breath of relief. No wonder Nolan had kept his texts brief—he'd been busy. Lilac wondered how Nolan and his dad had managed to get time off work to nurse Willow, or *if* they had.

"Landon, you know Tildy's rules about cleaning up messes, don't you?" Tanya asked as she approached.

Landon looked over his shoulder to a spot at a nearby crafting table full of construction paper scraps. "Ohhhhh-kay," he said, stomping his feet over toward the table.

Tanya watched him and then her eyes flickered toward the box. "Did you need me?"

"Ah, yes," said Lilac, standing up and snapping into action. She opened up the top flaps on the box, pulling out one of the pamphlets they'd just had delivered. "Gyu-ri and I are starting to spread the word about the big crossover event. She said you should have some at Tildy's Tots check-in for interested parents to grab. Maybe hand them out with receipts."

Tanya took the pamphlet, nodding as she looked it over. "Let's head back to my office," she said, turning.

Picking up the box, Lilac trailed after her. They went through another non-descript door hidden by a night sky painting and came out in a hallway that seemed familiar to Lilac, though she wasn't sure she'd spent much time there. They passed an open door to a large break room, a dozen fans spread out throughout the room to cool down the half a dozen people—some in costume, some half in costume, and some in Tildy Scout outfits—standing or sitting, eating or talking. She stared just long enough to see a woman with short hair smack a guy's shoulder over and over and point her way.

The guy in the sweat-covered undershirt, whose back was to her, turned, his phone in his hand.

Nolan.

Almost as if on cue, the phone Lilac had tucked into her pants pocket buzzed just then, but Tanya had slipped into a cramped office and looked back at her expectantly.

Lilac just nodded at Nolan and then made her way into the

room.

"Just put that on the desk," said Tanya, shutting the door behind them.

Her palms shaking—her heart had started beating wildly when her eyes had locked with Nolan's—Lilac slid her hand into her pocket and grasped her phone as she sat opposite Tanya's desk. Surely he couldn't have been messaging her at that very moment. That would have been too much of a coincidence.

"Can I ask you something?" said Tanya, bringing Lilac back to the present.

"Yes?" said Lilac.

"It's about... You and Earl and HR."

Of course. Lilac didn't know when, if ever, she'd be able to escape that shadow over everything she did here, but she supposed it was too early to hope for otherwise.

"I... I can't say much while it's still under investigation," she said. Her lawyer had even had her file a police report, but that hadn't gone far—they'd interviewed Earl and he'd protested his innocence, of course—so it was up to HR now. But the lawyer had insisted it would still help having it on record.

"I figured," said Tanya, her lips in a thin line. "I just wondered if... Well, would it help if I went to HR, too?"

Lilac straightened in her chair. "Sorry?" She wasn't sure if she'd heard her right.

Leaning back in her own chair, Tanya sighed. "Earl hasn't touched me—he probably knows what I'd do to him if he did—but he's made a few inappropriate comments. His eyes have certainly lingered here and there." She waved her hands around the room, though Lilac knew the "here and there" were probably her legs and behind in those shorts. Even in the lamest of Tildy Scout outfits, Tanya was gorgeous. "If I got enough women who've experienced the same to come forward..."

"Yes!" said Lilac excitedly. "It certainly couldn't hurt. But my lawyer said few people would probably want to risk their jobs."

Tanya snorted, threading her fingers together. "I don't know if

Tildy Corporation wants the kind of lawsuit a dismissal of multiple women could cause," she said. She frowned. "I'm just sorry I didn't say anything earlier. I... You're not the first girl who's worked with Earl. Three in the past few years alone. And they always get quiet —isolated—and then just up and vanish without so much as a goodbye."

There must have been something on Lilac's face at that—something disturbed—because Tanya chuckled. "They do go on to other work, I mean. I'm friends with two of them on Facebook, though we haven't really talked much since they left." She opened a drawer to pull out a phone and started scrolling through it. "I'll... I'll reach out to them. Tell them what I do know about what's going on, ask them if they might help."

"That would be amazing," said Lilac, tears forming in her eyes. She laughed then even as she cried and Tanya jumped up from her chair, swapping her phone for a tissue from a box on her desk and coming around the side to hand it to Lilac.

"Thank you," said Lilac, taking the tissue and dotting her eyes.

"No, thank *you* for doing what one—or a dozen—of us should have done ages ago." She sighed and sat on the edge of her desk, picking the phone up again. "I can't make any promises on behalf of anyone else, but I promise you I'll see HR. Today."

"Thanks," said Lilac. "That would be more than enough." She reached a hand out toward Tanya and she took it, squeezing tight.

Tanya looked over her shoulder at the box of pamphlets. "You leave those here. I'll take care of it. And then I'll prep the troops for the big camp sleepover in the Ballroom."

Gyu-ri had told Lilac that Tildy's Tots staff typically worked to ensure the kids' happiness and safety during the overnight. And that they only sort of looked forward to it, overtime or no.

Lilac cringed as she stood. "Sorry," she said.

Tanya waved a hand. "We're used to it," she said. "We've got workers of steel in Tildy's Tots." She looked Lilac over. "If you ever get tired of planning events and running errands, you're welcome to join us."

"Thank you," said Lilac, flattered. "I'll... I'll keep that in mind." She turned to exit then, remembering the phone in her hand and turning on the screen to check her messages. There *was* a text from Nolan amidst all the older notifications from her friends.

I want to help, it read. *Have dinner with me?*

She opened Tanya's door and there, a little ways down the hallway, he stood, his hair damp against his forehead, his body hidden beneath the furry plush bodysuit that belonged to Silly.

"I think you've lost something, Silly," said Lilac as she sauntered over toward him.

Nolan grinned, though his smile faltered somewhat. He took a wing and pointed it over his shoulder. "DeShawn has my head," he said, and Lilac noticed a handsome, brown-skinned man laughing with someone in the break room, Silly Sandgrouse's oversized head tucked beneath his arm against his side. "And he's the boss around here, so I don't have more than a moment before he snaps that sucker on me, mid-conversation or no."

Without thinking, Lilac reached out and took Silly's plush wing in her hand. It was soft, like her threadbare Tildy plush back at Aunt Frankie's. "I got your text," she said. "I can't believe you want to help—"

"Why wouldn't you?" he asked. "I'm sorry I didn't think to ask earlier."

"No, it's fine." Lilac shook her head and continued to stare at the plush wing.

"You know that's been in two toddlers' mouths this morning alone. And I might have accidentally rubbed some forehead sweat with it." He fanned himself with the other wing. "Dang, it's hot out here."

Smirking, Lilac pulled him back inside the break room, where the fans blew. She took note of all the eyes on them immediately, but she kept dragging Nolan toward one of the blowing fans. "Better?" she cooed once they'd come to a stop.

Nolan looked back and forth at the staring eyes and turned a bright shade of crimson. "Yeah," he said quietly.

"I heard about your sister," said Lilac. "Why didn't you tell me?"

Nolan cocked his head. "How? Oh... Landon?"

"I ran into him on the way here. He said his sister protected him from a bully."

At that, Nolan's eyebrows scrunched together. "Dad said she got into a fight with some kid and both she and Landon fell, but Landon only got a tooth knocked out."

Shrugging, Lilac ran her thumb over the soft wing she refused to let go. "He said she protected him from a bully. Didn't he tell you that?"

Nolan shook his head. "It's been crazy," he said. "And despite Willow's injuries, the kids are both still so hyper. But I'm glad. Willow gets a bad rap, but she's a good kid."

Lilac laughed then at the idea of a little girl with a "bad rap," though she'd likely witnessed some of that at the mall a few weeks ago. A lifetime ago.

"I want to stand up to a bully, too," said Nolan. "Can I... What if I told HR what happened that day when I bumped into you in the hall and all those pens and pencils went everywhere? Would that help?"

That was unexpected. Lilac actually had to strain to think—she remembered that moment clearly, remembered how a jolt of something like magic had ran through her when she'd locked eyes with Nolan, when their hands had brushed each other's as they'd scrambled to pick the writing utensils up.

How Earl had said something and Nolan had stood up for her.

How she'd actually failed to really thank him for it.

She hadn't even thought of that day. Hadn't told her lawyer about it. There'd been so much to discuss about that other day...

She let go of Silly's wing and took both of Nolan's cheeks in hers. "You'd be a hero in sandgrouse armor," she said, and then she kissed him.

The fans couldn't drown out the hoots and hollers that echoed around the break room, but Lilac just kept kissing him.

CHAPTER EIGHTEEN

Nolan had never spoken to a lawyer before. Even when a ton of pamphlets had arrived in the mail following his mom's accident, his dad hadn't wanted to deal with them—ambulance chasers, he'd called them, and he hadn't had the heart to deal with them with everything else to consider.

So Nolan had kind of expected it to go like a courtroom scene on TV. Instead, a friendly enough—if a touch robotic—guy asked Nolan to walk through his story with him, then Nolan and Lilac had went out for a bite to eat—*just* a bite to eat for now—and the next day, Nolan had sat down at HR and told him exactly what the lawyer had told him to say. It was the truth—Nolan wouldn't have abided otherwise—but the lawyer had had suggestions for how to word it and how to frame the scene that had set Brad the HR rep's mouth into a grim line. Brad had witnessed at least part of that scene himself.

He'd even sighed as he'd pulled out a thick file—complaints against Earl, apparently, though he hadn't said from when—and had Nolan put his signature to page.

After that, it was just a matter of continuing to wait.

Cheryl knew what he'd done and apparently, she'd told the others, too. Come Thursday, Angie, who wasn't even assigned to him this week, she was with Leah Llama, shimmied in between Eddie and Jo—not hard to do, since Jo was barely speaking to Eddie—and wanted to know the details.

"Rumor is Earl sexually harassed you," she said. "And you reported it?" She didn't look as if she were joking.

Jo rolled her eyes. "How did the truth get spun into that?"

"Is it impossible to imagine a *man* could get sexually harassed at work?" spat Eddie, his lips pouting into a frown.

Jo sat up as fast as a lightning bolt, grabbing her plate and stomping across the room.

Eddie hesitated, but he sighed and stood.

"Watch that mouth of yours if you want to get laid," said DeShawn, chomping on a Twizzler.

"Or if you ever want any woman to take you seriously," added Cheryl.

Eddie looked between Angie and Nolan. "You want to pile it on, too?"

Angie shrugged. "I think men can get harassed, too."

"That's not the point right now, though," said Nolan.

Eddie smirked. "And depending on who's doing the harassing..." His voice went high-pitched. "Oh, no, Ms. Assistant Manager, please don't kiss me in front of everyone." He clapped his hands against his cheeks.

DeShawn stifled a laugh and Cheryl raised her eyebrows but looked pointedly to Nolan for his reaction. Nolan didn't remember if Angie was present when it had happened, but the way the rumor mill was going, it was a wonder she didn't think they'd fornicated in the middle of the resort buffet, Silly suit and all.

"It wasn't me who was sexually harassed," said Nolan, not willing to joke with the guys about something that had really hurt Lilac. "And as to the other matter... We've just gone on a couple of dates. That's all."

Eddie was losing interest as he scanned over his shoulder for signs of Jo. He spotted her leaving, probably headed for the locker room, where he couldn't follow her. He quickly turned back to the table. "Well, nice work scoring *that* one," he said. "You'll have to tell me how that happened sometime." He rapped his knuckles on the table and then was off after Jo. "*Baby...*"

Cheryl scoffed as they disappeared around the corner.

"Trouble in paradise?" asked Angie. She seemed overly interested in watching Eddie go. Because of course some guys just never seemed to run out of options, crude as they could be.

Nolan wondered if that was how the Earls of the world were born. Perhaps the man had been handsome once or maybe that didn't even play a factor. Maybe he just felt powerful and entitled and "grandfathered in." Nolan imagined if Eddie had done half the things Earl had, HR would have worked a lot faster to give him his pink slip.

Nolan scrolled through the string of text messages he'd been exchanging with Lilac since the night before.

My hero, she'd called him in one.

Which had made Nolan feel a bit sick. He hadn't done anything that he shouldn't have thought to do immediately—that he shouldn't have done immediately, even if Lilac had originally seemed hesitant. Why hadn't he acted sooner? He might have been able to save her from what had happened in the first place.

"Well, everyone's saying a whole slew of women have been in HR the past few days," said Angie. She shrugged. "Luckily, I never spent more than a second or two with the guy."

"Really?" asked Cheryl, incredulous. "But that wasn't long enough for him to give you the creep vibe?"

DeShawn grimaced. "Now, hold on. I'm not denying the guy's a sleaze, especially with so many people coming forward, but you're saying he never did anything dirty to you, and you just *felt* he was a creep? That's biased."

Patting her lips with her napkin, Cheryl shook her head. "Sometimes you just know."

DeShawn met Nolan's eyes. "Damn if the odds aren't stacked against us."

"Oh, you have no bad *vibes* coming off you, D," said Angie, leaning forward across the table. Nolan wasn't sure if she meant to show off the barest bit of her cleavage—from an undone button on her Tildy Scout shirt—as she did, but he wasn't the only one who noticed.

DeShawn pointed toward the spot. "Every button fastened," he said, clearing his throat. "Costume regulations."

Oh-so-innocent, Angie smiled as she leaned back, slowly and methodically fastening her button.

"Oh, please," said Cheryl, crumpling up her napkin. "Get a room."

Angie stood, still taking an obnoxiously long time to fasten that button. "He can call me anytime he wants one," she said, sashaying back toward her llama across the room.

"Was that sexual harassment?" DeShawn asked, his face as stricken as if he'd seen a ghost.

Nolan opened his mouth and then shut it. "I... I don't know."

Cheryl cocked her head. "Did it make you uncomfortable?"

"Well," said DeShawn, tugging at the Tildy Scout scarf around his neck, "yes, but probably not in the way you're asking..."

"Does she have a position of power over you?" continued Cheryl. "Like, could she get you fired if you said no?"

"No," said DeShawn, "but she could if—"

Cheryl held up a finger. "Don't say she could if she made up the fact that you did something to her when you didn't. I'm positive it happens, but not as often as men seem to think." She stood, turning to Nolan this time. "I'm glad you helped out. I didn't realize you were *seeing* her on top of everything else—"

"But that's not why," Nolan said. "Not the *only* reason why, anyway."

"I know," said Cheryl. "But you'd be surprised how much farther a man's account can often go."

"But HR is pretty much eighty percent women," said DeShawn. "I'm calling b.s."

"And I'm telling you how it is." She tsked. "What are they teaching you boys in school, I wonder?"

"Definitely not Sexual Harassment 101," said DeShawn.

Yet so many guys seemed to pick that up anyway, thought Nolan.

"Heading to the ladies'," said Cheryl. "See you around."

Nolan nodded, his eyes back on his vibrating phone. A new message had just popped up.

"It's enough to almost make a man vow to be celibate," said DeShawn, letting out a deep breath. "Hey, five minutes, okay? Then you suit up."

Nolan grabbed DeShawn's arm as he stood, stopping him in place.

"Lilac's in trouble," he said. "I know you said five minutes..."

His lips pinched, DeShawn nodded as he shrugged himself free of Nolan's grasp. "Go," he said, but this time he grabbed Nolan's arm. "But you owe me."

Nolan ran toward the table where Silly's head rested beside the rest of the suit and grabbed it, shoving it at his Tildy Scout caretaker for the day. "Keep it prepped and ready," he said. "I'll be here as soon as I can."

If I still have a job when it's all over, he didn't say aloud.

———

It took far too long for Nolan to get to the parking lot, where Lilac had told him she was texting from inside her car.

I've been told to go home early, she'd written. *Earl is being let go and they figure it's better if I'm not on site when he has to clear his office.*

Then... *He's here*, the text wrote. *He's in the parking lot. He saw me.*

Lilac apparently had had the misfortune of parking just two cars down from Earl, Nolan could see as he approached. The man's trunk was open, a box half sticking out, but he was over at Lilac's sleek new hybrid, his face red, his hands flailing as he walked back and forth behind her car.

Basically, it looked as if he were *daring* her to run him over to try to escape.

"Hey!" shouted Nolan, bolting into a run. "What the hell is

your problem?" He held his phone up to the man as he came up beside him. "I'm going to call the cops."

"The hell you are," said Earl, lunging for the phone and successfully knocking it to the ground. It cracked and went scattering under Lilac's car.

The door to Lilac's car opened as Earl and Nolan locked hands, Nolan pushing as hard as—harder than—he got but not wanting to resort to punches. The guy deserved more than a few, but he didn't exactly want blood on his hands, even if it was shitty blood. The guy was older than his dad.

"Stop it," said Lilac, her hands out toward Nolan's arms.

"Stay back," said Nolan through clenched teeth. "Call the cops."

"Don't you *fucking* dare," said Earl. "Do you want to get fired, too, bitch? Huh?" He turned and spat on the back of her car. The loogie dripped down her license plate. "Bringing cops to a Tent Tildy parking lot, that'll look good on your performance review."

"Do it," said Nolan. "I'll take responsibility."

Lilac dialed and then put the phone to her ear. "Security?" she said, and Nolan didn't know whether it was a good or a bad thing that she'd gone for security before the police. "There's an issue in the West Tent Tildy parking lot—"

But Nolan didn't hear anything else she said as Earl roared then, putting his all into shoving Nolan forward. The shock made Nolan unprepared and his back slammed into a Chrysler parked nearby.

He grunted in pain, then went to kick at Earl, anything, but Earl was dropping his grip on Nolan's hands now, turning toward Lilac—

But before he could turn, a small, pointy dress shoe came up between Earl's legs and slammed right into his crotch. He winced and his hands went to his balls as he fell to his knees. Nolan scrambled up and went to Lilac's side, not caring that his foot "accidentally" kicked forward into Earl's thigh as he did.

"Are you all right?" he asked Lilac, taking her by the shoulders.

"Better than all right," she said. "He just gave me cause to kick him in the balls." She tucked a stray strand of hair behind her ear as her face took on this devilish grin and Nolan wanted to slam her lips to his and never stop kissing her. "Self-defense and all."

"Or saving me." Then he did put his lips to hers, gently nibbling on her bottom lip, sliding his tongue just slightly inside, grazing the tip of her tongue as shivers ransacked his whole body.

"If you're *fucking* her," said Earl between breaths, "you can forget any complaint you made up to use against me." He smiled, even through the tears watering his eyes. "That's right. I *know* it was you who went to HR about me."

Reluctantly, Nolan pulled away from Lilac's lips, although he kept his hold on her upper arms. "Half the staff filed a complaint about you."

"Because of *her*." Earl pointed toward Lilac, his finger shaking with rage. "*No one* had any complaints until you did—"

Lilac's nose went up in the air, the perfect example of the uptight, mature businesswoman Nolan initially thought her to be. "You can speak to my lawyer," she said just as the security Jeep pulled up.

"Oh, I will," said Earl, leaning on Lilac's car to stand himself up.

"Get your hands off her car—" Nolan started, but Lilac put a hand on his chest and shook her head, as if to tell him to let it go.

"I'm going to get a lawyer, too," he said. "And tell them she *fucked* her way into getting help to make up this whole case against me."

Lilac took a step away from Nolan as the security guys got out of their vehicle and Nolan waved at them. She crossed her arms, staring Earl down. "Now I'm confused. Was I *leading you on* or did I *make the whole thing up?*"

Earl spit again—this time at Lilac's feet. She jumped back. "Both, bitch."

One of the security guys shook his head in exasperation and went straight to Earl without even being told. "You were told to clean out your office," he said, as if he'd been fully aware of the situation. "And to wait there for an hour before you left."

Earl stepped back out of the man's grip, waving his hands toward him. "Like I'm going to do what they say? What are they going to do if I don't, huh? Fire me?"

The second security guard said some code gibberish into his walkie-talkie.

"Okay," said the guard nearest Earl with all the patience of a Tildy's Tots Tildy Scout speaking to a child camper, "let's take a ride to our office."

"Like *hell*," said Earl, jumping back and wincing. His junk probably still ached.

"Sir," said the walkie-talkie guard, "we have jurisdiction under the state of Florida to detain people on-site in the event of an incident."

"Detain *them*, then!" shouted Earl. "They assaulted me!"

"Uh, no," said Lilac, all-business. "He tried to keep me from leaving," she said, "and then *he* assaulted Nolan first."

"Sir, are you aware that keeping someone from leaving a place they desire to leave can be charged as kidnapping?" said the officer who reached out to grab Earl's elbow.

"*Kidnapping? Kidnapping?* You have *got* to be kidding me," Earl said, but he let the man guide him toward the Jeep. "I didn't lay a fucking *finger* on you."

Lilac scoffed. "Not today anyway."

"You asked for it," he said as the guard opened the Jeep door. "You think a sorority bimbo like you would get a job like the one *I* offered you if you hadn't *asked* for it?"

"I wasn't in a sorority," said Lilac. "But I'll thank you not to throw the term around as an insult." She checked out her nails then, as cool as a cucumber.

Earl was still shouting something unintelligible as he got into the Jeep and the guard shut the door closed.

"Do you want to file a report?" asked the walkie-talkie guard. "We can call in someone from the county."

Lilac exchanged a look with Nolan. "Yes," Nolan said. Lilac seemed unsure. "At least... I do."

The man turned, talking into his walkie-talkie once more.

"I don't want..." said Lilac. She sighed.

"Hey," said Nolan, putting a hand on her back. "You didn't ask for any of this, I know. But it's here and... We ought to make sure he gets what he deserves."

"He's fired," said Lilac. "That's enough. Plus, his wife kicked him out." She shrugged.

"And if he tries to use this incident against you?" asked Nolan. "Against us?" Oh, boy, would he have some explaining to do to his dad. "Let's get the papers filed. We don't have to press charges."

Lilac turned around, both her hands resting on his chest. "I've got you," she said. "My lawyer... Whatever you need." She looked up and met his gaze then and Nolan felt, surprisingly, that she was *all there* in the moment with him. There wasn't a shadow weighing her down. There wasn't the cavalier jovialness of a girl just looking for a casual fling. She had his back. Whatever that meant, as friends... As something more... She understood him now. She cared.

And despite how he'd tried to keep it casual for her sake, there was no question that he felt the same way.

He took her into his arms, resting his chin lightly atop her head. "Let's start over," he whispered as the walkie-talkie guard finished talking to his partner and made his way back toward them. "Let me take you on a date to Tildy World."

Lilac chuckled then—hard. "Is that a joke?"

"No," said Nolan. "Just you wait and see."

CHAPTER NINETEEN

It'd been a harried few days. Calls to Lilac's lawyer and reports to file. Lilac hadn't wanted to press charges, and Nolan had followed suit. Ironically, Earl had wanted to pursue charges, though the guards and police had directed him to an attorney rather than doing much of anything themselves. Nolan vouched for Lilac and Lilac vouched for Nolan—no one cared that Earl was shouting obscenities about them being a couple. Plus, there was security footage, so Earl was toast.

A couple. Lilac hadn't ever thought of herself as one half of a couple. It was too final, too confining.

Only now, she actually felt freer than ever. "What are you up to this fine Saturday morning?" Gavin sipped a coffee casually as he gazed into his phone's video camera from a place Lilac had never seen before.

"Um, where the hell are you?" asked Lilac, her tone more playful than her words suggested.

"Nowhere special," said Gavin. "Just the boss' townhouse." He took another sip but kept his eye on the camera, waiting for the reaction.

"You little Jezebel," said Lilac, making Gavin actually spit some of his coffee back into the cup. "So you and Gabriel are... a thing now? A full-fledged official thingy?"

Gavin wiped his lips. "Well, when you put it like that, it's suddenly ten times less romantic."

Before Lilac could say more, Pembroke of all people dialed in, asking to join the call. Gavin welcomed her, curiosity plain as day on her face. "Hey, Pem," he said.

"Hi," said Pembroke, grabbing hold of a swath of blue hair that flew at that moment across her eyes. Wherever she was, it was windy.

"Where are you?" asked Gavin, studying her image.

Lilac instead focused on the bigger issue that came to mind. "Did you change your blue streaks into entirely blue hair?"

Pembroke laughed and sat back on something. If Lilac didn't know better, she thought she saw the handle of a roll-on bag behind the girl's back. "Chicago and yes, I went all-blue." Her gaze traveled over the camera. "Though I don't know why. Bad enough I got all the stares with the blue streaks. I'm getting twice as many glances with an all-blue mop."

"You know you look fabulous," said Gavin. "Eat it up, Broke." He frowned. "But what are you doing here without letting me know you were stopping by?"

"Yeah... Sorry about that." Pembroke cleared her throat and looked around her. Lilac saw more people go by with suitcases. "It was kind of impromptu. And I won't be here long."

"You're in front of Union Station," said Gavin. "You're going on vacation?"

"Sort of," said Pembroke. "I... I actually don't really have a destination in mind."

"Okay, hold up, don't you go anywhere," said Gavin. "I'll be there in..." He looked over his shoulder and a man with a pretty tight body walked by behind him, a towel around his waist. He paused, almost frozen in the spotlight. He looked way too young to have his own successful marketing company, but then Lilac supposed he could have come from a trust fund like she did. She could have created a marketing company and hired Gavin to run it.

She should have thought of that.

The hot towel-toting boss came closer to Gavin and then pressed his lips to Lilac's best friend's. "What have we here?"

Smiling sweetly, Gavin returned the peck and then turned back to the camera. "Gabriel, meet my bestie, Lilac, and my other sweetheart of a friend, Pembroke." All that was missing was Brielle, but her messages had grown curt as of late. Gavin had surmised she'd broken it off with her comic book celebrity paramour about a week before.

Lilac waved *hi* and told her nether regions to behave as the sexy man leaned forward to get a closer look. *Nolan. And Gavin. Down, girl.*

"Doll, can we head to Union Station?" Gavin asked Gabriel. "Pembroke's there now."

"Sure." Gabriel nodded and pulled back, disappearing from view.

"*Someone's* got his boss wrapped around his little finger," said Lilac, snorting when Gavin turned scarlet.

"*Anyway*," said Gavin. "Chat later, 'kay, Li? When are you meeting Mr. Sandgrouse?"

"He's picking me up at three," said Lilac. Which was pretty late for a Tildy World date, but who was she to complain? It wasn't like she wouldn't have a zillion and one other chances to check out the park. Unfortunately, Christian had been named Earl's replacement, though whether it was because of Earl's situation or his lack of proximity to the man, he hadn't given off any skeevy vibes in the day since. They'd agreed to let her keep setting up shop at Gyu-ri's and to check in with him at least once a day on her progress with the big Tent Tildy/Ballroom crossover. That suited Lilac just fine.

"Have fun," said Gavin. "And you better remember *all* the details."

"Not until you tell me the story of how, precisely, you wound up *there* last night."

Gavin grinned widely and signed off.

"You have a date?" asked Pembroke. Lilac had almost forgotten she was on the call.

"Yeah," said Lilac. "The guy in the Silly Sandgrouse suit."

"That's great," said Pembroke. "I hope you have a fun time!"

"Thanks," said Lilac, feeling the awkwardness hang in the air even with hundreds of miles between them. "And you have a nice trip... Wherever you're going. Traveling can broaden your world."

Pembroke scratched her cheek. "I'm not leaving the country or anything."

"Even so," said Lilac. "It's a first step. An important one. Maybe someday you'll head to Japan, too." Lilac's parents had moved on to Taiwan this week—or maybe it was Hong Kong by now. Lilac could never be sure.

"Maybe," said Pembroke, her smile faltering.

"Hey, if you're ever serious about it, let me know," said Lilac, a genuine idea popping in her head. "I could foot the bill and maybe we'd invite Gavin and Brielle—"

"Oh, no, I couldn't." Pembroke's already-pale face looked ashen. "I mean, not that I'd mind going with all of you, but I couldn't have you pay for it."

"Well, think about it," said Lilac. "And tell me how your trip goes."

"Lilac?" asked Pembroke, just as Lilac was about to end the call.

"Hmm?"

"I'm glad you're okay," she said. "Whatever exactly happened, I'm proud of you for standing up for yourself and happy it all turned out okay."

Lilac felt her stomach turn sour, though the subject didn't make her quite as dizzy as it once had. "Thanks."

"I don't know if I'd have been brave enough to do what you did," said Pembroke.

"You would be if you turned to your friends, Pem," said Lilac. "If you ever need to talk to someone—or if you just want to go kick a man in the junk, I'm your gal."

Pembroke broke into laughter at that and they said their goodbyes.

"Lunch is here," called Aunt Frankie from inside the house. Lilac stood and grabbed her iced tea from the table on the patio. Frankie had ordered them some Thai.

And though her stomach was still spinning—largely because of the countdown to her first official date since she and Nolan had decided to start over—Lilac felt entirely happy and at home as she sat down to eat with Aunt Frankie. It was a feeling she thought she might never experience again, but it was there, and though the shadow of her pain would never entirely leave her, she felt like she'd managed to banish it to some dark corner of herself, a dark corner almost obliterated by the rays of sunshine from those who cared about her the most.

———

"You can't want to go on the Tildy Whirl for a third time," said Nolan. His legs were genuinely shaking as they exited the ride.

Still, Lilac tugged him back toward the growing line. "I always rode the Tildy Whirl three times," said Lilac. "Then Tildy's Cavern Adventure twice and if I had time, Tildy's Never-Ending World about four or five times."

"And you thought a date at Tildy World would be boring," said Nolan with a sheepish grin as he stepped back in line with her.

"No," she said. "That could never be the case." She draped her arms over his shoulders and leaned up for a quick kiss. "I'd just... Forgotten what it looked like on this side of things. Without the Tildy Scouts and the cramped hallways and the hidden doors behind the murals."

Lilac let her gaze wander around the park at the employees. She actually didn't know that many out here in the park proper because she'd been so caught up in the rather small worlds of Tent Tildy and Queen Animaliao's Ballroom. Most of the employees still wore Tildy Scout outfits out here since camping was an important enough theme in Tildy Tapir cartoons, though some wore costumes more thematically tied to the specific attractions where they worked. Like the Tildy Scouts—they still had that name for employees, regardless of what they wore—at Tildy Whirl wore clown outfits.

That had made Nolan shudder almost as much as the rocking and rolling whirling carts themselves. "Well, I'm just glad we're going on these rides before dinner," he said.

"You're being awfully coy about dinner," said Lilac. "How much time do we have left before we should get going?"

Someone cleared her throat as the line moved and Lilac spun around, taking Nolan's hand in hers as they moved to fill in the gap that had appeared. "We won't have to go far," said Nolan. "And dinner is at eight, so if we hop on a shuttle by about 7:30, we should make it with plenty of time to spare."

"A shuttle?" asked Lilac.

"Of course," said Nolan. "You don't honestly think I'd take you on a Tildy World date and not treat you to a meal at Queen Animaliao's Ballroom, do you?"

Queen Animaliao's Ballroom—he had to mean the Royal Dining Hall. *The* finest dining spot in all the theme park. There was only room for five parties a night and they booked up months in advance. Her parents could have easily afforded it but certainly hadn't cared enough to bother. Besides, they'd told her, that place was for grownups. Kids ate downstairs at the Palace Kitchens.

"How...?" asked Lilac, her jaw hung open.

Nolan bumped his arm into hers as they took another few steps forward. "I have friends in high places," he said. "Furry friends. And the queen herself."

A thought made Lilac's stomach drop. "But I'll pay," she said. "It can't be cheap—"

"Hush," said Nolan, laying a finger across her mouth. "Don't ruin the magic. Since when does Tildy discuss finances?"

"There was that one cartoon where she almost lost her cabin

because of the queen's new tax," said Lilac. "Her Majesty was under the influence of the dark shadow," she added.

Chuckling, Nolan wrapped an arm around her as he leaned closer to her ear and Lilac shivered from head to toe. "Okay, Ms. Tapir's personal archivist. But no dark shadow helped or hindered me. I get an employee discount." He kissed her temple then and Lilac about melted into goo.

By the time they staggered off their third turn at the Tildy Whirl, she took advantage of Nolan's need to regain his land legs by stepping aside and making a phone call to arrange a little employee benefit of her own.

———

Nolan had gotten them *the* best-positioned table at the finest restaurant at the best theme park in the world. Apparently, there'd been a cancellation and sometimes Tent Tildy threw that out to its staff to see if they wanted the chance to pick it up before they made it available to the public, but even so—Lilac was going to believe it was all a little Tildy Tapir magic that had aligned everything so perfectly together.

They sat nearest the window that overlooked all of the park and she could see everything from the peak of the mountain hiding Tildy's Cavern to the cabin in Tildy Town where Tildy Tapir supposedly hung her hat each night. The evening had settled in and there was a thin line of amber glow retreating over the horizon.

"To Tildy," said Nolan, holding up his champagne glass.

Lilac laughed and picked up her own, clinking it against his. "To Tildy," she agreed, taking a sip. Then she held it out again. "And to Silly Sandgrouse and the handsome, patient, supportive man who wears his head."

Embarrassed, Nolan seemed the spitting image of his foolish sandgrouse companion then as he raised his glass to hers. "I'll drink to Silly," he said. "But as for the rest... I'll just drink to a beautiful, kind, and supportive friend."

Lilac's smile faltered at that one, but she took a sip anyway. "Just a friend?"

One of Nolan's eyebrows cocked mischievously. "Did I say who that friend was?" he asked. He snickered as he put his glass back down. "I'm sorry. I did mean you. But that doesn't mean I don't want us to be more than that. Just trying to keep it casual."

He picked up his fork and dug into his salad.

Lilac exchanged her glass for her fork and looked out at the park, thinking over her own words thrown back at her. "This is a new beginning, right?"

"Right," said Nolan. "Though I don't think we necessarily got off on the wrong foot before."

"The thing is, I might have booked us a suite," said Lilac. "The Tent Tildy penthouse."

Nolan actually dropped his fork at that. "That's for honeymooners."

"And yet no one had booked it this weekend." She casually picked up several leaves of greens with her fork. "I know you work tomorrow and if you need to go home first, I understand—"

"Nope," said Nolan. "I cleared it with my dad. We're all good."

Lilac grinned as she wrapped her mouth around her first bite. "You hoped you'd be out all night?" she asked. "Did I ruin plans to take me elsewhere?"

"No," said Nolan, clearing his throat as he took a sip of water. "I mean, I was going to ask—maybe get us one of the economy rooms at Tent Tildy. Or a hotel off-site or..."

That was one drawback of the both of them still living with family.

"Well, it's my turn to treat you," said Lilac. She put down her fork and bent down to grab her purse, sneakily slipping out just the tip of a very familiar wrapping. "I brought strawberry again," she teased.

Nolan's grip nearly slipped on his glass of water, but he caught it in time before it made a big mess.

Lilac tittered and stuffed the condom back into her purse just as the waiter came back to fill their glasses with more water. Nolan handed his to the server sheepishly, his gaze flickering from Lilac to the window and back. His elbow went on the table and he cradled his face with his hand. Lilac wanted to crawl across the table and smash all of Queen Animaliao's finest china to the ground to replace that hand with her lips.

But she could stay civilized for another hour or so. Nolan *was* making one of her dreams come true. She picked up her champagne glass and stared out at the park again as the park came to life, an electric array of lights against a black sky.

"Wait for it," said Nolan.

And then that sky lit up in a great cacophony of scarlet as Tildy's nightly fireworks show began.

"We're in the best seat for this," said Lilac, her mouth open into a perfect 'o' as her jaw dropped.

The colors shifted to blue and green as more fireworks shot up from the lagoon beside the castle.

"I know," said Nolan. "I'm loving this view."

Lilac shifted her gaze back to Nolan to find him staring unabashedly in her direction. She groaned, but she laughed, too. "Cheeseball."

Nolan looked comically affronted. "I've seen the fireworks," he said. "Let me enjoy you."

Lilac scooched her chair around the side of the table so she could slide her arm through his. "Later," she said. "Back at Tent Tildy."

He took her chin between his thumb and forefinger and pressed his lips to hers. "That's to hold me over," he said.

Lilac leaned her head against his shoulder, feeling a sense of warmth and comfort wash over her from head to toe. He was everything she wanted—who cared if she was older than him by

EPILOGUE

"Nolan would like me to translate for him," said Angie as she walked over to Lilac, arm-in-wing with Silly Sandgrouse.

Arching an eyebrow, Lilac kept swinging the hands of the elementary schooler who'd glomped on to her for the past half an hour instead of making the rounds through the Ballroom to engage in all the Tent Tildy camping activities. "I don't see Nolan anywhere," she said smugly, trying to meet Silly's eye. She didn't imagine Nolan could see her that well. She'd asked him to put the head on her in the break room about a month back and she'd quickly panicked—everything was a mesh-covered blur in there. She knew now why so many of Nolan's co-workers preferred working as Queen Animaliao or Prince Beastly, but Nolan knew Silly inside and out. He hardly ever got placed on another shift, whether he wanted one or not. He got more photographs as Silly than anyone.

"Silly!" said the girl who'd been dancing with Lilac's hands. She ran over and hugged Silly Sandgrouse by the yellow legs. Silly patted her back and Lilac cocked her head, waiting for Nolan to turn on the Silly charm and make the girl laugh, but she was off like a bolt before he'd done much more than give her a pat.

Angie leaned conspiratorially toward Lilac. She liked Angie.

just a bit? Maybe she'd gotten the formula flipped this whole time. Baby-faced college boys had suddenly become her thing.

"Does Tildy really make dreams come true?" whispered Nolan.

"She does," said Lilac. "But I'm thinking I owe this night all to Silly."

Silly Sandgrouse was nowhere to be found that night in the Tent Tildy penthouse suite, though. That was all Nolan—and Lilac felt some new dreams spring to life that night, dreams she would work to make reality, with or without her tapir fairy godmother's help.

They'd been out for a few drinks over the past few months. She had her claws dug deep in Eddie, but apparently, that had caused some drama in the break room before Eddie's ex, Josephine, had left to start college a few years late. Jo had told Lilac dryly once that she had Eddie to thank for finally getting her "act together" and setting out for "greener pastures" in the form of a liberal arts school. Somehow Lilac didn't think Eddie had lovingly encouraged Jo to focus on her studies forthright.

"He says your legs look great," whispered Angie.

Lilac stared down at her bare legs—this was the first time she'd gotten to wear the Tildy Scout outfit. It seemed appropriate for the weekend of the big Ballroom/Tent Tildy crossover event. Tonight was the first of two sleepovers and they had scads of daytime activities for the kids just dropping by, too.

"He did *not* say that," said Lilac, staring accusingly at Silly. Silly Sandgrouse didn't speak.

Angie nudged Silly with her elbow and Silly jumped, waving his hand. He was totally off today. He probably wasn't used to the Ballroom venue.

"We have our own secret language," said Angie, and she slid her arm around his wing again. "See you around!"

Lilac nodded and resisted the urge to pinch Silly in the butt. She didn't think it'd do good to have any kids witness her digging around under the goofy bird's tail.

She'd only turned around a second before she heard someone call her name.

"Landon wants you to look at his dreamcatcher," said Willow, her arm wrapped around another little girl's shoulder. "This is Bev," she said.

"Hi," said Lilac. Landon had checked in with her every half hour at least throughout the day. He loved telling her about kindergarten. Whenever she came over to their house to have dinner or hang out—not too often, but it'd happened at least half a dozen times since she and Nolan had officially started dating—Landon literally managed to get between her and Nolan, sitting one leg on each of their laps on the couch or pushing his little chair with a booster seat to squish in between theirs at the table.

"Are you having fun?" she asked the girls. Willow had just gotten her casts off not too long before and she'd certainly wasted no time in running around like a triathlete, despite the physical therapy that was supposed to be necessary to have her fully back on her feet.

"Yeah!" said Willow and Bev at once. They giggled and wove their fingers together, Willow's free hand reaching to grab Lilac's. "I told him I'd go get you."

Lilac allowed herself to be dragged along to the crafting table, where Landon was sitting, holding his dreamcatcher high above his head. His grin was so adorable with that missing tooth.

Lilac slid in beside him at the table as Willow and Bev took off toward Tildy Tapir in the corner. Tildy waved to everyone around her as she stood by Cheryl, who was passing out S'mores.

"Nice," Lilac said, allowing Landon to put the dreamcatcher in her hand.

"That's for you," he said, then he picked up some supplies to start all over again.

"Thank you," said Lilac, ruffling his hair. "Take it home and give it to me when I come over, okay?" She nodded at Tanya, who was seated a few spaces away, leading the kids collected there in crafts.

"Looking forward to more of this next week?" asked Tanya.

Lilac beamed. She'd accepted Tanya's offer to work at Tildy's Tots—pay cut and all. She'd just wanted to finish out the summer planning this big event before she'd be ready to transfer. Christian hadn't minded at all and had offered Jillian the position of assistant manager. The woman had become much less frigid toward Lilac in the days since that conversation had taken place.

"You bet," said Lilac and she and a little boy across from her just stared at each other, smiling.

He was having fun. Everyone was having fun. Her event was going better than she'd imagined it. And she was about to put her degree to use—a little different use than she'd initially expected, but to more appropriate use than being the assistant manager of a resort. And she'd still be at Tildy World.

It had just felt right.

Someone tapped Lilac's shoulder and she turned. Gyu-ri, also wearing a Tildy Scout outfit for the first time that Lilac had witnessed, gestured over her shoulder. "Time for your break," she said. "See you in half an hour."

Lilac nodded and stood up, assuring Landon she would be back shortly—though it took some distraction from Tanya to avoid the waterworks—and she headed for the entryway, which took her to the hidden door leading back to the offices. She sat down in Gyu-ri's office, relaxing in the near-silence of the empty rooms. The echoing boom of the music from the Ballroom had faded to a mere buzz this far removed from it all.

She closed her eyes and rested a moment before her phone started buzzing and she picked it up, checking the screen. A group text from Gavin. *You busy?* he asked. *Lilac, I know you have your camp ball thing today.*

Lilac snorted. *Queen Animaliao's Campside Ball*, she typed, correcting him. *And I'm on break.*

Pembroke was already joining the chat. She typed, *Sounds fun! I'm sure you did an amazing job!*

Wish you all could be here, typed Lilac, wondering why Pembroke's journeys hadn't yet taken her down to the Sunshine State. *Though it's mostly for kids anyway.*

Take pictures, typed Gavin, though that went without saying.

What? typed Brielle, joining the conversation. *Sorry. Busy. Papers flying everywhere. Mom having epiphany.*

"Damn," said Lilac aloud to no one but herself. "Someone's having a busy day." She knew Brielle was working a museum job in her hometown now—and that she'd gotten back together with that hot pseudo-celebrity some months back. *Off work and about to shag hot comic guy?* Lilac typed, always happy to tease Brielle.

Basically, wrote Brielle, not even denying it. *Why, your dorky mascot still in his costume and you're trying to fill the time while he gets his handler to get him unstuck?*

Shut up, wrote Lilac, though she was grinning. She added a grinning emoji for good measure. *No one gets him out of his costume but me.* Not entirely accurate, given the sanctity of the dressing and undressing ritual Nolan and his crew adhered to, but Lilac's friends didn't need to know that. Sworn Tildy Scout secrets and all.

Okay, dirty ladies, wrote Gavin. *Can we move on please? I gathered you here today for a very important announcement.*

How are we 'gathered' anywhere exactly? wrote Lilac, in a mood to be snarky.

First... wrote Gavin, not rising to her bait. *Pembroke has something to say.*

Pembroke started working on her line of text, but it took her a little while. Lilac had time to take a sip of water.

I think I'm in love, wrote Pembroke at last.

Lilac stared at the phone in shock. She'd talked to Pembroke a bit during her travels this summer and the girl had seemed so uninterested in the idea of finding someone to shag in every port. Lilac sent a few questioning emoji her way. *How?* she wrote. *I thought you weren't into romance.*

She isn't into sex, wrote Gavin. *Big difference.*

That made zero sense to Lilac. *Maybe for you*, she wrote, her toes curling as she thought of the way Nolan had grabbed her by the wrists and pressed her against the bedroom wall of their new condo just the night before. They were supposed to be unpacking their things, but they'd gotten as far as putting together the new bed the previous weekend and that had been about all they'd needed thus far. *Told you you just hadn't found the one, Pem.*

That's not how it works, said Gavin. Always the one to take on the mediator role. *Lilac, open your mind already.*

Scoffing, Lilac took another sip of her water. Brielle used the space to speak up. *Guys. Can we let Pembroke talk please?*

She did, after another pause. *I still don't want sex. But I don't know... I kind of like kissing. Maybe someday.*

Lilac didn't know what to think about that. Maybe? How much planning did kissing take?

Pembroke kept typing. *I'm romantic ace, I guess. I don't have the rest defined.*

The rest? asked Brielle.

Questioning, wrote both Gavin and Pembroke.

Lilac was dying to know more, but she'd ask Gavin when she had him alone later.

In any case... wrote Brielle. *Glad to hear! Happy for you.*

Lilac felt like she should say something, though she didn't quite understand. *Yeah. Good for you.*

ANYWAY, wrote Gavin then. *I'm super happy for Pem, but I wanted all three of you here at once to ask you one thing: Will you be my groomsmaids? Boyfriends, partners, and dorky mascots welcome to come as guests.*

Lilac dropped her phone. The thing actually slipped free of her fingers and fell to the ground.

SHUT UP, she wrote the instant she scooped it up again. *How could you not tell me you were getting married?* She was ecstatic for him, though bewildered that so little time had passed since he'd started dating Gabriel—hot, hot Gabriel, who'd come to Orlando for Labor Day weekend with Gavin to meet her and Nolan. But mostly she was just a *tiny* bit pissed Gavin hadn't told her first.

Holy cow, wrote Pembroke. *You just started dating!* It'd been a few months, but true enough. Who got married after a few months? Then again, she *had* moved in with her boyfriend after a rather short amount of time herself. Lilac was happier and more settled than she'd ever been and yet... The idea of marriage made her head spin.

Um, yes! wrote Brielle and it took a second for Lilac to even figure out what she meant. Yes, she'd be his groomsmaid.

...So only Brielle is going to stand beside me? Gavin sent a frowny face.

UM, I'M THE MAID OF HONOR, RIGHT? He owed her that much for not coming to her first.

I'd love to! typed Pembroke. It didn't seem like anyone would be competing with her for it.

Congrats, wrote Brielle. *Send more details soon. Sorry, got to go!* She logged off.

I should get going, too, wrote Pembroke. *Got another train to catch.*

Pictures, please! wrote Lilac. Pembroke had been sending her pics from her travels and having her guess where she was.

Pembroke sent a winky face and logged off.

That just left Lilac and Gavin. She had so any questions, so many things she wanted to discuss, but she caught the time on her phone and knew she needed to get back out there.

Li, he wrote. *Are you angry with me?*

Why the hell would I be angry? she typed as fast as her fingers would allow. She stood up then, typing as she walked down the hallways.

For not telling you first. He could read her like a book.

Just a touch miffed, she admitted. *But, Gavvy, I'm so happy for you. Gabriel's amazing.*

Gavin sent a laughing face. *Don't ever tell him I hated his guts earlier this summer, okay?*

Lilac sent an emoji with one finger to its lips. *You never hated him*, she wrote. *He just drove you crazy. I should have known that was a sign you were in love.*

Ha ha, wrote Gavin as Lilac reached the door that would take her back out to that magical world. The music was louder now—a campfire song instead of the classical music that often played in the Ballroom.

Break's over, she wrote. *But we are having a LONG conversation sometime this weekend. After my Ballroom sleepovers are over.*

Gavin sent a thumbs up. *Yes, ma'am. Now get out there and dance with a campfire or whatever it is you do in a camp ball!*

Snorting, Lilac slipped the phone into the pockets in her shorts. She liked these uniforms. Unlike with her dress pants, you could always count on them to have pockets. Stepping out into the entryway and making her way back to the Ballroom, she arrived just in time for the music to cut out.

"Everyone," said a voice over the loudspeaker—Gyu-ri's, Lilac noted, and not the usual pre-recorded message. "Please stand at attention to welcome Her Majesty, Queen Animaliao, and her princely consort, Prince Beastly!"

A spotlight hit the royal chamber doors and Lilac wondered that she hadn't passed whoever had been preparing to step out while she'd been on her way out, but she *had* been focused on her phone.

The royal couple stepped out, hand in hand, their Tildy Scout caretakers to either side of them. Eddie stood with Queen Animaliao—Lilac recognized the queen as Cheryl—and DeShawn was with Prince Beastly.

But if Eddie and DeShawn are the caretakers, who...?

Lilac's mouth dropped open. Nolan was Prince Beastly.

Nolan was a literal cotton-pickin' *prince*.

Well, not a *literal* one.

Angie slid in beside her, her arm still wrapped around Silly's wing. "Surprise!" she said, grinning. "He asked me to make you think nothing was out of the ordinary."

"Who's in there then?" asked Lilac, staring Silly down. No wonder he'd seemed off.

"I don't know what you mean," said Angie, a finger tapping the side of her nose. "This is Silly Sandgrouse." She guided her fluffy mascot off toward the crowd of kids gathering to greet the royal couple.

Nolan looked *hot* as Prince Beastly. So elegant, so regal... So sophisticated. Not at all like the sweet and down-to-earth silly goof she knew him to be. But he looked like something from her dreams—her old dreams of what a happy future might look like. The voluminous blonde wig was smoother than his usual shaggy hair and made him look older.

He locked eyes with her and grinned. "A moment, please, my lady," he said to Cheryl, bringing her gloved hands to his lips, then quickly dropping them so she could wrap a waiting child in a half-embrace.

Prince Beastly tapped the shoulders of kids shouting out his name as he made his way across the ballroom floor. Lilac stood there, shell-shocked, as he approached and Nolan grabbed for her hand, pressing his lips to her knuckles. "My lady tells me we have you to thank for this evening of merriment," he said, every syllable resounding. Lilac had never heard him speak in character—any character—before.

Lilac tried not to laugh. "A gift for my queen and her consort," she said. "And the many children and animals who live in her lands."

Prince Beastly moved her hand to the side and wrapped his other hand around her waist. Lilac worried about the kids seeing him dance with anyone but the queen, but she was taking pictures now. DeShawn was staring straight at them, nodding.

"Looks like the prince has begun the dance!" he shouted, looking over his shoulders to get the kids excited. He twirled his hand above him as if holding a lasso and within ten seconds, the music started once more. "Let's dance!" Willow and Bev appeared beside him, Bev taking DeShawn's and Willow's hands in hers. Lilac quickly took note of the resemblance between Nolan's supervisor and Willow's little friend.

Kids all over the Ballroom started shimmying and as Prince Beastly whirled her around the room, Lilac caught sight of Landon dancing with Tanya and some other boys near the craft table.

"When did you learn to dance?" asked Lilac, amazed at how light on his feet Nolan was.

"My mother and father had me instructed," he said, his voice still halting and stiff. "As a mere lad. In anticipation of my royal courtship."

Chuckling, Lilac resisted the urge to put her cheek to his. The kids were dancing, but she wouldn't risk any of them catching sight of Prince Beastly making romantic gestures to another woman.

Still, she chanced a small movement to lean her lips closer to his ear.

"You know you're going to have to take me dancing again now," she said. "This time without this costume between us."

Nolan's lips twitched just slightly. "Prince Beastly doesn't dance in the nude," he said, his voice low.

Lilac snickered. That wasn't what she'd meant and he knew it.

"But Nolan Gregosky does," he said, his voice no more than a whisper.

Four friends. Four college grads. Four people figuring out that life doesn't always turn out the way you expected.

Brielle Reyes may not have post-college life planned out like some of her friends do, but she figures she'll work for her mother's home cleaning service while job hunting for something that makes use of her history and philosophy degrees. It'll work out as long as she doesn't fall in love. Her last relationship was a disaster and she has no idea where she'll be in a few weeks, let alone the rest of her life. Since the only guy in her age range she sees now on a regular basis is cantankerous if handsome client Archer Ward, she probably won't have a hard time sticking to that vow. Probably.

Archer Ward likes very few things: illustrating as a somewhat-celebrated comic artist and his privacy. When his meddling mother hires him a cleaning service on an almost daily basis because she doesn't fully trust her son to live on his own with his disability, he's at first annoyed—even if his house cleaner is the most beautiful woman he's ever spent more than a few minutes with. When he realizes her dreams may take her far outside of his restricted orbit, he has to decide whether to stifle his interest in her or risk messing up her plans to explore if there's something more between them.

Neither can deny they're growing a little fond of each other, even if falling in love just now makes no sense whatsoever. But how often does love ever make perfect sense?

Watch for the release of Stay in Touch Book 3 (*Touch of Comfort*, Gavin's story) and Stay in Touch Book 4 (*Touch of Romance*, Pembroke's story)!

Kiss. Marry. Kill. Nineteen-year-old June Eyermann has always known exactly which of her favorite Byronic heroes goes where. She'd kiss moody and possessive Rochester from *Jane Eyre* and marry prideful but repentant Darcy from *Pride and Prejudice*, leaving obsessive and spiteful Heathcliff from *Wuthering Heights* to be chucked off a cliff—but no. She couldn't leave any of her heroes behind. She lives for her favorite fictional worlds.

But June is about to get a serious wake up call when she returns home for the summer after her college freshman year. Stuck somewhere between feeling like a kid again under her parents' roof and being forced to start acting like an adult with worries about her future career, June looks at the library volunteer position offered to her as a way to keep her sanity for the next few months before she can go back to school.

What June doesn't expect to find at the library is her favorite romantic heroes brought to life—all in the same man. Obstinate, prideful and even a bit rude, Everett Rockford shouldn't exactly be "dating material," even if June's heart rate accelerates whenever she's near him. But after discovering his enigmatic past and witnessing a few fiery moments of tenderness, June can't help but see Rochester, Darcy and even Heathcliff in Everett. If she's going to make it through the summer without becoming a tragic heroine in her own story, she has to separate the man from the ideals of fiction in her head. Because if there's one thing she knows about Byronic love stories, it's that they don't always end happily ever after.

Lose yourself in the magical forests and charming towns of the Pacific Northwest, where picturesque Victorian homes hide mysteries spanning decades, faeries watch from the

trees, and romance awaits... for those bold enough to seek it.

Cass is a drifter. When she inherits an old Queen Anne Victorian in rural Oregon from her great-aunt Alexandra, all she wants is to quickly offload the house and move on to bigger and better things. But the residents of the small town have other plans in mind. Her neighbors are anxious for her to help them thwart the plans of a land developer eager to raze Alexandra's property, while a mysterious girl in the woods needs Cass's help understanding her own confusing, possibly supernatural abilities.

And though little surprises Cass (thanks to her own magical powers of prediction), she never could have anticipated her newfound feelings for the handsome fourth-grade teacher at the local elementary school—feelings that she thought she'd buried long ago. Cass has sworn off love, but Matthew McCarthy is unlike anyone Cass has ever met. If she isn't careful, he could learn her secret. Or worse—he just might thaw her frozen heart.

But falling in love could spell danger for both of them. Because it's not just the human residents of Riddle that have snared Cass in their web. Cass's presence has caught the attention of the fae that dwell in the woods. They know she has the Sight, and they don't want to let her go...

With its unique blend of small-town romance, cozy mystery, and light fantasy, the Northwest Magic series is sure to delight anyone who believes in faery gifts and happily-ever-afters.

MISTLETOE SO SWEET: A MOUNT HONEY GROVE ROMANCE

Christmas. A charming small town and a Scrooge that might have potential.

Cassie Paige threw herself into her business — Cassie's Confectionary & Cafe — after her husband left her a year ago, but she's decided to make this a great Christmas on her own. Then her childhood crush arrives in Mount Honey Grove for the holidays, stirring up emotions she hasn't felt in years.

There are two things Trent Ellis dislikes — his hometown and anything related to Christmas. While home for a visit, a family crisis has him helping out at the local bakery. The owner, even with her love of Christmas, is making Mount Honey Grove a bit more appealing.

Can Cassie help Trent find joy in the holidays again? Will that be enough to heal her heart and bring them love under the mistletoe?

If you love sweet romances in a small town filled with Christmas joy, you'll love A Mistletoe So Sweet.